RAIDER FELT
A BLINDING BLOW
AGAINST HIS SKULL.

He wobbled backward, momentarily stunned, his ears ringing and his brain fogged.

"Ready to quit?" the redhead taunted. Then he threw another crushing right to Raider's jaw. The fist whistled past his chin as Raider plowed his own cocked right into the man's ribs.

"Soon as I finish you," Raider told him between gasps.

They began trading punches, their arms churning like pistons linked to the same shaft. He was powerful, Raider admitted, as he drove another hard right into the side of the man's head.

CHAPTER ONE

My God, it's hard to be comfortable on horseback when you're thoroughly hung over. Raider was definitely, distinctly, thoroughly uncomfortable. And hung over.

The straight-shouldered grulla he was riding did nothing at all to help. The straighter the shoulder, the harder the jog; and if you want to cover ground, you go it at a jog. Raider wanted to cover ground. He did not particularly want to do it with his eyeballs feeling like they were about to drop out of their sockets and finish their job of trying to make him bleed to death one small capillary at a time. Every time the fool horse took a step it was like a tomahawk blow to his head, and every fresh lurch on the rough road the grulla was covering caused another fresh churning of the nausea in Raider's gut.

There were times, Raider was thinking, when he was not entirely sure that so much fun was good for a person.

That was a foolish damned thought, he quickly corrected himself. It had sure-God been fun.

A week and a half in Denver with his pockets full of shining yellow double eagles—provided by a generous soul who had not necessarily intended to be so generous but who was not half the gambler he thought he was—and no reason at all why Raider should not put all of it

5

to the fullest use. His business with Allan Pinkerton had been concluded, and the Agency had owed him some time off.

Well, he had certainly put the time to use. No rotgut bar whiskey this trip. Instead it had been champagne by the bucketful, raw oysters and pressed duck laid out on white linen, candlelight and the company to go with it.

That company. In spite of the repeated stabs of pain piercing his skull with every step his grulla took, Raider had to grin into the emptiness of the road that faced him.

No indeed, neighbor, no dollar whores or chance of the clap for this old boy, he thought. Not this trip. This time it hadn't been Wide-ass Wilda's collection of cribs. This time it had been the brocaded, chandelier-hung elegance of Juliet LaRue's genteel establishment, and the company of Janine and Milly and Pamela, and once—a rare distinction—of Juliet herself.

It was Milly, though, Millicent Gardinier, pronounced with a well deserved "yea" on the end, that he remembered the best.

Milly was quite a woman, a big girl, almost as tall as Raider himself, and with a body that would teach a mule skinner to pray just from looking at it. Raider had done more than just look. He had wallowed in her excellence, romped all over the LaRue featherbeds with her, felt himself locked hip-deep between those long, powerful, sleek thighs that could pull the loving out of a man like no human female ought to be able to do. He had enjoyed every minute of it, and by the time his money was about gone, she was admitting that she enjoyed it as much as he did.

That sort of compliment from a whore is not exactly the thing to make a man's chest puff out in pride as a rule. Generally speaking, a compliment like that is a come-on for repeat business, never mind how the rutting bastard smelled when he crawled into the saddle or how rough he bucked when he got to bumping bellies. When a whore tells you you're good, if you are smart, you first check your wallet and next swallow three grains of salt.

With Milly he really didn't think that was the case. She sounded as if she meant it. More important, she backed it up with a last night of uninterrupted screwing at no charge. A freebie.

Now *that* was sincerity.

Yes, Raider was in pretty good humor on that regard. But Milly wasn't with him now, and that hangover was. It was going to be a long, long ride from Denver down to Santa Fe.

He did not exactly *have* to go to Santa Fe at the moment; he still had a few days' time coming. But Doc Weatherbee was in Santa Fe and had sent Raider a wire in Denver. The wording had been vague—with Doc there was probably a good reason for not wanting to put anything down that someone else might read and understand—but apparently the old boy had something working. If Raider could get down there and join him, it would be easier for him.

Raider had no idea what was up, and he was not yet officially on the case. If he had been, he could have taken a train at Allan Pinkerton's expense. As it was, he was having to go the hard way. Allan was too much of a pinchpenny to let him use Agency funds without a formal assignment. And after Milly, Raider was too broke to get to Santa Fe by rail out of his own pocket. Doc would just have to wait a few days for his partner to join him.

That was all right with Raider. He and his friend would manage with or without Allan Pinkerton's help. Maybe that was why they made such a good team. In fact, he was no longer sure he could handle an investigation without the obstinate, fussy old bastard siding him.

Right now, though, Santa Fe was still an awfully long way away, and Raider really was not much in a mood for communing with other, non-hung-over men or even —a true mark of his mood—women.

The road running south along the Front Range paralleling the rails that Raider could not afford to take was a fair piece of highway, everything considered. It was also heavily populated and more than a little civilized.

Things were not so depressing that a man couldn't have a good time, which was why Raider was so thoroughly hung over. The first day south of Denver he had made Colorado City, a place mostly given to miners and such rowdy types. Raider had stopped there early enough to have some time to kill. The cards had been good to him, good enough so that he came out roughly even, which was very good indeed, considering the company he was keeping. But the whiskey had been a deep stack of cuts below the quality he had gotten used to in Denver when Milly was doing the pouring for him. Hence the hangover and the accompanying foul humor.

Ordinarily he might have held the grulla to the well-traveled road down through Pueblo, but the morning had been even more uncomfortable than the afternoon was proving to be, and so he had not really wanted to see or talk to another person if he could at all avoid it. He turned the rough-trotting horse onto the old military road—there were those who said the Spaniards had first used the route in their early explorations around here— that would slip over into the foothills and bypass the people who insisted on cluttering up this part of the country with their houses and shops and their pigpens and dairies. Bastards—under the dark haze of Raider's current mood and condition they were all bastards, including the best of them. Including most of all Allan Pinkerton, who rightfully should have given Raider rail fare.

The old military road, poorly marked and rarely

traveled nowadays, swung west along the foothills and would, he knew, eventually plunge through several canyon passages before rejoining the main road. That section, the tag end of the Santa Fe Trail winding up into and through Raton Pass, would be unavoidable. But he would not hit that yet for another day or two, and by then it might be bearable to suffer the jeers and joking of the freighters and muleteers who still managed to find some business in spite of the railroads that were building everywhere you looked these days.

Raider splashed across the shallow, deceptively tame-looking stream that was the Arkansas River here and paused on the south bank to dismount and shove his pounding skull beneath the murky water. The agony of moving so much and bending over proved to be more trouble than the cooling relief the water offered, but Raider did not know that until it was too late.

He muttered a few carefully selected curses and crawled wearily back into the saddle. He winced and cursed some more when he sat down. The saddle was a good one, but at the moment Raider felt like his ass was one large boil that might erupt at any time. He nudged the grulla and shifted his weight forward, and the animal resumed its harsh jog. At least that was one good thing he could say about the horse, poorly built though it was. It was a well-trained animal that did not have to be kept on the bit and reins all the time.

In midafternoon he forded another stream, barely a trickle of water, and climbed an embankment that was more loose, gray gravel than soil. The horse topped out after a brief scramble, and Raider paused to let the animal catch a breather and to resettle his own hat. He did not feel quite as bad as he had earlier in the day, but still his Stetson felt like it was made of steel bands that added a pound and a half of weight and was bolted half an inch tighter with every mile that passed.

He took a Denver-bought cigar from his shirt pocket

and dipped two fingers into his vest for a match to light it. Earlier, he had not felt like adding that normally delightful taste to the fur that was coating his tongue, but he thought he could stand one now. He was feeling almost human enough to believe that he might be able to stand living again.

"Oh-ho, you ugly ol' bastard," he told his horse. "Looks like you might have some company an' I might have someone else's cooking tonight."

On the hard ground beneath the grulla's feet was a beaten line of tracks made by so many animals that an impression had been left even on this rocky soil. The few marks placed in ground soft enough to leave a record of the passage showed that it was a herd of driven cattle that had passed the place, and not too long before. There were no bugdrags or wind drift in the depressions, which surely meant that he was close enough to the outfit to catch it and cadge a meal.

He still was not anxious to be in anyone else's company, but the prospect of a proper meal prepared by a trail cook beat the idea of facing his own cooking.

The trail joined the old road for about a mile, but there it turned off to Raider's right and into the mountains that rose abruptly there. Raider pulled the grulla down to a halt and stopped for a moment to puzzle out what that meant.

He was still a little hung over and a little slow, and it took him a moment to realize what was wrong.

This was pretty late in the year. The high country was about dried up, and the grass at the higher elevations was poor. Ranchers wintered their cattle on the low ground and summered up high. Whoever was driving this herd seemed to be going in the wrong direction for so late in the season. He ought to be pulling his animals down out of the mountains, not pushing them up still higher.

Funny, Raider thought.

Maybe not so funny.

He checked the prints again. Even with a hangover he could not have been *that* wrong. The beeves definitely were being taken up higher. He stood in his stirrups and tried for a better look at what lay above him to the west. There was, he thought, the possibility of a notch immediately above the turnoff the cattle had taken, maybe with a hanging valley or a wide cirque above it. From down below he could not tell for sure, and he never would have spotted the opening from a casual look. It had taken a definite search to find anything suspicious about the notch that might or still might not be there.

That being the case, there was a fine probability that the fellow driving these animals was not the fellow who had bought and paid for them. When a man takes beef into a high, hidden valley at the wrong time of the year, that possibility was likely.

"Old horse," Raider muttered out loud, "you don't give a shit anyhow, an' I'm not so anxious for someone else's cooking that I figure to get shot over it. Why don't you and me keep on the way we were going and leave these boys alone. The way folks like to treat rustlers around here, I think they got troubles enough without us adding to them. And I damn sure got troubles enough without *them* adding to mine." He supposed he probably should have done something law-abiding about it, but the truth was that he just didn't feel like it. It wasn't his case anyhow.

He touched the horse with his heels and put it back onto the old road toward the south and, eventually, Santa Fe.

The road came quickly to a drop and had to curl in a switchback toward the bottom. Raider had just made the turn and was preparing to go down to the bottom of the narrow cut when he heard something that sounded depressingly familiar not far overhead.

He looked up and sighed. He had been right about that sound.

There was a dark-haired, dark-eyed young yahoo standing on a rock not far above him with a Spencer carbine in his hands and a downright hostile look on his face. What Raider had heard was the sound of the weapon being cocked. The Spencer was aimed downhill in a direction that Raider did not like at all. It was aimed at his chest.

"Afternoon, sonny," Raider called in a deliberately pleasant voice. "If you're looking for deer, I ain't one."

CHAPTER TWO

"I seen you looking at them tracks, mister."

"Uh huh." There was no point in denying the obvious. Raider could save his lies for later, when they might do more good. "I was thinking 'bout trying to bum a meal," he added truthfully. That much honesty was about enough, though. "I figured it might be too far off the road to go out o' my way. Any idea how far those boys are ahead of me?"

"Shit," the boy with the Spencer said. "Do you expect me to believe any of that crap?"

"I reckon you ought to. It's the truth."

"You look like a liar to me," the boy prodded.

"Son, I don't even know what a liar is supposed to look like. I sure don't see how you could have that matter figured out at your tender age."

"Tender age, my ass, mister. An' if you make any more cracks about my age, I'll blow a hole through your gut big enough to pass a watermelon through."

"I don't think so," Raider commented in an agreeable tone of voice. "But that isn't getting us anywhere. Jawing at a person rarely does. Why don't you just put your gun aside, and I'll go look somewheres else for my supper."

"You'd like that, wouldn't you?"

"Damn straight I would. So would you in my place."

13

"But I ain't in your place, mister. I'm the one as has the rifle here, and don't you be forgetting it."

"I swear, sonny, first you get upset because I don't ride straight on by, and now you seem upset because I figure to move along. Just what is it you *do* want?"

"I want you to stay put, mister, while I decide whether to kill you now or wait so someone else can do it later."

"Those are hard words, son, and right at the moment I don't have a whole hell of a lot of patience. I'm hung over and feeling kind of foul, so leave me be. You mind your business, and I'll mind mine." It seemed a perfectly sensible idea to Raider.

"The hell you say, mister." The boy waggled the muzzle of the carbine. "Get down off that horse an' climb up here," he ordered.

The kid looked really nervous, Raider could see. He licked his lips and swallowed hard several times. That was a pretty good sign, Raider decided. The boy intended to shoot. And about the time Raider got a leg flung over his cantle and was balanced on one stirrup—sure, that would be a fine time to pull the trigger. The kid was young and obviously inexperienced at killing people or he wouldn't be so nervous, but it looked like someone had taught him the basics very nicely indeed.

It was a shame the boy wouldn't live long enough to make use of that education he had already gotten a running start on.

He still had a chance, though.

"Son, I'm in no mood to argue with you, and I damn sure won't put myself at a disadvantage by stepping off this horse at your say-so. What I think you ought to do is to lay that gun aside before I think you're threatening me with it. Should that happen, son, I reckon I'd be forced to hurt you. Maybe even kill you. Have you been in many gunfights?" Raider did not wait for him to answer. "I don't know what you've heard about it. Probably something dramatic. And stupid. The fact is, when you face a man who figures to shoot back, you can't take time to aim real close. You can't draw a fine bead an' try to wound the other man. You have to go for the big, soft parts of the body. Those are the places that will kill him. Put him down with a hard shock and kill him. So I'm telling you, son, don't try me because I won't have time to be gentle with you. I'll have to kill you. I'm sorry about that. It isn't good to have to kill young'uns, especially those with promise. But if you force me, I'll have to do it."

"I'm the one holding a gun on you, you know. It ain't the other way around here."

"True enough," Raider said mildly. He was hoping the boy would drop it there and let him ride on. He had no quarrel with this kid or with anyone he might be trying to protect, presumably the same bunch who had driven those cattle in the wrong direction for an honest man to be going. Wearily, thinking to help educate the kid and nothing more, he added, "You know, son, it ain't who's holding the gun that counts, it's who is doing the most damage the quickest."

That, he quickly saw, was the wrong thing to say. The boy's grip tightened on the stock of his Spencer. *Oh shit,* Raider thought. *He's going to.*

The boy shifted the muzzle of the carbine again, looking for a good, hard, killing first shot.

That was a mistake. He didn't have that much time.

Raider palmed his .45 and loosed three fast, belching spears of flame and lead into the boy's chest and belly.

"I really am sorry, sonny," he said to the corpse that lay on the rock above him. "I didn't want to do that."

He thought about climbing up there to see if the kid had anything that Raider couldn't live without— like a fistful of money he wouldn't need any longer— but decided the risk was not worth the reward. The boy might have friends nearby. The prudent thing to do was to leave. Now.

Raider kneed the well-trained, hard-riding grulla ahead, directing it by shifts of his weight and the pressure of his knees, and rode down the trail while he ejected the empties from his Colt and thumbed fresh cartridges into the chambers. A man just never knew.

Three miles down the road, Raider figured he should be in the clear. He heard no sounds of pursuit behind him, and the noise of the gunshots would not have carried far. Everything should have been just dandy.

Raider was wrong.

One moment he was riding peacefully along the old, seldom-used ruts of the military road. The next moment he was surrounded by a bunch of town-dressed yahoos carrying shotguns.

"Afternoon, gents. Anything I can do for you?" He touched the brim of his hat, and when he was done, kept his right hand well clear of the polished walnut grips of his Colt. With a single man, even a grown and nasty son of a bitch, he might argue. With a whole posse of folks carrying shotguns he was not going to quarrel at all.

"Bet your ass you can do something for us, mister," one of the riders told him. "You can set right there with your hands as still as them mountains. Jesse, take a little weight off'n the gentleman if you would, please."

Another of the men climbed awkwardly down from his mount, carelessly swinging the muzzle of his double-barreled scattergun in an arc that threatened at least half his friends with instant annihilation if his finger happened to tighten by accident. The man, Raider decided, wasn't very familiar with either firearms or saddle horses, but it looked like he didn't have to be. He was in the driver's seat, and Raider was the one under all the guns.

The man called Jesse walked to Raider's side and removed the heavy Colt from his holster.

"Be careful with that," Raider advised. "Soon as you gentlemen work out that I ain't who you think I am, I'll be wanting that back."

"Who do you believe we think you are, mister?" the first one spoke up again.

Raider shrugged. "Damned if I know, but it can't be me. I never done anything down this way to be ashamed of. Since you boys have the look of a duly constituted posse on some sort of serious business, I figure you must be after somebody. I also figure it isn't likely to be a Pinkerton agent, which I happen to be."

"Don't buy that bullshit, Luke. That's him," another of the possemen broke in immediately behind Raider's speech. "Look at that red shirt and leather vest. You saw him too. That's him, all right."

"Whoever you're looking for," Raider said, "you can't have gotten a very close look at him or you'd know it wasn't me. Listen, damn it, half the men in this part of the country wear red shirts and leather vests just the same as I do. Hell, boys, you can't convict a man of anything by his choice of clothes. Not when they're so common. Besides, I told you, I'm a Pink. We play on the other side of the fence."

Luke grinned. "Did you hear him try to weasel out of it, boys? He knows we didn't get a good, close look at him because he saw us coming the same as we saw him going. He's not only a thief, he's a smart thief to boot."

"I don't think so," one of the men said. "He's a smart-ass maybe, but if he was so damned smart as he'd like us to believe, he wouldn't be here fixing to be hung, would he?"

"I guess he wouldn't at that," Luke agreed. "Climb down off that horse, mister. No, wait. Jesse, lead him over by that tree." Luke chuckled. "No point in making the poor fellow walk when he can ride."

Jesse was no cowman. He had to be a city type, for instead of getting onto his own horse and leading

Raider's grulla, he took the reins of both animals and led them afoot the seventy or eighty yards to the nearest trees.

"Now you can get down," Luke invited.

"So you can give me a fair trial before you hang me?" Raider asked sarcastically.

"Exactly," Luke agreed. He seemed not at all put out by Raider's tone of voice.

Well, Raider realized, there was no need for him to be.

"Do I get a chance to defend myself?" Raider asked.

"Hell yes," another of the posse members said with a grin. "It wouldn't be any fun otherwise."

"Jesus," Raider said. "There's probably ten thousand people in this state, most of 'em perfectly sensible men. And here I go and stumble into a flock of idiots." He shook his head and crawled off the grulla. One of the possemen took a rope off his saddle and began tying a hangman's noose.

CHAPTER THREE

"Does any of you boys want to defend the gentleman before we hang him?" Luke asked.

There was no response from the dozen or so posse members who were watching. Nor, Raider noticed, was there any apparent reluctance on their part to look him in the eye. Oh, they were convinced, all right. They had their man.

Luke looked at Raider and shrugged. "You see how it is, mister. I expect if you want some defending, you'll have to do it yourself."

"From what I can see," Raider told him, "there's not much point in me trying. You already got me figured for hanging. An' I don't even know what it is I'm supposed to have done, damn it."

"You know that well enough," one of the men spat. "Shithead."

"The point is, boys," Raider answered calmly, "I don't. Whatever it is, you got the wrong man here. All I'm doing—or *was* doing—was riding through on my way down to Santa Fe. I been up to Denver for a few weeks. You could check that easy enough. I could give you the Pinkerton office address there. Or you could ask the girls where I spent the most o' my time. Hell, there's lots of ways I could prove where I been and who I am."

"Uh huh," Luke said in a bored tone of voice that

19

also said he neither believed Raider's story nor cared to hear it.

"Listen to me, you idiot bastards," Raider insisted. "I don't know what it is you want from me, but you got the wrong fellow here. Now that's the simple truth of it. I ain't done a damn thing around here that you could get mad about, much less hang me for."

Raider tried to put all the world's sincerity into those few words. He was hoping that this crowd had not seen him shoot that boy back down the trail. He did not see how they could possibly have found out about that and gotten in front of him by some route he did not know. Their horses did not look lathered or even mildly sweated the way they would have if they had run to jump in front of him from that point three miles back. But still . . .

He looked at the faces around him and was not at all reassured by what he saw.

Raider was a man who liked to gamble, but this was a bit much even for his sporting blood. And the stakes were a hell of a lot higher than he wanted to play against, with a deck so obviously stacked against him.

"Listen, damn it," he said. "If you want to have your trial, that's gonna mean telling me anyway. So what is it that I'm supposed to have done to get you so upset?"

"You know," another of the men said dully.

"No, Pete, that seems a fair enough question," Luke said patiently. "And we do want to be fair here. We'll give the man a trial. The whole works, right?"

He drew a round of nodding approval from his friends. They seemed to be looking forward to the charade.

"Climb down, boys," Luke said. "We'll get this over with and then go home to our families."

The men dismounted and stood with their reins held loosely and, Raider thought, awkwardly in their hands. These definitely were townsmen, not a bunch of punchers. In a way that was a shame, because Raider understood the ways and the emotions of men of the open country a lot more than he ever would these store clerks who now surrounded him.

"Somebody tie this man before we get down to business," Luke ordered. "It wouldn't hardly do to let him get into any more mischief." The man might well have noticed Raider eyeing the shotguns and few gunbelts in the crowd. Those were handled about as awkwardly as the horses were. It had been a faint hope at best, but . . .

One of the men actually took a pocketknife and sliced a length from the catch rope hanging at his saddle to provide a piece suitable to tie Raider's hands with.

Raider could scarcely believe that he had seen such a thing happen. *No one* cut up his own rope, for crying out loud. No one but a complete damn fool, anyway. Both the horse and the rope had to have been borrowed, and by some yahoo who didn't realize what he was doing when he cut the thing. The wonder maybe was not so much that he did it as that he had had a knife in his pocket to do the job with.

Be that as it may, the piece of tough manila was wrapped securely around Raider's wrists, and his hands were tied behind his back. From what he could feel of the job, the men doing it were aware of their own inexperience and were going to some pains to make up in bulk and tightness what they lacked in expertise. Raider would not easily shed the bonds, even if he managed to find some time to try.

"That hurts," he protested at one point.

"It won't for long," the rope cutter responded cheerfully.

"Jesus!" Raider said.

"Too late," the one with the knife said, just as cheerfully.

The men finished tying Raider and tugged painfully at his arms to test their work. "All done, Luke," the rope cutter said. "He ain't going anywhere but to the end of Harry's noose."

Harry was the noose builder then. Raider stared at each one of the men, trying to memorize names and faces to the best of his ability. If he managed to get out of this, he would want a chance to discuss it with them again, one by one, where there would be no witnesses or interference. And if he *didn't* get out of it, by God, he intended to come back and *haunt* the bastards. One by one.

"My nose itches," Raider said.

"Tough," one of the men told him coldly.

"So scratch it," another said with a laugh.

"You boys are all heart, you know that? Shit. How about somebody lighting me a cigar anyway? I oughta be entitled to that much." He glared at the lot of them gathered in a circle around him.

It was Luke who stepped nearer and took a cigar from Raider's pocket. From his own vest he produced a fancily engraved and very handsome little tool that nipped the twist from the end of the stogie and a match to light it with. He put the cigar between Raider's teeth and held the flame to the end until there was a good coal glowing there.

Raider breathed the rich smoke deep into his lungs with something close to satisfaction and deliberately neglected to thank the man. He was not exactly feeling gratitude toward Luke or any of the others at that moment, and he certainly was not going to beg or grovel his way into their good graces. They could kill him, but they were not going to break him first or so much as make him bend.

"Nothing to say about that?" Luke taunted.

Raider shrugged. "It's a good cigar. What the hell do you want, a recommendation?"

"No, I suppose not," Luke said. To the other men he added, "Let's get on with this, boys." He motioned one of them forward. "Leonard, you got the best look at him."

The man nodded.

"Is this the same fella you saw after you heard the shooting?"

Again he nodded.

"You're sure of that?"

"I am."

"Sure of what?" Raider injected. "You heard what shooting? You saw what man? What the hell happened, anyhow?"

"Be quiet," Luke told him patiently. "You'll get your chance."

"Harry," Luke went on, "you were the only one who took time to ride over and get a good look at Charlie's body. You're sure the boy is dead?"

Harry, the one with the nearly finished noose in his hands, spat a stream of brown tobacco that splattered Raider's boots and nodded vigorously. "Damn straight the kid's dead," he said. He was glaring pure venom at Raider while he spoke. "Shot him right between the eyes, he did. Split the kid's skull open like a fucking melon. Brains and gore all over the place. Flies crawlin' inside the kid's head, laying maggot eggs already. Yeah, I seen him. Yeah, he's dead. Yeah, this bastard done it." Still staring coldly at Raider, he added, "That boy would have been fourteen this winter, mister. We all of us liked him real good. When you hurt him, man, you did piss us off. Now we figure you can pay for it."

"Mister," Raider protested, "I still don't know what the fuck you're talking about. All I done to deserve this was to ride down the road. I never killed any kid in my life, and I don't figure to. I'll trade lead with any man an' some women, but I never done what you think I did. I reckon if I had, you would be right to string me up. And when I get loose from here, if I get the chance,

I will help you hang the man that did it. Without even the regular fee to Pinkerton's. But it wasn't me."

"Bullshit," Luke said mildly. He was by far the least emotional of all the men.

"I still don't even know what this is all about. Why would anybody want to shoot a kid?"

"You tell us," one of the men said angrily.

Raider glared at him and did not bother to respond.

"Still want to play pretend, do you?" Luke asked with a tight-lipped smile that carried no humor at all. "We have you cold, mister. That's a fact."

Luke stood directly in front of Raider and crowded close, sticking his chin out and looking up into Raider's eyes. The man was a good six inches shorter than Raider and reminded him of a bantam rooster on the prod the way he stood there defying Raider to disagree with him.

"That herd you boys hit was our town herd, mister. The meat for all our tables this whole coming winter long. Taking the beef roast off my table and out o' the mouths of my old woman and babies, that was bad enough. "But the boy we'd hired to tend that herd, mister. His name was Charlie Ramage. A damned good boy he was, too. You wouldn't know about that, I don't suppose, or care if you did know. But that was one good kid. Didn't have any folks. They died of the flux on the way out here, all of us traveling together with our wagons. Building together when we got here. All but the Ramages and a few others that didn't make it. But we took Charlie in like he was one of our own. Gave him a roof and a bed and work to do, treated him like he belonged to all of us. And he appreciated it, too. He wasn't some kind of upstart. He was a good kid, a damned good kid. All the way around, he was.

"When we let him handle the town herd for us, it was like we was giving him a present. He wanted to be a cowboy in the worst way, and this was his start on it, he figured. He wanted to strap a gunbelt on and wear gauntlets and gloves like the drovers do, but we wouldn't let him do that. By God, mister, I wish now that we had let him. Maybe he'd have blown a tunnel through your gut if we had. We were trying to be good to him and not let him get into trouble, and now he's dead. Mister, that don't set well with us. We figure to make up to him for it. Pretty damned quick now, too." Luke paused for breath. He too was becoming emotional.

"We can almost understand a thief, even if a thief is a low son of a bitch that takes what ain't rightfully his. But we can understand a man wanting to eat. We'd chase a thief, we would. But sòme miserable bastard that would kill a kid like Charlie, well, there just ain't no end to the earth as far as catching him is concerned. So we're awful happy to have found you so easy. By God, we are."

"Mister," Raider said levelly, "I sympathize about it. But I ain't the one that shot that boy. If I do something, I'll own up to it. This time it happens that I ain't guilty of anything. Except like I said, riding down the road on my way to Santa Fe. I don't figure to allow you to hang me for that."

"Allow? Mister, there ain't any 'allow' to it. We got you, and we figure to hang you. Harry, you done with that noose yet?"

"Ready any time you are, Luke."

"Good. I think we better use it before I get upset here and do something un-Christian, like slice this man's fingers off before we hang him. That wouldn't be a right thing to do, and we aren't going to drop down to his level. Not for a minute, we ain't."

Harry nodded his approval and handed the reins of his horse to one of the other men. On foot he moved under the nearest tree and began trying to flip the noose over a projecting limb fourteen or fifteen feet above ground level. He had trouble getting it over, but on the fifth try he managed. Raider did not feel particularly proud of Harry for his perseverance.

Harry ostentatiously fussed with the swinging noose until he had it positioned to his satisfaction. He turned and grinned at the other posse members. "All set, boys."

The men turned as if on command toward Raider.

Raider spat the stub of his cigar onto the ground. "I was kinda hoping for something more than this," he said. He made a mighty effort to yank his hands free from the ropes that bound them behind his back. The posse watched him without trying to interfere. They seemed to be enjoying his discomfort thoroughly. Slowly they began to drift toward him, the circle closing a slow step at a time.

If I had any sense, I suppose I'd be pissing my drawers now, but I guess I've never been that bright, Raider thought. And I don't figure to warn them to tie my feet too. If I'm lucky, one of them will get close enough that I can kick his fucking throat to pieces before I go under, because they can kill me, but they can't make me quit.

CHAPTER FOUR

Jesse was the one closest to Raider, and he apparently was not content to let the punishment go with a simple hanging. He wanted to see some pain first. He stepped in to a good swinging distance and launched a vicious right into Raider's unprotected belly.

Raider had felt worse, but it had been a hell of a long time ago. The fist landed with enough force to double Raider over against the sharp, sudden gout of pain.

By then another one was hammering his kidneys from behind, and one, Raider never saw which, looped a punch over Jesse's shoulder to explode against Raider's temple.

Raider knew from past experience that the impact of bare knuckles against the hard bone of his skull would have split the man's hand open, but the knowledge did little to dull the pain of it. He could feel a flow of blood begin to stream moist and sticky down his jaw.

The blows continued to fall, so many that the feel of them became a steady, constant blur instead of a series of separate pains. Raider gritted his teeth and concentrated on keeping his balance. They had him tied. They could beat him if they wished, but they could not bow him. He would *not* grovel before them. And he would—

27

he swore it—remember these men, each one of them, for as long as he might be capable of memory.

Luke's voice cut through the confusion of the flurries of punching and swearing.

"God damn it!" the posse leader was shouting. "Back away there. Damn you, get off him. Jesse, Pete, Ansley. Get the hell off of him. We ain't a pack of dogs here. We're gonna hang the son of a bitch, but we ain't gonna savage him like a bunch of animals first. You got that? Have you *got* that, damn it?"

The blows stopped falling, and the men began to back away. They still looked angry, though, and not at all abashed in the face of Luke's anger.

"He deserved it," one of them—Raider thought it was Harry—muttered in an undertone.

"We aren't a bunch of killers here," Luke said patiently. "We're a duly constituted posse enforcing the law. Now you boys remember that. We are better than this murdering son of a bitch. We aren't going to drag ourselves down to his level."

Luke's interference in their fun had come quickly but not quickly enough as far as Raider was concerned. After just those few moments of it, he hurt like hell, and that was the simple truth of the matter. If he had been alone, he would have been bent double from the pain in his back and his belly, but he was not going to let these bastards see him react to what they had given him. He had entirely too much pride for that. His eyes flashing cold fire, he stared at them, one by one, and knew they could feel the bite of his raw disgust.

A cut inside his cheek filled his mouth with blood, and he spat it out at Luke's feet. "Proud of yourselves?" He spat that out too, like a gypsy's curse. There was venom as well as blood coming from his mouth.

"Shut your mouth, you murdering prick," Luke shot back at him. "I stopped these men for their sake, not yours. We're good, honest men, which you wouldn't understand, I'm sure. And we'll hang you by the neck until you're dead. Then we'll go home to our families and put you out of mind, mister. There won't be anybody mourning your grave. I mean to keep it that way too. Harry, shove this bastard up on his horse so we can drop him clean."

"We could haul him up just as easy," Harry suggested. "Pull him up slow so it'll take him a long time to die, you know?"

"I know, God damn it, and I said we'll drop him clean. We're gonna do this civilized and decent, by God. We ain't going to act like criminals when we hang a criminal."

Harry and the others did not like it, but Harry shrugged. He took Raider by the arm and led him, not gently but without any excess roughness either, toward where the grulla was standing. It had been left with its reins knotted and thrown over the patient animal's neck.

"He'p me hoist him up, somebody," Harry asked, and immediately there were a dozen willing hands clutching at Raider and lifting him into the air like a sack of meal.

It was a strange feeling. Raider was helpless in their grip. So many of them were able to shift his body as if he were a child. He had not been lifted like that since he was a small boy, but the feeling now was not one of warmth and affection. There was no one to throw him overhead and catch him and listen to him squeal. He, by God, was not going to be doing any squealing where any of these bastards might hear him. Never.

The grulla was standing almost directly under the free-swinging noose. The rope with the thirteen twists in the coil that formed its loop was there before his eyes as the posse lifted him easily and planted him astraddle the grulla.

He could see the waiting noose in hard silhouette against the clear, crisp blue of the sky and the darker greenish purple of the mountains that rose above them.

It was an ugly sight, but Raider gave it a long look as they positioned him in his saddle. He would not bow to the men, and he would not bow to the noose that waited to snuff out his life.

He looked at the rope, and his throat tightened despite the effort of will that kept his features calm and apparently unconcerned. In his imagination he already could feel the grating scrape of the harsh rope against tender throat flesh and the sickening drop and white-hot stab of pain that was sure to come when his neck snapped.

Raider had seen enough men hang before. A good many of them had come to the gallows quietly and stoically. Very few begged and whined at the end. But all of them ended the same once the trap was sprung.

The drop was sudden. The rope always stretched farther than anyone could have believed, and it gave off a low, thrumming sound that reached inside the guts of the spectators as the hemp was pulled nearly to its breaking point by the sudden weight.

There was a sharp, distinct snap of the breaking vertebrae when the hangman had done his job well and the bulky knot—its bulk was the reason it was tied that way—was positioned correctly below the ear to help push the head over with a snap and thus to assist in the breaking of the neck.

Raider had seen it often enough. Often enough they had been men that he and Doc had helped send up the thirteen steps to the gallows platform. He wondered briefly whether Doc would ever learn what had become of him. He thought that Weatherbee probably would. When Raider failed to arrive in Santa Fe, Doc would wonder. And what he wondered about, Doc generally managed to learn about. Weatherbee almost certainly would find retribution for his friend, but that would be damned small comfort for Raider. By then he would be long dead and soon enough forgotten.

He was not afraid, though, not really. If he had a regret at all, it was that he was not to have enough time to get back at these possemen who were going to hang him for something he had not done.

That was the rub. He hadn't done it.

It would have been different, he thought, if he was guilty of the murder they thought he had committed. He could pay for anything he had done. He was no coward and no shirker. If someone caught him fair and square for a crime he had committed, he could go under without hating him for what he did to him.

But not, by God, for a crime he had not done. That was another cat altogether, and this ugly act he could not accept.

He stared at the noose and felt a quick sense of shame that these bastards would so soon see him the way he knew he would be.

It was invariable. In all the hangings he had witnessed, he had never known of one man to fail to do it after that loud, exceedingly ugly noise of the neck bones popping apart.

Every time without fail, the man's bladder and bowels emptied, and for yards around there would be the biting, acrid stench of fresh shit, and the rank wetness would spread down the poor bastard's pants legs.

Perhaps even more than death, Raider loathed the idea that these puling town bastards would see him reduced to such a condition before them. It was one thing to die. It was another thing to die without dignity, and Raider's pride was still strong as he glowered at the noose that was to end his life.

"Sorry hog fuckers," he snapped at them.

"Gag him. Somebody gag him," Luke ordered.

Raider was seated on the grulla now, his legs gripped by the men who surrounded him and the animal.

The men began to curse him from their positions on the ground beside him, and once again one of them reached up to begin pummelling Raider's unprotected kidneys.

Another whipped off his bandanna and took hold of Raider's sleeve to yank him down lower and shove the makeshift gag into his mouth.

There was anger and confusion on the men's faces, and the others began to punch him too. But to reach him with their fists, they had to release their holds on his legs and on the grulla.

Raider was seated deep in the sturdy stock saddle, and for a bare instant there was only one hand grabbing at his left leg while the others tried to hit him.

He saw the opportunity, and he drove the steel of his spur rowels into the belly of the well-trained grulla. Raider screamed out his rage and defiance like a catamount roaring into the night air or a silvertip grizzly challenging the sky.

Startled, the possemen recoiled as the grulla dropped its jaw in reaction to the unexpected pain and wrung its tail. The horse's haunches bunched and exploded in a surge of power and ripped Raider from the midst of the posse.

The man who had been clutching his leg was too slow to react, and his fingers slipped off the rough denim of Raider's jeans. His pull was hard enough to twist Raider in the saddle, but the high-backed cantle kept Raider from falling.

The dangling noose before him slapped Raider cruelly in the face. The loop was standing open, and he might well have hanged himself when the lunging grulla bolted forward. But instead, the bulk of the heavy knot cracked painfully against his ear and was gone.

Behind him men were shouting, and within seconds he could hear the dull explosions of gunfire.

Raider bent forward over the grulla's neck and hung on with his knees. He had no time to seek the stirrups, and his balance was poor with his hands tied behind him, but he had a chance. A ghost of a chance to be sure, but the horse was running free and fast, and with every strong bound of the pumping legs he increased his lead over the posse that he knew would be pounding in pursuit behind him within seconds.

Raider stabbed at the flopping stirrups until he found one and then the other. With that to aid him, he shifted his weight sharply to the right, and the horse responded by turning to stay beneath him.

"Run, you fucker," he yelled into the wind. He raked the grulla again with his spurs and threw his weight to the left, trying to guide the animal onto the road, back the way he had so recently come. "Run it, boy!"

CHAPTER FIVE

With his feet socked home in the stirrups, Raider felt a lot better; but he would not be comfortable until he could get his hands free too, and that would take some time. Ten minutes, five, at least one lousy little minute of peace down off this bouncing, jolting grulla's back so that he could concentrate on getting his hands loose.

He did not have that kind of free time. The possemen were jumping for their horses. He swiveled his neck to look. Some of them had already grabbed the reins and were swinging onto their mounts. One was already seated and spurring. Raider did not take time to try to see who he was. One was as bad as another.

A few of them were trying to shoot and mount at the same time. Raider wished them good luck—like maybe shooting one of their own horses or something. The range was already on the long side for short-barreled scatterguns, which fortunately was what these town-type fellows seemed to prefer. A far-reaching rifle could have made cold beef of him pronto.

And it wasn't over yet. A misstep by the grulla or a moment of inattention by Raider, even the unlikely possibility that one of those city dudes would have a horse fast enough to run him down—the grulla was not the greatest animal he had ever owned, but Raider knew better than to ever mount himself on a dog-slow horse—

and that would be all she wrote for one Mr. Raider, late of the Pinkerton National Detective Agency.

The grulla thundered around a bend, momentarily out of sight of the pursuers, and the temptation was strong to send the horse crashing into the underbrush and thick stand of trees that lay to the left, against the precipitous foothills that rose so sharply toward the high country.

He was tempted, but he was not stupid. Crashing into that brush with his hands tied behind his back, unable to guide the horse except by shifting his weight, unable to twist and bend and fight his way into the limbs, he could easily be swept off the grulla—and if that happened, he was almost certainly a dead man.

The first of the possemen was around the bend now and back in sight. The lead man did not seem to be gaining on the grulla, but he was not losing ground either.

Raider kept the horse on the road and raked it repeatedly with the cruel steel of his spurs. It was a hell of a way to treat a stout-hearted animal, but better the horse should bleed than Raider.

Raider twisted his neck around and got another peek at the man who was nearest him. Whoever he was, the fellow was short and seemed to be pretty light. In a long chase at such speeds that would give him an advantage, for Raider was tall and although he was lean, he was solid muscle and definitely no lightweight. His deep-seated saddle also was built for durability and comfort rather than for light weight, and the pursuer would have a real advantage when it came to the weights the two horses were carrying. The other posse members already seemed to be lagging a little to the rear, but this rider was not being left in anyone's dust.

Raider cursed and restrained himself from raking the grulla again. The animal was already giving him its best, and he did not want to do anything to add to its stress.

The calmer it ran now, the longer and harder it would run in the long haul.

The two men pounded north on the old road, rounding bends and taking the hills and dips at a hard gallop. Much of the time now, the rest of the posse was too far behind to be in sight except on the rare straight stretches. They were definitely falling farther back. The race now belonged to Raider and the rider sixty or seventy yards behind him.

They dropped down into the coulee where Raider had had the run-in with the carbine-carrying youngster, and Raider groaned. This was going to be a rough ascent if the scrambling grulla made it at all. The switchback turns rising to the top were sharp, the footing was loose gravel, and there were a thousand things that could go wrong.

The horse leaped the trickle of water that lay at the bottom of the depression, and the jolting lurch of its jump was nearly enough to unseat Raider. Stark fear kept his legs clamped like vises around the horse's barrel and saved him, barely, from taking a fatal tumble.

Up the steep trail the grulla raced. At the first switchback Raider was not sure that the animal saw that it had to turn, for it kept running full-tilt along the rising roadbed toward the drop-off at the outer edge of the curve.

Raider wanted desperately to fling his weight onto the left stirrup to turn the horse, but he did not dare. The footing was too bad and the drops too long for him to risk upsetting the grulla's precarious balance with his own 185 pounds.

At the last possible instant the grulla dropped its haunches into a sliding stop and dropped catlike down in the front end. That unexpected manuever nearly upset Raider. The horse darted violently to the left, leading with its head the way a fine cutting horse will do. Before Raider had time to adjust to the new direction, it was racing forward again, but on the opposite direction of the switchback.

They swept beneath the rock where the body of the boy probably still lay. In any event, Raider could see no sign of the youth or the Spencer carbine he had been carrying. Both must have been out of sight because of the higher elevation of the rock slab where he had fallen. At that moment Raider would have given almost anything for that boy to be there still, alive and on the prod, because he almost certainly would have started throwing lead when he saw the posse coming at a run behind the fleeing fugitive.

The grulla made the final turnback in the same heart-stopping fashion again and, back on level ground, picked up the pace without Raider having to use his spurs.

Raider glanced back. The lead posseman must have had some difficulty negotiating the climbing turns. Perhaps it was only that he had control over his mount and was not in the helpless position Raider was and so could use his own good sense to avoid the rocky death a fall would have meant. Whatever the reason, he was now a good twenty or twenty-five yards farther back.

"Come on, you pretty little oat muncher," Raider urged. "Get us out of this."

They raced north along the old Spanish road, and Raider recognized the landmarks around him. Coming up was the place where the cattle had been driven west toward the mountains.

It took no great time or thought for Raider to make his decision. If the rustlers—and they must have been the same crowd the posse thought they had found when they caught Raider—were up this trail, they might well have another guard posted somewhere ahead.

Finding a guard point or the beef herd was the only slim hope Raider had of getting out of his hands-tied dilemma.

He threw his weight into the left stirrup, and the horse dutifully responded by swinging off the roadway and heading west. The country rose gently here, and for a moment Raider was afraid he had turned off the road too soon and might miss the trail laid down by the passing cattle.

Soon, though, he saw what he was looking for. The yucca and the sparse grasses were knocked down and trampled in a line stringing out ahead of him, pointing toward a notch in the mountain walls that looked like just another fold in the jagged rock faces of the Front Range.

"Not much more now. I hope," Raider told the horse through gritted teeth.

The posseman was still behind him, holding his distance at about a hundred yards. There were no others in sight now, but one was enough to pull a trigger.

The grulla seemed to sense that they were following the trail of the cattle. The animal must once have been a trail horse, and probably a cutter at that. It lined out along the marks of passage left by the herd and followed the trail around a series of upthrust rock spires that rose red and daggerlike from the gravelly soil.

Behind him Raider heard a gunshot. The posseman must have thought he was in danger of losing Raider in the country they were entering and was firing wildly in the general direction of Raider and the grulla horse. At this range he could have scant hope of hitting either horse or rider.

The trail curved around a clump of the blood-colored rock spires and climbed abruptly into a deep pass that Raider had not suspected would be there. The pass seemed now to be an easy way up into the mountains, but it could be seen only from a high, close position in among the foothills.

The footing was bad, and once the tiring grulla stumbled. Raider could not fault the horse. They must have come a half a dozen miles already at a pace that would have made a racehorse proud. The question was whether it was going to be enough.

The single close pursuer got back into sight around the last sharp turn and again let loose a haphazard shot uphill toward Raider.

The grulla topped out on the climbing trail and charged straight ahead into the narrow, rising pass. A creek bed meandered through the cut and made the footing impossible for such speed, but Raider did not dare try to slow the grulla. He was risking the horse's legs at such a gallop, but he was risking his own neck if he slowed.

Throw the dice and pay the piper what he's due, son. A gambling man can't beg nor back off either one, he thought.

He spurred the horse on through the melon-sized rocks in and near the creek bed.

Off to one side Raider thought he saw a flash of color that might have been a late-blooming clump of mountain wildflowers or might have been something else. He could not take the time to look, but he had a clear impression that the color was not from flower petals. He hoped against hope that it was not.

Seconds later he heard the sharp crack of rifle fire, completely unlike the hollow thud of shotgun shells. The firing began and burst forth into a short, wicked little fire fight much like the skirmishes he had heard so many times during the war years—a sudden flurry of heavy firing that ripped out with a crackle like cloth being ripped. And then there was silence again.

Thank goodness, Raider told himself. A guard point keeping the posse off the herd. It had to be.

He sat back against the cantle and leaned his weight back to signal the grulla that the run was over.

"Whoa, boy. Whoa it down now."

Raider felt weak. His legs were quivering with fatigue

and the aftermath of fear. His hands, he realized suddenly, hurt like hell. He must have been yanking against the ropes while he rode, although he had not been aware of it.

He did not really care. The cards seemed to have been reshuffled for a new game, and he was more than willing to exchange this one for the last. No matter what this crowd was like, they had to be better than that posse of idiots.

The grulla came to a halt, sweat-lathered and heaving, and Raider slumped wearily in the saddle. He was content to wait until the rustlers came to collect him.

CHAPTER SIX

A dozen men or more, at least as many as were in the posse outside the entrance to the steep-walled cut, came fogging it out of the flat, hanging valley that Raider could see ahead of him.

These riders were no town dwellers. They were rough men, unkempt in appearance and heavily armed. They rode tough, scruffy ponies already hairing up for the coming winter, and they rode them with the casual, confident grace of Comanches. And that, Raider realized, was a high compliment indeed.

At least half the men or more had the dark hair and dark flashing eyes and swarthy look of Mexicans or half-breeds. Each of them carried at least two revolvers and a carbine. Several had additional pistols slung in flapped military-style holsters on their saddles. This was a fighting crew, Raider could see.

Two of the men stopped beside his blowing grulla, while the rest thundered on toward the opening of the cut where the firing had been coming from. There was no more gunfire to be heard now, and Raider guessed that the posse had not had the guts to tough it out in a pitched fight against well-entrenched riflemen.

It was one thing to chase an unarmed, firmly tied fugitive who would be easy prey for a hangman's noose when he was caught. It was quite another thing to

41

charge a nest of determined riflemen who had the advantages of cover and high, hidden positions.

It took a man with determination and a peck of grit in his craw to ride into the face of an enemy position. It made a man feel naked and hollow in the gut to do that, and the town posse, whoever they were and wherever they had come from, did not seem to have the willingness to die on someone else's behalf. They were willing to kill, not to die. Therein lay the difference.

The two who had pulled rein beside Raider sat easy on prancing horses that had been gigged into sudden action but had not had enough of a run to work them out of that sudden agitation. The ponies pranced and curvetted beneath their riders, but the men rode them without seeming to notice, much less to mind the shifting mounts between their knees.

"*Hola, amigo,*" one of the men greeted Raider with a flashing display of teeth.

"Howdy."

"A lovely fall day, is it not?" the bandit asked politely.

"Lovely indeed. And a fine place you have here from what I can see of it. Only one thing wrong with the whole thing," Raider said. "I can't seem to reach my cigars." He pointed with his chin toward a breast pocket. "I'd like to offer one so you can join me, but. . . ."

"Of course." The Mexican shifted his horse nearer in a pretty side pass that Raider had not even seen him signal to the horse, so slight was the required knee pressure. "Let me help you, by all means."

He took a cigar from Raider's pocket, used a Bowie with a foot-long blade to lop a quarter inch of twist from one end, and placed the stogie between Raider's teeth.

"Join me?"

The Mexican nodded and took cigars for himself and

his friend as well. The second man struck a lucifer and got all three lighted. Raider angled the cigar in his teeth to keep the curl of smoke out of his eyes and said, "I was hoping this could be a bit more comfortable, you know?"

"I know. But perhaps not yet, yes?"

So he was not going to automatically untie Raider's hands. Raider shrugged. He was a hell of a lot more comfortable at this moment than if he had stayed with the posse.

They heard a clatter of shod hooves on rock and turned to see the main body of bandits returning. At the head of the pack was a squat, powerfully built man whose face looked like antique leather and whose hair and drooping moustache were streaked with gray. The man was less heavily armed than the others, carrying only a single revolver with an unadorned walnut butt and a single, slender knife at his belt. Yet it was obvious from his carriage and the calm certainty of command etched into his features that this man was the leader.

In Spanish, he called without any hint of brag or bravado, "They flew, my friends, like blackbirds leaving the rushes. I think they will not return, welcome though they would be at any time. Perhaps we shall send them this message."

"Perhaps we have already sent them this message," one of the others offered.

"You may be correct, my good right arm," the leader said. "And so, Miguelito, what have you found here?" He pulled up beside the cigar-smoking Mexican and Raider.

The bandit sat a little straighter in his saddle when he responded. "A gringo, *mi jefe*. Somewhat indisposed." Miguel pointed toward Raider's firmly bound hands.

"You have had some troubles?" the leader asked—unnecessarily, Raider thought—in English.

"A small disagreement with your blackbirds," Raider told him. "They seemed to think I had stolen something from them. It is not polite to argue, so I left."

The tough-looking graybeard laughed. "Very wise, I think." He did not seem at all upset that Raider might have died for one of the bandit leader's sins. "Allow me to introduce myself to you. I am Juan Mace, and this place of great comfort is known as Mace's Hole." He bowed with false modesty. "In my honor, it is said. Perhaps since no one else seems to come to my little valley." He extended a hand toward Raider, offering it to be shaken, realized that his guest was still tied, and grinned. "Let us release you so we can talk in comfort," he said. With his own knife Mace cut Raider free of the rope.

Lord, but it felt good to get his hands back for his own use. Raider took a moment to rub his wrists. The blood on his wrists and hands where he had tried to wrench himself free of the bonds was already drying. The wounds were mere scrapes and should not be serious.

"Thank you," he said. And he meant it. He extended his hand and shook with Mace. "I'm Slocum. John Slocum."

It was the first name that popped into his mind. Certainly he could not use his own. He seriously doubted that a Pinkerton man would be welcome here, and Slocum's name had been one of those mentioned recently by Wagner as a potential troublemaker for the agency. Raider himself was not so sure, but the name was fresh in his mind, and he used it on the spur of the moment.

Mace nodded, and for a moment his eyes narrowed in thought. "John Slocum. I have heard of you, I think. Would this be the first time you have disagreed with the members of a posse?"

Raider shrugged. "Perhaps not quite the first time."

He hoped to hell there was no one in Mace's camp who had ever met Slocum.

"I thought not, yes." Mace tapped the brim of his wide hat. "In here it is good to keep the memory alert. Very helpful at unexpected times. You should remember that."

"I will, thanks." Raider took the cigar from his teeth, admired the ash that had been building there, and carefully flicked the ash away with the tip of his little finger. "Small pleasures are greatly appreciated at such times, are they not, Juanito?"

The familiar form of address caused several of Mace's riders to suck air in through their teeth in astonishment and probably in anger as well, but Mace himself did not seem to mind. He reached forward to grasp Raider by the forearm and gave him a friendly shake. "I like you, John. Your day has been a troubled one. Come join us for a meal."

"Thanks, I will." Raider grinned at him, replaced the cigar between his teeth, and took up his reins. It felt damned good to be able to do so.

They rode at an easy lope back into the spreading valley from which Mace and his men had so recently boiled. Once they were beyond the confinement of the entrance, Raider could see that the valley was much bigger than he had expected, a beautiful little hole set against the side of the mountains, with a cabin and set of outbuildings beside a creek near the entrance and a great deal of grass available in the distance. There were cattle grazing beyond the buildings, and someone had gone to the trouble of planting corn and some other crops. The bedraggled remains of the corn stalks showed inside a scantling fence and a number of empty rows where something else must have grown but had already been harvested.

"Mighty pretty," Raider complimented.

"Thank you. It is our home. It has been so for many

years now. Our needs are simple, you see. We work a little, play a little, spend our winters in comfort eating and enjoying ourselves. A little corn for the tortillas. A few beans and chilies to fill the tongue with flavor." He grinned. "And very good beef. We do so dearly love our *carne*, you know?"

"I know," Raider said with a laugh. It was perfectly obvious that the posse members had supplied Juan Mace with his winter's beef. So much easier than tending a herd all summer long just so you would have something to eat later.

They turned the horses loose—still saddled and with their cinches tight—in a corral that looked somewhat tumbledown until a closer inspection showed that it was tightly constructed, even if it did seem to have been repaired and added to frequently over past years. The men tied their reins up but left the horses bridled, ready to leap into and take off at a run without notice if the need should arise again. It was an interesting precaution, Raider noted, and said much about both the man and the place. He hoped he would never have to come back here in the line of duty. It would be a hard place to take.

"This way," Mace invited. "It should be ready for us. We were preparing to eat when we heard the sound of the rifles."

Raider filed with the others into what at first glance he had thought was a low-roofed shed. Instead it proved to be a dining hall, most of it dug into the ground with only the top half of the log walls protruding to form a partial dugout, partial building. It would have been very easy to keep warm in the winter, he realized, which must be a problem once the hole was closed in with drifted snow. Once that happened, the community here would be completely isolated, possibly for months at a time, unless a person had snowshoes or some of those long wooden slats known as Norwegian snowshoes.

The place was dominated by a long table big enough to accommodate the whole of Mace's crew. It was already set with stacks of tin plates and cups and steaming pots of stew, and it smelled a lot better than it looked. The mixture had a pleasantly spicy aroma that set Raider's nostrils twitching and his mouth watering.

"It's been a while since I smelled anything that good," he said. Even the elegant meals he had taken in Denver had not had that kind of solid appeal.

"I hope you will enjoy it," Mace said courteously. He waved Raider into a chair at the right of the one massive armchair placed at the head of the long table where Mace himself would obviously sit.

"That is my son's place," he volunteered. "But he is now at work protecting us, you see. He will not be here until tomorrow unless he sees the posse leave and realizes that they are no more a danger to us."

Raider nodded. He sat and began to reach immediately for a plate and the tempting stew ladle but stopped himself when he realized that none of the others were digging into the meal. There must be some formality at Juan Mace's table.

Mace smiled approvingly at him and then nodded briefly down the length of the table. All the men ducked their heads, and most of them crossed themselves quickly. There was a short undertone of moving lips and muttered voices—praying perhaps—and then the table erupted into activity as the men grabbed for the ladles and began heaping their plates with savory chunks of beef and beans and onion floating in thick gravy.

"Mighty fine," Raider said. "You're a generous host."

"It is with pleasure that I share my modest table with so famous a man as John Slocum," Mace demurred.

"Famous? I sure was hoping to avoid that. A man in my business can get along better when he ain't so well known," Raider said with a smile. *That* was true enough, even if he was flying false colors.

"I understand this, of course, but I assure you, you are a welcome guest here at any time. The things I have heard of you I admire."

"Again, Juanito, you are very kind."

The meal tasted every bit as good as it had smelled, and Raider loaded his gut until he could not pack in any more. The eating was not done at a leisurely pace. The men bolted down their food and left as soon as they were through. Within ten minutes or so, Raider, Mace, and the man called Miguel were the only ones remaining in the place.

Miguel had been seated at the far end of the table. He moved down to sit on Mace's left side when he was through eating.

"A cigar, gentlemen?" Raider offered.

"You have only the two of them left," Miguel said. "I remember this from before."

"Sorry. But I reckon I do have enough for the two of you then."

Mace accepted the offer calmly, as if such courtesies were his due, but Miguel declined. Raider lit the stogies for himself and Juan Mace. He drew the rich smoke into his lungs in contentment and leaned back in his chair.

"Now that right there is the satisfaction that life is all about, you know?"

"Indeed, John. It has been a great length of time since I had a smoke the equal of this one."

"Cuban," Raider said. "I picked them up in Denver. Fifty cents apiece and worth every bit of it."

"Indeed," Mace said appreciatively. "Perhaps soon I should send to the city for a case of them."

For all the ragged appearance of the place, the old boy hadn't quivered at the price, Raider noticed. He must be making out pretty well in this little hidey-hole at the edge of nowhere. Perhaps well enough to justify

Allan Pinkerton's attention. Certainly enough to justify a report to the home office about it.

A slatternly woman, scrawny and with long black hair that was ropy with an accumulation of grease, came into the dining hall and began to pile the dirtied dishes into the pots that still held the remains of the stew.

Miguel absently fingered the cheeks of her ass while she worked at their end of the table. She did not seem to notice.

"That," Mace said, "is la señorita Angelica. Unlike her name, perhaps, but useful. You are free to enjoy her if you wish. There is no fee for such things here. In fact, please do not offer her any coins if you should feel the need for relief. Such a thing could only cause troubles, you understand?"

"Whatever you prefer," Raider said noncommittally. The truth was that he could not imagine himself so hard up that he would want to roll with the unlovely Angelica. Not after having spent so much time with Milly up in Denver.

He chuckled at the thought. Be honest about it, man, he told himself. There's been times enough in the past and probably would be again in the future when Angelica or a scag even uglier than her would be enough to get him so hard that a cat couldn't scratch it. When you haven't had any for a while, all it has to be is a warm place to stick it. At times like those, you close your eyes and ignore the smell of the last customer's sweat and come, and you let 'er rip.

Mace must have caught the hint of smile that flickered over Raider's lips, for the bandit leader grinned and said, "Exactly. A woman is a woman, no? And we have had the poor fortune to lose two of them recently. It was terrible, but I have no doubt that we shall be able to find replacements before the snow comes. If not," he shrugged, "I personally will give the sweet Angelica a crock of grease to assure her comfort." He laughed, and

Miguel laughed with him. Raider thought, though, that perhaps Miguel's laughter was not so easily delivered as Mace's.

"Come, my friend," Mace said, rising from his padded armchair. "You must be weary now. I will show you where you can sleep." He hesitated. "It would not be good for you to try to leave us during this night," he cautioned. "In the light of morning, when you are rested and your thoughts are in order, there is a thing I would discuss with you. An assistance you might render to me. And to yourself as well."

Raider nodded. He had been fairly warned, he took it. If he tried to get back to the road, he would be fair game for the men still on guard there. And that posse might still be hanging around waiting for just such a second chance at any of Mace's men foolish enough to put their noses into the trap. This seemed a poor time to be bucking tigers.

"I'll go unsaddle," Raider said.

"Very good," Mace said. "Join me inside my house when you are ready."

CHAPTER SEVEN

Raider slept poorly that night. The bunks were scattered out in a number of small half-dugouts, with three or four men to a building instead of the whole crew being in one large structure. It made sense when Raider thought about it, because any nocturnal attacker would have his troubles trying to bottle up so many different structures, while with a single bunkhouse a few men with rifles or shotguns and a couple burning torches could cause real havoc. Raider had seen it done that way, and he appreciated Juan Mace's thoughtfulness on the subject.

In the shelter where Raider was shown a bunk there were only two other men, one a Mexican who went by the name of Cabbo for no reason that Raider could comprehend, the other an American gunnie called Slick. Both were tough, competent-looking men who had little to say and tried to make no great show of their own importance.

While his companions for the night were not disturbing, his lack of a Colt certainly was. Raider was used to sleeping with a revolver close at hand, and his was still in the possession of the posseman they called Jesse. Or at least it had been the last time he saw it. He missed the comfort of knowing it was there if he should need it.

Instead he slept with his hand on the bone hilt of his

heavy Bowie. The posse had not bothered to take that from him. Probably they had no idea how much damage a good man with a knife can cause, and so they had not thought it important to take his away. But still, a knife is scant protection against men with guns, and Raider was rarely comfortable without a gun, even among friends. With strangers, as these men were, he was definitely ill at ease. He spent much of the night wishing that the Bowie knife had a cylinder with six large chambers and one of those dinguses underneath to make the thing go boom. He always slept lightly, ready to wake at the slightest noise or disturbance, but this night he passed more awake than asleep, dozing only occasionally in short snatches of rest. He was glad to see the morning sun arrive.

He got up at the first hint of dawn and pulled his hat and boots on without waking Cabbo and Slick. He let himself out of the solidly built, tight-fitted door and up the slight incline to the level ground outside.

No one else seemed to be up yet. Raider reached automatically for his breast pocket, then remembered that he was out of cigars again. He cursed a little under his breath, but only mildly. It was not that important.

He walked to the creek, removed his hat and shirt, and used the icy flow of sweet water to wash his head refreshingly clear of the night's uneasiness and scrub away the stink of fear-sweat he had collected during that run-in the day before. He felt much better after the partial bath. He smoothed his wet hair back with his hands and returned his hat to its accustomed place.

The morning air, even without the cold water, was chill enough to be bracing. Between the two he was wide awake now and ready for anything.

He checked the grulla and saw that it was fine. His saddle hung apparently unmolested on the top fence rail where he had put it the evening before, and the hay bunks were freshly loaded with well-cured stems of good mountain grasses. Probably, he thought, cut on one of the natural meadows along the streams that cut down into this hanging valley of Mace's.

He made no move to go near the grulla. The hay bunks had been filled not too many minutes before so that it was plain there was someone else awake and shifting about already. Raider did not want anyone to think he was going for his horse in an effort to slip away while the occupants of Mace's Hole were asleep. That would not do at all.

Instead, satisfied that the animal was properly tended, he turned toward the dining hall, where he hoped he might find a cup of coffee to start the day with.

Inside he surprised Angelica at her chores. She was dealing a stack of tin plates to the table settings as an accomplished gambler would deal cards to the points of a felt-covered table.

She seemed startled when he appeared unexpectedly. She jumped a little, and Raider gave her a smile of apology.

"Sorry," he said. "I just came in hopin' to find some coffee."

The woman nodded and inclined her head toward a curtain-hung doorway that led into a hole toward the back of the big room. "It's prob'ly ready now. If I set it out too early, it gets cold. Th' men don't like that."

"Thanks."

Raider entered the tiny, almost entirely underground room that seemed to serve as a kitchen. He had seen closets bigger, but there was an iron stove against one wall and a workbench on the opposite wall. At the rear was a genuinely lovely old sideboard of dusty and scarred but obviously fine-quality rubbed mahogany. The doors on the front of the massive old piece had been carved in bas relief by a craftsman who had known his business, and above the doors there were small insets of a lighter wood with garden scenes painted on them—pictures of beautifully gowned women in swings amid lacy-looking greenery, while other ladies and some gentlemen in tall hats and cravats and choker collars used some sort of long mallets to hit little round balls into wickets stuck in the grass. Raider was intrigued enough to kneel close in the poor light of a single lantern to make out the pictures beneath the dust and grime that had accumulated on them. He wondered how Juan Mace had ended up with such a fine piece of furniture. To call it simply out of place here would have been a monumental understatement.

A huge pot of coffee was on the stove directly over the firebox. Raider could hear the purr of a well-laid fire inside the metal and the soft boil of water inside the pot. He used a rag to protect his hands from the heat of the pot and poured himself a cup. The coffee was weak, not yet fully boiled and ready, but he was ready enough for it that he did not care if it was ready for him. He took a sip and felt the warmth burn down his gullet and spread into his belly. On a crisp morning that was almost as bracing as a knock of good liquor.

Griddlecakes and slabs of fresh beef coming up for breakfast, he observed with satisfaction. The makings were laid out neatly on the work counter, where they would be ready at hand when the cook piled into them. The cook seemed to be Angelica since there was no sign of anyone else around. He wondered if she had had to fill the hay bunks before starting breakfast.

Raider carried his cup out into the much bigger and better-lighted dining hall and slouched into the same chair he had used the night before.

"Pretty day, isn't it?" he offered in an effort toward politeness.

The woman grunted. After a moment she added, "If you're wanting to fuck, I already promised Bruce for after eatin'." She gave him a hooded glance and said, "You're a likely lookin' one, ain't you. If you figure you can't wait your turn, it's all right. I could take keer of you before I ring the bell. There won't be none of them moves anyhow until I call that it's on the table."

"I can wait," Raider said. He was still a long way from needing anything of this sorry bawd.

She shrugged. "Suit yourself." She finished preparing the table, set out some bowls of brown sugar and lard to spread onto the griddlecakes, and disappeared into the kitchen.

Raider could hear her busying around, and a few moments later he caught the delightful aroma and heard the soft sizzle of frying meat. She couldn't finish soon enough to suit him.

The door to the dining hall swung open, and one of Mace's men entered. Raider had seen the fellow the night before but did not know his name.

He was one of the Americans, a burly fellow with bright red hair and a mass of shaggy red fur covering his face and peeking out at the throat of his shirt. He wore a .45 slung at his right hip and another in a cross-draw holster on his left side. As far as Raider could see, he was not carrying a knife. He did not seem at all pleased to see Raider in the room before him.

"What the fuck are you doin' here?" he demanded immediately.

Raider lifted his coffee cup toward him. "Taking the chill off." He did not like the man's manner. Raider gave him a tight, humorless grin and challenged, "That bother you some?"

"Damn right it does," the redhead responded. "I got the first hump on ol' Angie this morning. So get the hell outta here an' wait your turn."

Raider cocked his head to the side and eyed the man. "You'd be Bruce in that case. She said you were first." He shrugged. "I'm in no big hurry. You do what you want. I figure to finish this cup of coffee an' have my breakfast."

"You admit it, by God. You tried to butt your way in ahead o' me, didn't you? Bastard! You'd already o' been slopping up her cunt if she hadn't wanted me better. Prick."

Mildly, Raider told him, "Think what you like, mister, but was I you, I'd be cautious what names I use to strangers. If I got mad, I might take a notion to shave that beard of yours. Usin' tweezers."

"I'll call you what I damn well please, any time I want to," Bruce threatened. He looked positively delighted at the opportunity for a fight. "You ain't wearing a gun. Is that what's makin' you so brave? Figure I won't shoot a poor little pipsqueak that ain't armed?"

"I don't suppose I need to ask you for any favors. You'd be easy enough to take without that."

Bruce threw his head back and laughed. "B'God, I think you're gonna get me all warmed up an' ready for ol' Angie. Busting your head open is gonna be fun." He flopped his arms around to loosen them and flexed his muscles. Even beneath the cloth of his shirt, his arms looked like coils of thick rope. "Mace gave us the word we wasn't to kill you 'less you tried to run. He never said nothing about busting your ass in two."

Raider continued to lounge in his chair with the coffee cup in his right hand. He eyed the redhead closely and wondered if this time he might have bitten off more than he wanted to chew. With a gun it would have been no contest, but the bastard was a big one and seemed fit and ready.

"What're you waitin' on?" Bruce demanded.

"Not a thing." Without any warning in his tone of voice or his expression, Raider sent the still-hot contents of his cup curving through the air toward Bruce's eyes. He launched his own much more substantial weight behind the hot coffee and gave the redhead a solid head butt in the solar plexus that knocked the breath out of the big man in a loud, explosive gush.

Raider knew exactly how he intended to finish it—
and quickly—with a series of boots to the redhead's
head and throat as soon as he went down from the first
rush.

But Bruce had been there before. He had not gotten
the scars on his knuckles from punching blocks of wood,
and he was no stranger to rough-and-tumble.

No sooner had the head butt been delivered than
Raider felt a powerful smash against the side of his jaw.
Bruce had been unable to stop Raider's attack, but he
had sent a fist slashing down viciously.

Raider wobbled backward, momentarily stunned, his
ears ringing and his brain fogged. The big bastard was
quick, much quicker than Raider had guessed.

Bruce went sprawling backward as Raider had intended, and for a moment the redhead was on the ground
on his back, where Raider's boots could have finished
him. But at that critical moment Raider was in no
condition to continue his attack the way he had expected. Instead, he was reeling in the opposite direction,
shaking his head and trying to get his senses back in
order.

Bruce scrambled to his feet and stood for a moment
doubled over, gulping for air to refill his rudely emptied
lungs. Raider leaned against a rock- and log-faced wall
and shook his head again. The cobwebs seemed to be
clearing a little.

For a time the two men stood staring at each other,
trying to take the other's measure.

The redhead snarled. "Now you *are* in for it."

"You got to earn it, mister," Raider said. "I don't
come free."

Crouched, their fists balled, they began shuffling toward and around each other, each looking for an opening. If he got the chance, Raider would cripple or kill
the redhead. He was sure the other man had the same
intentions toward him. Fighting between grown men is

not the same roly-poly good fun as it is between small boys.

Raider dropped his left shoulder, leaned forward quickly, and then, just as quickly, drew back.

Bruce launched a crushing right hand toward the spot where he had expected Raider's head to be. The fist whistled past Raider's chin a good four inches wide of its mark, and Raider used the opportunity to pile his own cocked right into Bruce's ribs immediately beneath the man's armpit. The blow landed solidly and well. Raider could feel it shaking his own frame. Being on the receiving end of that one must have been discouraging.

Once again, though, the redhead was not going to roll over and die just because Raider had asked him politely. Having missed with the right fist, Bruce flung his arm in a backhanded sweep. His knuckles connected with Raider's head, on solid bone too high to do any damage, but hard enough to bring tears of quick pain into Raider's eyes.

He was a powerful shit, Raider conceded, and awfully quick.

They squared off as they had before and continued their shuffling circle around each other.

Raider gave him the same shoulder feint for the second time and, exactly as he had before, followed it with a right. But this time the right too was a fake. When Bruce crossed with a hard left that would have taken Raider on the point of the jaw, Raider twisted his body abruptly to the left and brought his right boot flashing up in a kick that barely missed Bruce's kneecap, landing instead on the slab of muscle covering his lower thigh.

Sharp pain drained Bruce's face of color even from that misdirected kick. The redhead bawled out his rage in a loud roar and, dropping all notions of finesse or fighting skill, charged directly at Raider.

There was no way to avoid a rush like that, and for

several long moments the two men stood chin to chin, trading punches, one chopping body shot after another, their arms churning like pistons linked to the same shaft. Both were taking heavy punishment. A steady rain of fists like that could not be maintained long by any man.

They broke apart, each stepping backward at the same time, as if they had sat down and agreed in advance just how many punches each was willing to sustain. Both men were breathing heavily.

"Ready to quit?" Bruce taunted.

"Uh huh," Raider told him between gasps. "Soon as I finish you."

"Then you got a long ways to. . . ." The words had been a ruse. Bruce interrupted them with a renewed attack aimed at Raider's breadbasket.

Raider darted away lightly and looped a hard right over Bruce's shoulder, catching him on the side of his head—Raider had been hoping for his jaw—solidly enough to send the bruiser to his knees.

Raider stepped forward to plant a finishing boot to the man's head. He never delivered the kick.

Instead, he found himself being plucked off the ground by both arms and lifted bodily away from the redhead. He had not noticed anyone else entering the building, but then his attention had been focused elsewhere.

"Stop! Now!" It was a command with the sharp ring of authority behind it.

Miguel, Raider saw now, Juan Mace's second in command. Miguel had Raider by the left arm, and Cabbo had him by the right. When he saw who they were, Raider quit trying to struggle against their grasp.

Bruce began to launch himself from the floor, but Miguel's outthrust palm was enough to pull him up short.

"No more," Miguel said.

Bruce did not like it, but he accepted it. Discipline was tighter around this outfit than Raider had suspected from the little he had seen before.

"Leave this one alone," Miguel ordered, staring at Bruce. "He may be one of us. You know Juanito's rule."

"And if he is not?" Bruce demanded. He screwed his mouth into a face and spat. There was blood mixed with the sputum that hit the floor.

"Then it is your affair," Miguel told him. To Raider he said, "We do not permit fighting among our people. Remember this."

Raider nodded. Hell, he was ready to quit. He'd been able to get Bruce onto the ground, set for finishing, once. He was not at all sure he could do it again.

"*Angelica!*" Miguel called. "Food. Now!"

CHAPTER EIGHT

Bruce bolted a skimpy meal and was the first to leave the dining hall. Raider got the impression that he was not especially popular with the man, and perhaps Bruce would have preferred someone else's company. The redhead did not even wait to claim rights to Angelica but growled something to her on his way out.

Raider took his own good time, finishing off his steak and a pile of the flour griddlecakes and then another hunk of meat before he sat back with a final cup of coffee. By then the last of the rest of the men were leaving too.

Mace had not made an appearance during the meal. From the conversation around the table, Raider gathered that this was customary at the morning meal.

When only Raider remained at the table, Angelica emerged from the dark little hole that was her kitchen. She brought a pot of steaming hot coffee. The tin pitchers of the stuff deposited on the table before the meal were cooling by now.

She took Raider's cup out of his fingers, dumped the coffee from it into one of the pitchers, and then poured him a fresh, much hotter cup.

"Why, thanks." He had not been expecting any such treatment.

The woman sat at the table opposite him, where Miguel had sat the night before.

"I was listenin' a while ago," she said. "I heard you tell Bruce that I'd held you off o' me. I don't rightly know why the silly son of a bitch woulda believed you, but I reckon if he hadn't, he'd've been beating my ass 'stead of trying to whup yours. Anyway, what I'm sayin', mister, is that I thank you. I get bruises an' broke bones enough around here. You saved me from more of the same. I'm truly grateful."

Raider shrugged. "It wasn't any big deal."

"It was to me. If there's anything I can do for you . . . I mean more'n just pussy, too. You already got the use of that, same as the rest of 'em. But I mean *any*thing. You let me know, hear?"

"I'll remember that, Angelica. It's kind of you to offer." He meant that too. The woman had nothing, was nothing. A woman in her position really had nothing to offer a man except her body, and as she had said herself, he already had been given free rein with that any time he chose to use it. When you got right down to it, then, the poor creature really had nothing left to give except the feeble words of thanks, and most people depreciated those by overuse. In her case, he knew, it was the very best she had to give, and that was exactly the way he accepted it.

She must have been able to tell in his tone of voice the sincerity he felt because she blushed—until then Raider would have said that it was impossible for a slattern like Angelica to blush—and grabbing her apron in strong hands, wringing the cloth until he thought it might rip, she fled from the table and scurried back toward the security of her tiny kitchen.

As Raider left the building, he very nearly bumped headlong into Miguel, who was approaching at a fast walk.

"It is time you are finished, *amigo. El jefe* asks that you join him. He is at his home. Go now, please."

"Sure." Raider stuck his hands into his pockets and ambled across the bare, beaten earth of the compound yard toward Mace's neat little cabin.

Raider had spent a few hours there the night before, in a small, he might even call it cozy, little room tacked onto the side of the place. They had had a few drinks and had spoken of nothing important, and Raider had left Mace and Miguel alone there when he went to bed. There was an outside door to that small room, and he headed toward it now.

"Not to the side," Miguel called behind him. "Go into the house itself, please. That is where Juanito waits for you."

Raider nodded absently and shifted his course slightly. The front door was closed, and so he stopped and knocked before he entered.

"Come," Juan Mace called from within.

Raider let himself in and stood there for a moment in amazement.

The main part of the cabin, small though it was and rough on its exterior, was a study in elegance in miniature. He had seen grand rooms in St. Louis that were not nearly so well appointed.

The draperies at the windows were made of rich, plush velvet in a deep shade of red, trimmed in gold lace and gold tassels. The floors—they must have been smoothed wood, but he could not tell from where he stood—were covered with rich-looking carpet or rugs cut to fit, rugs carrying an intricate design that included old flowers and, he thought, dragons, mostly in cream and gold and yellow and tan shades.

The furnishings were even more heavily carved and constructed than the old sideboard he had noticed in the kitchen. They were upholstered and deeply padded and looked as if a man could sink into them and have to call in a pulley hoist to get himself out again.

There were no lanterns but lamps of pewter and porcelain with hand-painted milk-glass globes. Stemware and a brandy decanter stood on a small table beside the most massive of the several chairs in the front room. Juan Mace sat smiling in that chair.

"Is it too early for the brandy, John Slocum?" Mace asked.

Still stunned, Raider shook his head. "I might could use one as a matter of fact."

Mace laughed out loud. "You are surprised, yes?"

"I am surprised. Yes."

"Even the men, all except Miguelito and perhaps one or two more, they would be as surprised."

"You're a man of taste, Juanito." Raider crossed the expanse of soft carpet and accepted the snifter that Mace held out to him. Mace indicated a chair, and Raider sat in it gingerly, fighting back an impulse to brush off the seat of his jeans before he sat.

"I agree," Mace said. "I am a man of taste. Also of ambition. You know this feeling too, John Slocum?"

"I do," he admitted. "I never indulged it as deep as you seem to be doing. Not at any digs of my own, anyhow, though I enjoy quality whenever I can afford it. Which ain't real often." That was true enough on a Pinkerton's salary. It wasn't the money that kept him in the business.

"This I understand," Mace said with a sage nod. "I too wish for more such opportunity. I would help you achieve what you wish, as you may help me achieve what I wish. This is the reason I have called you here. I believe you may be a man with talents I can make use of, yes?"

"A gun?"

Mace waved the suggestion aside as if it were nothing. "Pah! Guns. A thousand men I can buy who can use a gun. Ten thousand. Some of them even brave men. No, it is not a gun that I need, nor even bravery, though I understand that you have this too, and it will be useful." He took a shallow sip from his glass. Raider did the same.

"Go on," Raider said.

Mace nodded. "In good time, yes." He took another small drink.

Raider decided that *el jefe* was not going to be rushed. For some reason he seemed to be enjoying this, relishing his thoughts the way he was the excellent brandy. Fine, Raider thought. It was his party. Raider sat back deeper in the luxurious chair and crossed his legs. He was in no hurry. Less of one than he had been in now that Mace had piqued Raider's interest with his surroundings and his hints of money to become available.

Mace smiled, a slow, catlike smile. He blinked twice, and the smile disappeared. "Forgive me. My thoughts have been elsewhere for the moment."

"De nada."

"We were speaking of guns and bravery, I believe. They are both simple matters and often found in simple men. What I want of you, John Slocum, is more than this. You are a man of intelligence. This I have heard and this I believe for myself. Our talk last night, it meant nothing to you, or so you thought. It meant much to me. I wanted to know the quickness of your mind. You showed it to me, perhaps without so much as knowing that you did so."

"If you say you were grilling me, then I reckon you were. But you're right. I never knew you were doing it."

Mace seemed to accept that as a high compliment. He smiled with pure delight. "Thank you. I am, you would then agree, not a simple-minded *jefe* of ruffians and *bandidos?*"

"I wouldn't have called you simple *before* we had this talk, Juanito. I damn sure won't now."

Mace shrugged. "There are many who would not agree with you, *amigo*. They know I am here. They regard me as a nuisance. They take me no more seriously than this, but they are wrong. In the years I have made Mace's Hole my home—and made it a famous if disreputable part of local history—they have not been able to defeat me nor to drive me away. They have come to accept me as a part of life. And to despise me as just a brigand, a man of no consequence."

"Self-defense," Raider said.

"What?"

"I said that's plain old self-defense. They can't whip you. I gather that they've tried. So if they want to keep their own self-respect, they got to find ways to look down on you. Beat you in their heads if they can't on the ground. Like I said, self-defense."

"Yes!" Mace yelped, almost bouncing out of his chair with his excitement. "Yes, exactly so. You *do* understand me, John. You *are* the man of the quick mind as I had determined. Self-defense." He grinned. "I must remember this." His face, lined with age and weather and the harshness of life, capped with steely gray as it was, looked almost youthful in his pleasure. "Self-defense. Yes."

Raider took another birdlike sip of his brandy. Damn, but it was good stuff. Equal to anything he had been served in Denver. Maybe better. Raider wondered again how Juan Mace might have come by anything so fine as his liquor and his furniture so deep in the middle of nothing as this pretty little mountain valley was. Hell, why not, he thought. He asked.

Mace laughed. "Simple," he said. "As simple as those fools think me to be. We are but a few miles below the Arkansas River, yes?"

Raider nodded. He remembered crossing it not long before finding the tracks that eventually had led him to Mace, albeit unwillingly.

"The river, John, it is the path the suppliers of the high mines must take. It is a road made by the hand of nature, yes?"

"Sure," Raider agreed. It had always been that way, probably always would.

"Along this road of the gracious Mother," Mace said, "passes all of the wondrous things the mines and the miners desire. Along it comes too the gold they send back out from the bosom of the Mother."

Raider nodded.

"I have been a careful man, John. There are people in my pay who will tell me what passes on this road. And when. I have chosen with care, without greed. I have taken that which I needed and that which I wished. Never, ever have I taken the gold the men ship out of the mountains. It has not been that I did not know when they would send it down, no. Although the fools who despise me have believed this to be so. No, John, I knew and I know that the gold is the thing they will most strongly defend and, if I take it, will most strongly protest. So I leave them their handfuls of yellow metal, and they leave me alone and think I am without value, not worth the trouble and the blood it would take to move Juan Mace and his men from this place." He laughed. "They know the road to my hole almost as well as I do. The inside of it they do not know at all."

"Patience," Raider said, "and wisdom. You haven't done badly here, Juanito."

"I have not done badly," Mace agreed. "I intend to do far better. With the help of some with guns and some with knowledge. Perhaps with your help, John."

Raider thought he knew where the conversation was going now. Not the details, to be sure, but the general direction. And information like that might well be of interest to the Denver office.

"Like you said yourself, Juan, those boys will get really pissed off if you go taking one of their shipments. It would have to be one hell of a load to make it worth your while. Or mine."

Mace laughed happily. "See, John? Did I not tell you? You are a man of wisdom as well as knowledge. A man with the quick mind. I like this. I respect it. But you are only guessing, yes? It is true. I would be tempted no more easily than you. You would like a sweet roll perhaps, fresh from the oven and sprinkled with cinnamon and white sugar?"

Raider looked at his brandy snifter. It was empty. And while his belly was still comfortably full from breakfast, it had been an awful long time since he had had a fresh-baked sweet. Besides, there was something about the look in Mace's eyes that said he wanted to serve one of the things. It wouldn't hurt to humor the old boy.

"I wouldn't mind that, Juanito," Raider said.

"Nor would I." Mace smiled again. In anticipation, Raider thought, although a bit of baked dough, no matter how good, seemed to Raider hardly a good reason for the kind of excitement that Mace was now displaying.

Over his shoulder, Mace called, "The sweets now, my sweet." He stood.

Puzzled, Raider rose also.

A moment later a door to the back part of the small house opened. Through it walked—a vision.

She could not have been real. There could not have been a woman this side of Denver, hell, this side of Boston, as fine as this one.

Raider began to feel his face coloring with embarrassment. He could feel the beginnings of a hard-on just from the first surprised glance, and his mouth was probably hanging open like a flytrap. He gulped and felt shakier than he had when fighting with the redhead.

Jesus! he thought. I'm dreaming or drunk or dead or all three.

CHAPTER NINE

The woman was a study in cream and gold. Complexion of the purest, finest cream. Hair of flowing gold, long and full and meant to form a sheltering tent as she bent to give herself to a man. Eyes a tawny hazel flecked with gold, catlike and mysterious.

She was a tall woman, slender and graceful but with a full swell of breast and hip and a tiny uncorseted waist between. It was maddeningly obvious that she needed no corset, for she wore a filmy peignoir set of some flimsy, sheer material that sent Raider into a pounding agony at the sight of her.

She was no shy, shrinking violet, either. She saw the bulge at his crotch, a massive upheaval that threatened to rip out the buttons of his fly, and her reaction was a peal of laughter that sounded like carillon bells playing. Her voice was throaty and seductive. "Juan, dear, are you sure you will be able to control this one? Just look at the poor man's reaction." She laughed again and moved to him. With one hand she offered Raider a silver tray of sweet rolls. With the other she flippantly patted the bulge at his crotch. "Down, please. We do try to be civilized here. And you do always have Angelica."

Mace laughed even louder than the woman had.

"You see, John, why I labor so. This lovely thing is my, uh, *enamorada,* Elaine Volnay. Is that the right word?"

Who the hell cares about words? Raider wanted to say. He did not. He was not at all sure he could say anything just then. My God, that was a lot of woman.

She stood nearly as tall as he in her high-heeled slippers. At this range he could not avoid knowing that she was wearing a delicate but penetrating scent of some kind that cut through him as sharply and deeply as a saber could ever have done. His senses were reeling, focused completely on the sights and scents of this magnificent creature.

How she might ever have come to be with a man like Juan Mace was beyond him. But since she was, it was perfectly obvious to him. She was here and therefore so must he bè. This woman he had to possess. One way or another, whatever it might cost him, he had to have her. He had to taste her body and touch it and feel the strength of her long, beautiful legs wrapped around him. If she would give herself to him, that would be wonderful. If not, he intended to take her regardless. Taking such a woman as this would not be rape, it would be necessity. He licked his lips, hoping that this time she would know why his mouth was so dry, and tried to get himself back under control before the old bandit took offense.

"My pleasure, Miss Volnay," he said. He was not a gambler for nothing. The words came out evenly, without any hint of the passion he felt. His erection began to ebb. There would be time for that later. Of that he was positive—there would have to be.

The woman offered her hand, and the touch of her fingertips sent a renewed wave of lust racing through Raider's veins. Her fingertips were softer, silkier, more exciting than the breasts or thighs of any other woman he had ever known.

She gave him a knowing smile that held within it the secrets of all womankind, and then she turned away.

Raider stood mutely with a sweet roll in his hand—he did not remember having taken it from the tray—and tried once again to regain control of himself. He shook his head, much the same way he had after the redhead had tried to scramble his brains earlier in the morning, and the movement drew another round of laughter from both Mace and his woman.

"We do have a few rules here, John. Among them, I am afraid—no, I insist—is that Elaine is not to be touched. She is not so much as to be talked about. You understand this?"

Back in command of himself now that she no longer stood so close to him, Raider said, "Of course I understand that, Juanito. If she was mine, she wouldn't ever be touched either. Or allowed to leave the bedroom. Ever." He smiled and took a bite from the sticky roll and complimented Mace on its quality without really tasting it. It might have been compressed sawdust for all he knew or cared.

"Good, John. I am pleased that you understand this, for anyone who does not. . . ." Mace shrugged and held his hands out in unspoken apology for the events that must inevitably follow any such violation of the chieftain's prerogatives. "Sit now, my friend. We must discuss the things I wish from you."

Raider nodded. Elaine said her goodbyes and left the room, and both men returned to their seats. Raider no longer really cared what Juan Mace had up his sleeve. A gold shipment, an ore theft, stealing a load of manure, it really did not matter. Whatever Juanito wanted, he was going to get from Raider. At least until Raider got that woman. Then they would see.

Mace, businesslike again, began to talk, rapidly and with certainty. He had given his planning a great deal of time and attention, and he described his intentions without any apparent reserve. Too completely, in fact, for him to have permitted Raider to leave with that knowledge if he had decided not to become part of the plan.

By the time Mace was done, though, there was no chance of that. There would have been no chance of it even if the woman had not been part of the equation.

Incredibly enough, by the time Juan Mace was done talking, Raider was excited about it to the point that he nearly forgot the presence of Elaine Volnay elsewhere in the small house.

"My God, Juanito, you're going to make history. Do you know that? You're abso-damned-lutely going to make history. *We* are going to make it. Nobody has ever pulled off anything half that marvelous since the first caveman clunked his neighbor in the head so he could steal some meat. I *love* it. And that ain't something I'd say to just anybody."

Mace smilingly nodded his acceptance of the praise. It was, after all, his due. Mace rose and walked to Raider. He extended his hand to seal the bargain. "You are one of us now, John. Remember my few rules and we shall all be rich men on a day very near."

Raider grinned and shook the old scoundrel's hand. "It's a deal."

CHAPTER TEN

Mace led the way into the dining hall for the noon meal, with Raider at his heels. The old man's appearance caused something of a stir in the place. Raider had already been told that he always took his evening meal with his men but otherwise stayed by himself in his house. Now that Raider knew why, he could understand it. That Elaine was something, and apparently most of the men did not even know about her. Keeping her secret would be some job around a crowd like this.

The bandit chieftain nodded and smiled, acting as if it were not at all unusual for him to be there. He took his place at the head of the table, and Miguel sat at the foot. Again Raider was waved to the chair at Mace's right. Apparently that was to become his proper place at the table, and apparently that sort of formality was important to Mace.

Before the old man allowed them to begin eating, he stood and got their attention with a thumping of his spoon on the table top.

First in Spanish and then in English he told them, "I have news that will please all of us here, my dear friends and companions. This man, John Slocum, is to provide the assistance we have been needing for the venture that is to come. None of you," he smiled and pointed with his chin, "except of course the incomparable Miguel Cervaisos, yet knows what this great and wonderful thing is to be, yet each of you knows its importance, yes?"

He waited for the round of agreeing nods that followed before he went on. "Of course this is true. You all are part of my heart and of my plans. You have helped me in this without knowing what the end of it is to be. You know I have been worried." He held up a hand, even though the men had offered no vocal protest. "Yes, even I have been worried. But John Slocum is to provide the one service that I could not, my friends and brothers. He is to be considered as one of us now. You will give him the courtesies of position behind only myself and Miguel. This is what I say to you. Now, eat." He sat.

Jesus, Raider thought. Number three. That's powerful. It was also, in a way, worrisome because it was pretty plain from the expressions he saw around the table that the delight was all Mace's. Even Miguel did not look overjoyed to hear that a stranger was being run in near the top.

Raider could imagine how the redhead called Bruce would be taking it. Raider still had a lot to learn about the rules and regulations around this place, but it was clear enough that fighting was not allowed. That sounded like a fine idea until you put it into practice around a hard-bitten crowd like this. Such a rule could lead to real blowups when the pressures got to be too much to contain. And Bruce was already about fit to bust if Raider could judge it from the last look he had gotten at the man that morning.

He looked at Bruce, careful to keep his face poker-plain, and did not like what he saw there. He was reasonably sure he could take the man in a stand-up fight with fists, knives, or guns. But when a man feels that strongly against you, he is as likely to throw one into your back in the darkness as to call you out. And there isn't one man alive who can protect himself from what he can't see. If a man wanted you dead badly enough, he would find a way to get to you. Anyone who didn't believe that could ask old Abe Lincoln. How much worse would it be if Bruce—and the others—knew who this new number three really was.

They all ate in their usual mad rush to bolt the food and be gone, although why, Raider could not really understand; there didn't seem to be all that much waiting for them elsewhere. This time even Mace was finished and gone before Raider was halfway through his lunch. Finally only he and Miguel were left in the place.

Miguel drifted up the length of the table and took the recently vacated chair beside Raider.

"So," he said. "Now you are a part of us. You have taken the oath?"

"What oath?"

"You have not taken the oath then. Forget, please, that I bring it up. It is not for me to decide."

"Even if you would have decided different?" Raider prompted.

"I said that it is not my place to decide. That is *all* I said. Remember this."

"I appreciate the difference," Raider told him. "I know what you're saying. Hell, Miguel, I don't blame you. Maybe you oughta know that. I didn't ask Juan for it. He offered. It was just plain too good to pass."

Miguel nodded. "Perhaps we can get along then. For as long as it is required of the both of us. But I warn you, do not press these men. Do not taunt them or try to rule them. You they will not obey. If you conduct yourself poorly, John Slocum, it could hurt Juanito. If you hurt Juanito, I shall surely kill you. This too you should know."

"I don't doubt that for a minute," Raider said with a smile. "I'm no damn fool. I want everything to go along just the way Juan wants it to. Then I'll go my way and he will go his. Okay?"

"*Si.* Okay." He reached into a shirt pocket. "You are without your cigars, I believe. Here. You know the storeroom? There are cases more of them there. Take as many as you wish. They are for all to enjoy. And anything else you find there. Juanito is a most generous man with his friends." He grinned. "And a most bitter enemy with those who are not his friends."

Raider accepted the evil-looking little rum crook. The penny cigars were not necessarily his favorites, but they tasted better than nothing. He bit the end off the thing —you don't care about the social niceties of tip trimming when you're smoking a rum crook—and accepted a light from Miguel. The two men sat and smoked in silence.

Mace stuck his head in the door a few minutes later. "Ah, Miguel. I have found you."

"There is something you need, *jefe?*"

"A thing of no importance, but. . . ."

"*Si?*"

"Geraldo. He was not here for the meal. It is not like him to be late for a meal."

"I don't know, *jefe.* I sent the men today to replace the guards and to call Geraldo and Lewis back in." He shrugged. "They have not yet come."

"As I said, Miguel, a thing of no importance." He smiled. "They are but boys. Boys have strange lusts and even stranger needs. Things that we old men with the gray in our hair have forgotten, no?" He said that with something of a wink.

After having seen Elaine, Raider needed no lengthy explanations about that.

Hell, he thought, there are a lot of old wives' tales about grayheads not being able to get it up. But then there were a lot more about practice making perfect and such.

Why, one of the things Raider remembered reading in the Bible was that Moses had died at one hell of an age—Raider could not remember what it had been, but it was powerful—and one of the few things it had said about the old fellow was that—how had they put it? —his natural force was unabated. When he had realized what they meant, Raider had had to laugh out loud. The old boy could still get it up. And that was one of the few things that had been thought important enough to be mentioned of Moses in his last days.

So, just in case Raider lived into old age, unlikely though it might be, that was one thing he probably would not have to worry about. It was for sure something that Juan Mace wasn't fretting over.

When Mace was gone Raider said, "Yesterday Juanito mentioned a son. Geraldo?"

"Yes."

"A thing of no importance, he said. Bull."

"A thing of great importance," Miguel agreed. "The son is his greatest joy. His greatest hope."

"Even more than, uh . . . ?"

"Pah," Miguel said. "To ask such a thing tells me one thing and one thing only, Señor Slocum. It says to me that you have no sons of your own."

Raider smiled. "It's the truth."

"But of course. It is obvious. A woman, any woman, is only a place for a man to spend himself. But a son, aiee, that is the way a man lives beyond the span of his own few years. This is the only true legacy a man can leave behind him. This you did not know, John Slocum?"

For some reason Raider answered the man honestly. "It is a thing, Miguel, that I have suspected but do not wish to examine too closely. If I know it to be the truth," he shrugged, "I must look inside myself in places I might not want to go."

Miguel looked at him closely, both surprise and interest evident in his expression. He said, "I think maybe, señor, I misjudged you yesterday. Juan has said from the beginning that he wanted a man with intelligence to do the job you will do. I did not think you were that man. Now I am not so sure." He shook his head. "Always I should know better than to disagree with *el jefe*. He is a man whose judgment and friendship I place value upon."

"I know what you mean. I'll take your change of mind kindly."

Miguel nodded. He rose from his chair. "And now I must go do the things *el jefe* wants me to do but cannot ask me to do, which is to search for his Geraldo, yes?"

"Is there a whorehouse near? Maybe one with a good bar attached?"

"Not for a very long way. But perhaps near enough," Miguel said with a laugh. He gave Raider a friendly wave and left.

Alone in the big, chilly room, Raider sat and contemplated the last of his cigar. He really did not want to think about the subject Miguel had raised. Children. A man's link with tomorrow.

There would be no children for Raider. No family. No woman he could look at in his bed and know that she would be there tomorrow and next year and frying his beef in his last days. Raider was no Moses in that respect either. And he had known it for so long now that he was able to pretend that it did not matter.

As for a continuation of a man's life into tomorrow, well, Raider's life had not been so grand that it ought to be prolonged past his own lifetime. Hell, no. And he didn't want to think about it.

He heard Angelica moving around in her kitchen, beginning to stir now that it sounded like the last of the men was gone.

On an impulse, ugly scag though she was, Raider left his chair and crossed to the front door. He dropped the bar into place over it and pulled the latch string inside.

He went into the kitchen and found her there. She smiled at him in a genuine welcome, and he ignored the pleasure on her face at his appearance. What he wanted from her now was not closeness and not gratitude. Nothing human, really.

He felt an urge, a strong and almost overwhelming need to couple with her, or with anyone. To hump her the way a wolf will shove it into any bitch in heat he comes across and for perhaps the same reasons. Right at that moment Raider did not want to examine any of those reasons.

He held a finger to his lips to silence the woman and pulled her roughly against him.

Angelica's body was thin. Not voluptuously slender the way Elaine's was, but the thin, scrawny, flat-planed body of a woman who had neither enough to eat nor enough rest.

He held her tight against him for a brief instant, and in that time he could feel the boniness of her ribs and pelvis and the faint flutter of her heartbeat reaching him through the rough cloth of his shirt.

He did not want to kiss her, did not want to make love to her. He took her by the arms and shoved her down onto the packed-earth floor. She lay there uncomplaining, not protesting or questioning him.

Raider threw her skirt above her waist to get it out of the way, and automatically Angelica spread her thighs apart to receive him. She was looking at him though, damn her, and there was a light of understanding and human kindness in her eyes. He wished that she would not look at him.

He unbuckled his belt and unbuttoned his trousers and let them drop around his ankles. He was only half erect in the confusion of the emotions he was feeling, and Angelica sat up and took him in her hands and then in her mouth to help him.

Damn you, woman, he thought. Don't be kind to me. Don't understand me or help me. I don't want to be close to you or care about you. I just want to fuck you. For me, not for you. Don't you know that?

As soon as he was erect, the stimulation of her lips and tongue doing what his own strange passions could not, he reached to take her by the hair and shove her away, but she had already felt his readiness and had stretched out on the floor again with her legs open. And this time with her eyes closed and her head turned to the side. She was making it easier for him, damn her.

Raider dropped onto his knees and, without preamble or gentleness, thrust himself deep into her.

He slid into her easily. She was already wet. He hoped to hell that it was the leftover come of someone else and not any form of eagerness on her part. He did not want that kind of participation from her.

He grabbed her by the shoulders and squeezed and drove himself again and again as deep within her body as he could force himself. He could feel the jolting impact of her ass against the unyielding dirt, and the knowledge that his power must be hurting her spurred him on to an even wilder frenzy of bucking.

He buried his face in the hollow of her neck and after a time realized that he was biting her too. He did not stop.

It took Raider only a minute or two to peak. He exploded with come in a climax that was an oddly sexless physical release. No more than that.

Grunting and sweating, he collapsed onto Angelica's thin body but almost as quickly rolled off her and sat on the floor beside her. She did not move for a time, not even to close her legs. She lay there just as he had left her.

Raider sighed. He reached out and, very gently,

tugged her skirt back down and smoothed it decently across her legs. He petted the woman's shoulder and smoothed her hair.

"Angelica. . . ." He did not know what more he could say.

"You needed me," she whispered. "Would you mind if I . . . I'll tell you anyway. I want you to know. John, you really needed me just then. I could feel that you did. Ain't nobody needed me for anything, *needed* me, I mean, in as long as I can remember." She opened her eyes and sat up to face him. "Thank you, John."

Raider squeezed his eyes shut tight and worked very hard to get complete control over himself. What he was feeling right now was for schoolboys and babies, not for grown men who should know better than to get taken down by maudlin regrets.

He reached out and put a hand gently on the back of Angelica's neck and pulled her to him, nestling her head against his shoulder and petting her quietly.

For a very long time Raider and Angelica sat like that.

CHAPTER ELEVEN

Raider had read some of the penny dreadfuls that were becoming so popular, including one about Texas bad-man Sam Bass that made him sound like some kind of Robin Hood reincarnated and returned to glorious life. According to those things, a life on the run must be one wonderful experience. Bullshit! As Raider well knew from the opposite side of the fence, the facts were more boring than anything else. Except when they were frightening, cold, hungry, and otherwise damned uncomfortable. At the moment he was bored.

After all, there is only so much a man can do of sleeping and eating when there are no good poker games going, no decent whiskey to drink, and, more important, no decent whores to chase. And he certainly did not want to be getting after Angelica again. Not after that first, last, and only time.

Mace was preoccupied inside the little house that was off limits—and with good reason—except by special invitation. Miguel was not a man Raider was likely to be too friendly with, and no one else around the camp was supposed to know yet what was going on. He was, plain and simple, bored.

He investigated the storeroom and found the supply of cigars, as Miguel had promised. He also found a supply of cased firearms, to which he cheerfully helped himself. A new Colt's revolver in .44-40 caliber instead of the tried-and-true old .45 Colt, and a Winchester lever carbine in a caliber to match. Raider liked that touch. With that pair he could pack a single type of cartridge and feed both weapons. Raider had never seen an 1873 Colt in the .44-40 cartridge before and was pleased. He had heard about them, but so far, even the Pinkertons did not have the weapons. At least Mace seemed to be right up to date despite his out-of-the-way location. In more ways than one.

Raider spent the afternoon becoming acquainted with the new Colt—and noticing that no one seemed to think a thing about his having a pistol on his hip again—but his thoughts were elsewhere.

Elaine Volnay. Elaine Volnay! The name kept running through Raider's thoughts like a tune he could not get out of his head.

Elaine Volnay was one hell of a woman, and Raider had to have her. He was still sticky—and disgusted—from his encounter with Angelica, but the thought of Mace's woman continued to pound into his skull. Mere physical release inside Angelica was not going to be enough to get Mace's woman out of his mind or beyond the driving urge in his groin.

Raider walked upstream from the camp. He assumed but had not been told that he was free to move around if he wanted to, but there was no point now in making anyone nervous by getting his grulla out of the corral. And walking sure beat lying around with nothing to do.

He found a depression in the creek bed where the water was deep enough to permit some semblance of a bath, and he stripped his clothes off. The thought of Angelica's juices on him was uncomfortable. He wanted to bathe them away, and with them perhaps the memories of his being with her.

He took his time about it, scrubbing at himself repeatedly until he was satisfied that he was as clean as he could get without hot water and soap. At that, it was one hell of an improvement. He arranged the new Colt, which seemed to shoot every bit as well as the old tried-and-true model, on the creek bank close to his hand and lay down to let the slow-flowing water wash over him. Raider wallowed in the gravelly creek bed for a time, not minding the sharp scrub of rock particles under his naked back, and fished in his shirt pocket for another rum crook and a lucifer. With a full belly, a clean body, and a cigar, he felt about as good as could have been expected under the circumstances.

The circumstances, he admitted to himself, were a bit odd even, or especially, for a Pink.

Here he was, traveling under a temporarily borrowed name, one of Allan Pinkerton's top agents, and damned if he hadn't been invited into what promised to be the biggest, the finest, absolutely the grandest robbery since the beginning of time.

That did present a few problems, not the least of which was that for the first time since—hell, probably since he was a kid—Raider was seriously tempted to overthrow his responsibilities and pitch into the plan with Juan Mace for real and not just as a dodge to keep himself alive until a squad of operatives could be brought down from Denver on the first available train south. Or a special damn train, this thing being as big as it was.

Well, almost seriously. He honestly was not quite sure yet.

If it turned out that Raider could not stifle his conscience—and he had never really considered a conscience to be a human frailty before now—there were other problems that had to be met.

Doc right now was in Santa Fe expecting Raider to join him and receive another, possibly ho-hum routine assignment that Weatherbee needed his help on. His not showing up would be cause for alarm in itself, whether he tossed in with Mace or played it for the Pinkertons. Either way, unless Doc's Santa Fe job was a *real* earthshaker, his partner would be launching a frantic if not very obvious search within another four days at the outside. And unless he had the facts, Doc helping or Doc hindering could either one be a problem. Weatherbee was just plain good. Almost as good as Raider was, he had to admit. And either way it blew, Doc could blunder into a part of this and mess things up for sure.

If Raider did play it straight down the line, he had that to worry about. And he had to think about trying to get word out to Allan Pinkerton up in Denver so that the Agency and hopefully Doc as well would be aware of what was going on. And to damn well stay clear until he was ready for the kind of help they could supply.

With the Mace camp being so tightly run, that in itself could be a major problem. Raider had no idea where the nearest telegraph office was.

Or—and it was a very big question—whether Juan Mace might include the telegrapher in that office among his helpful sources of information. If Raider tried to run a wire through the wrong set of Western Union-trained fingertips, he could wind up dead for his efforts. Now *that* really seemed like a waste.

No, he decided, if he wanted to get information out, it would have to be by mail. Slower but safer. At least then he would only be broadcasting the address for public consumption; and by posting his letter in a drop instead of in person at a post office, he could even avoid that. That was, he decided, by far the safest way to go. *If* he decided to tell the Agency about any of it.

He sighed. The haul from this job could run to several millions. Several *millions!* That wasn't a piker's take.

If he managed to foul it up on behalf of the Agency, he knew, Allan would have no trouble at all claiming a ten percent recovery fee from Juan Mace's unhappy victims. After a loss like that, they and their insurance companies would be delighted to pay the Pinkertons a hefty fee for services rendered.

And in return, he knew full well, a grateful Allan would authorize Raider a perfectly normal rate of salary. If he was really lucky and Allan was *really* in a good humor, the best Raider could hope for would be that his expenses would not be questioned as closely as they usually were.

Jesus sweet Christ, he thought, what a fucking problem a conscience can be.

By far the easiest thing to do would be to help Mace pull it off, pocket a healthy share of the take, plop that into a bank somewhere, and go on down to Santa Fe or wherever to find Doc and tell him that he had been taken drunk for the past however long and—sorry about that—he wouldn't do it again, cross his heart and hope to croak.

Again Raider sighed heavily. Whom did he think he was kidding? His problem was finding a way to write and post a letter, not how to pull a robbery. Maybe.

His thoughts were interrupted—he did not mind a bit as it turned out—by a loud crackle of breaking twigs and crunching fall leaves as someone moved toward him through the line of scrub oak that bordered the creek here.

Whoever it was did not bother to try to sneak up on him, but still Raider's hand moved almost of its own will to the butt of the Colt in its holster on the dry creek bank. He let his hand stay there while he searched the scrub in the direction of the noise.

A moment later he grinned and took his hand off the revolver.

"I'd stand up to greet you, ma'am, but, uh . . ."

Elaine Volnay smiled, and the sight of a happy-go-lucky amusement crossing those perfect features was very much like a whole bank of gaslights flaring into roaring brilliance all at once. It was as if her smile caused the whole world to come alight. "It would be most rude and ungentlemanly for you not to stand, Mr. Slocum," she said.

For a moment, so great was his confusion, Raider almost asked her who the hell she was talking about. He was used to wearing other people's names, or he should have been after so long, but this woman had a power over him that seemed to rob him of everything except the desire to possess her. Not the way he had just possessed Angelica—not as an object exactly—but to possess her nonetheless, perhaps in the way the ancient Romans had possessed their slaves. Not as animals but wholly owned, wholly within the master's power. He wanted Elaine that way, and he wanted for this to be by her will as well as his. That was the difference, he realized. He wanted to own more than her body. He wanted her to give him her soul as well, and that could not be bought or bartered. That could only be given, never claimed.

Raider looked at her and grinned. "All right, ma'am. I wouldn't want to be rude."

He stood slowly, uncoiling his long, muscular frame from the creek bed where he had been lying. He stood facing her, letting the cold water drip down the length of him and making no effort to cover himself before her.

All right, he thought, I'm hung and I ain't ashamed of it. If you've ever seen better, I'll be surprised. But I'm betting you haven't. His grin became all the wider, and he challenged her with it.

The woman stood there, not at all abashed by his nudity, and let her eyes run brazenly over him from head to foot and back again to the weighty meat that hung between his legs.

"Well?" he demanded.

"I can't say that I am disappointed." She laughed. It was no shy giggle but an out-and-out belly laugh.

"Now I just know you ain't laughing at me, Miss Volnay. I try to be modest, but there's times when that just isn't possible."

"So I see," she said. "No, I was not laughing at you, John. I was laughing . . . perhaps now is not the time to discuss it. If you don't mind?"

"Whatever you prefer. I can wait. For a little while."

She arched her eyebrows and turned her head coquettishly aside. But still, he noticed, her eyes remained fixed on him. "A little while? You should be able to do better than that. There can be danger, you know, in short waits. Or in impetuous actions. Surely you of all people should know that."

"Sometimes, ma'am, rashness is its own reward. Other times it leads to greater rewards. What do you think?"

She tossed her head, and her face lost the look of playfulness it had worn until that moment. She was still beautiful, astonishingly beautiful, but now she was not an enchanting woman but a goddess in radiant perfection. She stared at him with a look that probably was meant to be withering. If Raider had been less sure of himself, he undoubtedly would have been crushed by such a look. As it was, the long training and longer habits of playing other people's games and wearing identities that he slipped into and out of the way some normal men changed clothes helped him keep his eyes meeting hers without change. He looked back at her coolly and refused to drop his eyes; and after a brief moment that somehow seemed to be a struggle, the woman gave in.

"Have you seen my horse, John? He seems to have wandered away while I was examining some late-blooming wildflowers."

"No, I'm afraid I haven't."

"Pity. Never mind. If I can't find him, he'll wander back home soon enough."

"I could escort you back."

Would it be worth that to you?" She was taunting him now, challenging him. Her head tilted back and her chin rose haughtily. She looked quite regal, and very cold.

All right, he thought. You're used to having it your own way. You're used to men crawling at your feet and begging for a chance to lick the sweat from between your toes. Let's see what you do when the man isn't gallant and won't play your games.

"No," he told her. "There's no piece of ass worth that. Not yours nor Queen Victoria's with gold plating on it. Sorry."

He more than halfway expected fury as her response, but that was not what he received from her. Again she dropped her head back and let full blown laughter roll out of that beautiful throat and past those perfect lips. "Gawd, John. You'd make a horrid courtier. But you are hung, I'll give you that much. Go back to your bath now before you make me angry. Or foolish. Either one would be very bad for you." She turned away from him and walked back out of sight among the scrub oaks.

Jesus, but that was a bunch of woman, he thought. That one he just had to have. With or without Juan Mace's robbery plans. That one he had to have.

CHAPTER TWELVE

Raider wandered back toward the headquarters area, confused and curious and wondering how he should take this strange, self-possessed, and completely beautiful woman. And wondering even more how she regarded him. For some reason, that was important to him, more important than it rightfully should be.

Most of Juan Mace's men were lounging in the afternoon sunshine, some of them playing cards or noisily rolling dice. The games seemed to be undertaken more for the activity than the profit. That kind of game Raider could do without. If he was going to gamble, he was going to be out for blood—that was simply his nature—and such an attitude here would more likely lead to problems than to a heavier weight of coin in his profits.

He did not see the redhaired Bruce among the others and wondered briefly whether the man was inside the dining hall or perhaps one of the buildings taking his frustrations out on a defenseless Angelica. Raider hoped not. The woman already had more troubles than were her share. She really did not deserve to have to deal with Bruce. Especially not after what Raider had already done to her. He was embarrassed about that and slightly ashamed. If he was lucky she would be sensible enough, and kind enough, not to mention the incident to him again.

The peaceful midafternoon scene was disrupted by the arrival of a pair of lathered horses. Miguel was on one of them and with him the man, Raider did not at the moment remember his name, who had sided Miguel the first time Raider had seen this crowd.

The two went directly to Mace's elegant little log house and barged inside the side door without knocking. Whatever they were about in there, Raider decided, it must be serious.

Good Lord, he thought, it must be about Mace's son. The kid had not shown up when he was supposed to. And the start of this whole thing had been when that youngster out on the road had thrown down on Raider.

The kid was cold beef now, and had been long enough to start bloating. Jesus, if that was Geraldo Mace that Raider had had to shoot, there would be hell to pay in the Mace camp now. Wouldn't they be delighted to find the boy's killer right at hand. There was no telling what they might decide to do about it, except in the last resort. That much he did not have to think about too long to figure out.

Raider began to quicken his pace and head toward the house.

"Can I come in?"

Miguel gave him a look of clear disapproval, but Mace, seated in the one comfortable chair in the side room, nodded. "You may as well, John."

"Why would you want to?" Miguel asked him bluntly.

Raider gave the man a level stare and said, "Because from the look on your face when you rode in, there's bad news here. If there's any way I can help, I want to. And I'd wanta know about it too. I figure we're all together now here. Or isn't that so?" He directed the last question to Mace himself, ignoring Miguel completely.

"You are right," Mace said. "And the news is very

bad, but for me alone I think. Not for you or for our business together."

"It still concerns me, the way I figure it," Raider told him. "If a man's my partner and my friend, I expect I got to go with him all the way. So if there's anything I can do, just tell me. It'll be done."

Mace nodded. He seemed genuinely grateful. "The problem is my son an' his companion. They were guarding on the road. Now they are not to be found."

"Neither of them?" Raider asked. The answer was obvious, but he wanted some time to think for a moment. Two of them. Geraldo and a companion. Yet the boy Raider shot had been alone; he was positive about that. If there had been another, he certainly would have participated in the fight. Or come after Raider alone if he had not been close at hand when the boy threw down on the passerby. Hills and gulleys can do strange things to the way sound travels, but not so strange that the gunshots could not have been heard by anyone else on guard in the vicinity. Besides, if the partner had been anywhere in that area, he surely would have found the boy's body once he had realized that the kid was missing. No, there had to be some other explanation. Perhaps the boy had not been Geraldo Mace after all. Although, thinking back to the kid's conversation at the time, it definitely had been Mace's stolen herd of cattle he was guarding.

It was fairly certain that Raider had killed one of the two guards, either Geraldo or the other guard. The question, then, was which one Raider had killed. And what the hell had become of the other one. That part of it made no sense at all.

"Both are missing," Miguel told him.

"You searched for them, of course."

"Of course. Very well indeed."

"Could they have slipped off somewhere to get laid?" Raider asked.

"There is no place close," Miguel said. "None closer than Pueblo or Canyon City. An' Geraldo would not have gone without discussing this with his papa. Never. Most of all, never when he was to guard our passage."

Mace agreed. "He is a fine boy, Geraldo. I say this not because he is my son, although I say it with pride that this is so, but because it is the truth. He is a boy who would not shirk his duties. Never."

"And his buddy?" Raider asked.

Both Mace and Miguel shrugged. "A young one as well. A little wild maybe. A little quick with the pistol, quick with the bottle, quick to pull a señorita into the bed," Mace said. "But a good boy, I think."

"Very good. Very quick," Miguel agreed.

If so, Raider was thinking, it may well have been the buddy he had beefed and not Geraldo. Which really did not much matter at this point. Whoever was still alive —or presumably should be—was still missing. There seemed to be no reason for one to have been there and not the other. And Raider certainly could not ask which one he had shot.

"Boys, even good ones," Raider said, "sometimes can talk each other into things that one of them alone wouldn't do. It could be something like that."

"If it is, I personally shall take a belt to both their asses," Mace said.

CHAPTER THIRTEEN

The three men sat for a time in silence. Mace seemed to want to drop the subject of his missing son, and Raider could understand that. Miguel appeared to be very much in tune with his master's moods and wishes anyway.

After several minutes, Mace left his chair with a small groan of effort, reminding Raider, for probably the first time since he had initially seen the man, of Mace's advancing age and the toll hard years must have taken in his past. Mace was getting along toward the end of his allotted time, and although he acted like a young man, he was not.

The bandit chieftain brought a bottle and glasses from a cabinet near a small desk—this time quite ordinary whiskey served in plain glasses. There was no hint in this side room of the opulence to be found elsewhere in the house. He poured with a generous hand, and he sighed upon returning to the comfort of his chair.

"Life is not always so easy," he said to no one in particular.

"*Salud*," Raider offered, raising his glass with a sympathetic look.

"Yes, *salud*," Mace said.

Miguel grunted but said nothing.

A hint of noise from the main part of the house

caught Raider's attention, reminding him, as if he needed reminding, of the woman's presence there. He might well need to cover his own tracks, he realized. The woman was not supposed to be seen outside the house the way he understood it, and if she said anything about their creekside encounter—and Raider did not—Mace might begin to question his newfound partner. Considering his real identity, and most especially with the two youngsters missing, Raider could not risk that. He cleared his throat.

"Juanito," he began, "I had a pleasant surprise today."

"Yes?" Mace seemed grateful now for the distraction of some conversation.

"I was walking up the creek a while ago."

Miguel nodded. "So I had heard." Mace nodded as well.

Inside himself, his face showing none of it, Raider took careful note of their knowledge. So they had heard. Which meant that Raider, even in the guise of John Slocum, was being watched if not actually hindered. It was a damn good thing, he realized, that he had left the grulla in the corral. A move toward the horse might have elicited more reaction than he wanted or needed from these people.

"While I was up there, I saw Miss Volnay," he said. "I thought she stayed pretty much inside."

Miguel's face remained blank. This was no business of his. Mace, however, grimaced. It was the look of a strong man acknowledging an area of weakness.

"You know how this must be," Mace said. "The lady is no bird to be held in the gilded cage. There are times when she feels the need to move about. She says she loves the feel of the wind in her hair and the motion of the horse beneath her. This I can understand, although I cannot encourage it."

Raider nodded.

Wearily Mace said, "I ask her to move about only at night but. . . ." He shrugged. "What can I do? I cannot command the sunshine at night, and she says she delights in the sunshine on the mountaintops and the sight of the wind moving through the turning leaves. How can I deny her this?"

It was obvious that Mace would indeed have denied her the pleasure if he thought he could. Apparently the leash Juan Mace kept on his mistress was a tenuous thing, not the forged chain Raider might have expected. It looked, in fact, like Elaine Volnay had pretty well convinced this tough old bandit chief that she had the world's sole remaining pussy, and if he wanted inside it, there were some limits about what he could say and do with her.

Tied the old boy up like a kitten playing with a ball of yarn, Raider thought. A soft strand here and another there, and all of a sudden the guy couldn't do a thing about it. That too was mighty interesting to know.

"How indeed," Raider said noncommittally.

As if the talk about her had been a cue, there was a timid knock at the closed door that connected Mace's side room with the rest of the house.

It was Miguel who leaped lightly to his feet. "I shall inquire, *jefe*," he said in quick Spanish. Mace nodded.

Raider raised his eyebrows in inquiry, but Mace motioned for him to keep his seat.

It was, of course, Elaine at the door. She looked disheveled, her hair disarranged from the way Raider had seen it so recently. And she looked pale, and angry. She leaned forward far enough to peek into the room to see who was there, then moved close to Miguel's ear and whispered in a low, urgent tone that carried to Raider's closely tuned ears, although too softly for him to make out anything of what she said.

Miguel's expression hardened, and his face went white. While the woman was still talking, he spun and pulled a revolver from his sash. The weapon was cocked and pointed at Raider's chest.

"So, *amigo,* you admit that you did see the lady this afternoon?"

Raider sat unblinking, holding his still partially full glass of Mace's whiskey in his gun hand. His expression gave away nothing, although he noted that Miguel's draw had been slow and mechanical, not the motion of a really quick gunhand. If he had to, he could probably get his own still-holstered Colt into action at least as quickly as Miguel could put him under. On the other hand, there would be no margin for error, and Miguel would almost certainly be able to get lead into him while Raider was pulling and firing. Deliberately Raider slumped deeper into his chair. "I did."

He needn't have bothered. "No," Elaine protested. She stepped inside the room where all three men could see her. It was clear then why she had been hiding behind the door. Her blouse was torn open at the throat, and she was clutching the cloth together at her neck with one hand to keep from exposing her breasts. "He was not the man," she said.

Both Mace and Raider, seeing the condition of her clothing, came to their feet.

There was no hesitation of age or lack of youthful grace in Mace's movements now. Such minor infirmities were completely forgotten.

"What is this?" Mace demanded. *"Qué?"*

"It was on my way back," Elaine said. Her head was tipped haughtily back, and her eyes were flashing fire now. "After I had spoken with John here, I was in the brush looking for my horse. A man . . . saw me there. He was not a . . . kind man. He was very rough with me." To Mace alone she added, "Do you know what I mean, *mi caro?*"

Mace nodded. Raider would have expected Mace to be boiling and red-faced with anger, but he was not. He seemed completely calm and controlled. His expression had hardened, but there was no more outward indication of what he might be thinking or feeling than that. Such a degree of control gave Raider new respect for the man. Juan Mace was evidently brighter and deeper than Raider had been giving him credit for, despite the indications already presented by his excellent tastes. "I do understand," he said softly. There was a chilling quality in that very softness.

"You will tell me who this man was," Mace ordered. The words were definitely a command. Juan Mace might have had difficulty controlling this woman in some respects, but now he was fully in command. She lowered her eyes from his and seemed to be looking toward some vague, unseen place that was not part of this room or this house.

"I do not know the man's name," she said. "He was a large man and brutal. His hair was red and his beard full. Do you wish descriptions of a more . . . private nature?"

"I do not," Mace said. "Miguel, John, you know who she means?"

Miguel nodded firmly. Raider murmured, "Reckon I do too."

"Bring him to me. Do this quietly and without harming him. I would have a talk with this man."

Both Miguel and Raider nodded. Mace was already moving toward the woman to comfort her when Raider and Miguel marched out into the afternoon sunlight.

Raider glanced toward the western rim of mountains, where the sun was already sinking behind the high wall of rock. "He'll be running," Raider said. "It won't be long to dark."

"Long enough," Miguel said. "There are two ways he could try to leave. One you know. It is toward the open country, where he would have to pass the guards.

You know that way, so take it. There is another. Up there." Miguel pointed vaguely toward the mountains, perhaps in a direction slightly north of west, Raider noted. "I will look for him there. If he has passed through the common entrance, our people will have seen him go. If this has happened, take all but one of the men who are there and find him."

"And you?"

"I would need no assistance," Miguel said grimly. A side implication of that, Raider realized, was Miguel's belief that Raider—or John Slocum—might well need help where the Mexican bandit would not.

That was just fine by Raider. Being underestimated by an enemy, or a potential enemy at the least, was like being given an extra weapon if a fight were to come. That was a good thing to know.

"What if Bruce is smarter than you believe?" Raider asked.

"You mean what, *amigo?*"

"I mean you and Juanito expect him to be running already. This is a pretty good-sized hole up here. What if he goes to ground in it?"

"That would be of no consequence," Miguel said. "It would only delay, not change. Go now, please."

They had reached the corral. Miguel said, "The bay there. The saddle is a good one, and the animal is ready. Take it."

Raider nodded and reached quickly to yank the cinch tight. He unfastened the bay's loosely tied reins and swung into the saddle, but quick as he was, Miguel was mounted and away before him.

Raider hoped that no one would decide that he was stealing a horse and begin shooting. He did not wait to offer explanations to anyone, though. He wheeled the horse away from the rail where it had been tied and went thundering out of the enclosure on Miguel's heels.

Someone else could take the time to close the corral gate behind them.

And someone would, he was sure. There were enough curious heads already turning their way in response to the sudden rapid movement of two of the gang's top men. Or one of them. Raider still had not quite decided which.

CHAPTER FOURTEEN

Raider was still more than a little miffed by Miguel's assumption that a backwoods Mexican bandit could bring Bruce back without help while a top-flight Pinkerton agent could not. Not that Miguel knew he was an agent. He damn well better not, anyhow. And not that the resentment was a very professional attitude for Raider to adopt. Still . . .

The bay horse—it really was a good one—raced the length of the narrow cut leading into or out of Mace's hanging valley to the sentry station Raider remembered seeing there before. There were three men lounging in the shade of a precariously leaning slab of rock. They certainly looked unexcited, if curious, about Raider's approach. He was glad to see too that they did not immediately reach for their rifles when they saw who it was.

A few moments of conversation proved that whatever Bruce had chosen to do after his unwise assault on Juan Mace's woman—for which Raider could not really blame him, drunk or sober—the man had not tried to escape in that direction.

Shit, Raider thought, that meant Miguel would find him. Childish though it might have been, Raider resented that. He had wanted to be the one to bring Bruce back to the fold. Alone. Without the help of Miguel or any of the other Mace men. He repeated a few other choice profanities to himself, thanked the men at the mouth of the cut, and turned the bay horse back toward the camp at a much slower pace than he had used on the fast trip outward. Shit!

There was no sign of Miguel at the headquarters, nor had Raider expected there to be. The eastern pass was much closer than the high exit to the northwest, wherever it might actually be. Miguel would probably need much more time to find his man, and he might need help to subdue him. Raider thought about that and decided to ask Mace's permission to ride in that direction.

Mace, however, refused his offer.

"Stay here, John," Mace told him. "Miguel knows the country there as well as I myself. No one else is needed. And if he expects no one to be there but the red-bearded one, it would be foolish for me to place others in his path, yes?"

"Yes," Raider reluctantly agreed. Damn his own hurt feelings and wounded pride, but of course Mace was right. When a man thinks he is alone with an enemy and someone else steps into the line of fire, it is the newcomer's own fault if he gets his head blown apart in the confusion. And Raider was not entirely sure that Miguel would mind all that much having a reasonable excuse to put a bullet into Raider on the pretext that he thought Raider was Bruce. Raider definitely did not trust Juan Mace's number-two man, and he was fairly certain that the distrust was mutual.

"We will wait here," Mace said. "Now if you would excuse me, I wish to attend to the lady. She is badly. . . ." He seemed to be groping for the word he wanted.

"Shaken?" Raider asked. "She has a right to be."

Mace nodded. "Please, now."

"Of course." Raider left the side room of the odd little cabin where Mace lived amid such unexpected comforts, not the least of which was Elaine Volnay, and wandered back out into the yard among the collection of low-roofed shacks and dugouts that housed the gang.

The men began drifting toward him, sidling nearer with a great pretense of casual disinterest, the way a stray dog will approach a traveler's fireside. Unaware of it until, oh my, what are you doing here? Well, now that I'm here, maybe I'll sit down and let you scratch my ears and get rid of any stray scraps that would clutter your campsite.

Within five minutes after he found a bench to sit on, Raider had half the Mace camp idling within easy hearing distance.

Their pretense amused him, and Raider pretended in his turn not to notice them. He pulled a penknife from his pocket and chose a wood chip from among several littered on the ground at his feet. Slowly, taking great pains with his work and as much time as possible, he began to fashion a leering devil's face on the sliver of wood. It seemed rather appropriate.

Finally, one of the men could stand it no longer. He moved deliberately nearer and stared down at Raider's work in progress. "Kinda nifty," he said.

"I do needlepoint too," Raider said with a straight face.

"Uh huh." The man obviously did not know what Raider was talking about. "You, uh, went on a fast ride a bit ago."

"Sure did," Raider agreed. "Good horse, that bay."

"You were, uh, looking for something in particular?"

"Yes." Raider continued to give his attention to the bit of wood and the penknife in his hands. The tiny devil's nose was proving delicate to construct.

"Well?" the man demanded.

"Well what?" Raider showed him the wooden figure. "What d'you think so far?"

"Damn it, mister, you know good an' well what I'm asking you."

"Uh huh," Raider again agreed. "But maybe it isn't my place to say anything."

"Oh." That explanation seemed quite enough here. Once told it was Mace's business and not theirs, the men of the camp accepted the fact that they were out of it. They pretended to drop their interest in the whole affair and drifted away as silently as they had come. Only the one who had been bold enough to speak to Raider remained. After a moment more he said, "That really is a cunning li'l thing you're making."

"You like it? Here." Raider flicked the smoothed wood twice with his knife tip to create the eyebrows of the miniature monster and handed it to the man. The fellow's face split into a glad smile.

"That's damned decent of you, Slocum. Thanks."

"Sure." Raider really was not in a mood for casual conversation at the moment. He put his penknife back into his pocket, stood, and brushed the wood shavings off the front of his trousers. "I'll see you later."

"Sure."

An hour later Miguel and the redhaired Bruce returned to the camp. They rode side by side, with no sign of struggle or animosity, and Raider noticed at once that Bruce still carried a Colt in his holster. He noticed as well, though, that Bruce's cartridge belt was empty of shells, and he was betting that the Colt was as empty as the belt. The men of the camp were interested in their arrival but not aroused by it, and they evidently knew better than to ask questions. They watched with idle curiosity while Miguel and Bruce turned their horses into the corral and walked toward Mace's house. Raider joined them at the door.

"You had the good fortune, I see," Raider said.

Miguel grinned. Raider was willing to bet Miguel had been fairly certain of where he would find the redhead before either of them ever set out in search. Raider's role had been one of providing insurance in case Miguel guessed wrong. For some reason, that rankled him.

Bruce, Raider saw, looked quite nervous. His face was set into masklike rigidity, but he could not keep his eyes from darting back and forth to either side, and every second or two he ran a dry tongue over even drier lips. He carried himself stiffly, as if he were made of the same wood Raider had just used to make the small devil's head. There were, Raider decided, a number of similarities between the two.

Miguel knocked on the door only once, a sharp rap calling attention to his arrival without being a request for permission to enter, and opened it without waiting for an answer. He motioned for Bruce to enter first. Miguel followed, then Raider.

Mace was not in the room, and the connecting door to the rest of the house was closed. Miguel pointed imperiously to a straight-backed wooden chair, and Bruce obediently sat in it. To Raider, Miguel said, "Watch him. I have already promised him if he moves I shall blow off his *cojones,* but will harm nothing else. Keep this in mind, please, if he should want to leave."

Raider nodded. There was no doubt in his mind—and he was certain there could be none in Bruce's either—that this was exactly what would happen if Bruce were foolish enough to try to make a break.

Bruce sat as still as a cast-iron hitching post while Miguel was out of the room. It took only a moment before both Miguel and Mace were there.

Mace saw the silent captive and smiled. Except for the old man's eyes, the smile might have seemed a pleasant one. But the eyes held a coldness much like that of a rattlesnake. And there was something else in them—a sort of gleeful anticipation—that frightened even Raider. It must surely have turned Bruce cold and made him wish that he had accepted Miguel's gunfire while he had the chance.

"Welcome back," Juan Mace said politely.

CHAPTER FIFTEEN

Mace did not show up for the evening meal. Neither did Bruce for that matter. Raider ate his meal as rapidly as the rest of the crew and kept his silence. Mace's lack of violence was beginning to worry him.

That, he decided, was a strange way to look at things, but it happened to be the truth. He simply would have felt much better if the old man had turned loose the rage he'd obviously felt when he saw Elaine and learned about the way she had been treated. For a man in Mace's position to let such a thing go was unthinkable. For him to react so calmly was frightening.

When the first of the men finished eating and prepared to bolt for the door, Miguel held a hand up to stop him. "Wait. Keep your seat. And the rest of you."

There was a great deal of curiosity around the table now but no argument. Those who were still eating slowed to a quick halt, and within a minute or two the table was both silent and still, with no one moving or asking questions.

Jesus, Raider thought. The place was like a deep-rock tunnel with charges set and fuses lit but no one knowing when or where it would blow.

They did not have long to wait.

"You are finished?" Miguel asked. *"Bueno*. We go

outside now. All of us. *El jefe* would have a word with one and all this night."

Still there was no noise except the scrape of chair legs on the floor. Someone dropped a spoon onto his plate, and the clatter was loud enough to make the others wince. The man who had committed the error flinched as if he thought he might be struck for such a small thing.

Oh, yes, Raider thought, they can feel it around them even if they don't know what it's about. Hell, I know more than they do and I'm fretting.

The sun had already slipped below the high rock wall to the west, but the light was still strong. With no direct sunlight, though, it was becoming cool. If any of the other men noticed the chill, they paid it no mind; nor did Raider.

Juan Mace and Bruce were standing in the packed-earth yard when the rest of the men emerged from the chuck building. Bruce looked exactly as he had when Raider had last seen him. The man had not been beaten or abused in any apparent way, but he looked defeated, his shoulders slumped in hopelessness, his face haggard and slack, lacking fear or any other discernible expression. He really looked, Raider thought, as if killing him would cause no great change. It would just be a question of whether he stood upright or fell down. Nothing more.

Mace stared at each of his men as they exited the low dining shelter, and one by one they halted and grouped together in silence. When all were outdoors, Mace said, "To the corral. Sit on the rails. For this you must have a good view, yes?"

The men did not understand but they obeyed. They moved in a tight-packed body toward the corral, felt Mace's impatient eyes on their backs, and stepped up the pace.

Behind them, Mace crooked his finger for Bruce to follow and turned without bothering to see that the huge redhead was marching with him. He did not need to watch. Bruce followed as docilely as a pup, head down and eyes focused somewhere in the vicinity of his own boot toes.

Mace waited with his prisoner at the gate until all the men were seated on the corral rails. Then he led Bruce forward to the center of the hoof-churned arena.

His pointing finger sought out two of the men—both of them middle-aged Mexicans—and beckoned them forward. Those men would, Raider thought, be among the oldest and closest of Mace's companions.

Mace spoke to them in Spanish, too low for Raider to understand what he was saying. Whatever was said, Bruce did not react to it.

The two bandits trotted away and returned moments later with a sixteen-pound hammer and a number of stout wooden stakes, which they proceeded to drive into the ground in a rectangular pattern nine or ten feet square. Uh huh, Raider thought.

Next, one of them went to Bruce's horse and brought back the redhead's saddle rope. It looked like a good rope and a strong one. Here it would not have gotten much use, for if Bruce had ever been a cowhand, those days were long behind him. The Mexican cut the rope into four equal lengths.

Speaking loudly enough for all to hear, Mace said, "Take the clothing off, please."

Bruce, redhaired and naturally ruddy-complected, blanched almost dead white, but he said nothing and moved quickly to comply with what he had been told to do.

He was a powerful man, but naked he looked paunchy, his muscles sagging and his skin an ugly, mottled white. Without his clothes he did not seem at all the threatening bear of a man he was when dressed. Even a woman like Angelica could not have found him attractive with his gut and wrinkles and goosebumps on such public display. He looked diminished, both physically and emotionally. Bruce did not raise his eyes toward any of his companions, Raider noticed. He looked and must have felt humiliated. Mace knew what he was doing, Raider decided, because he had stripped Bruce of much more than his clothes.

For a moment Raider wondered why in the world a man like Bruce would submit to such treatment, but the answer to that was obvious. He was clinging to a small, dim hope that by doing this and whatever else Juan Mace demanded of him he might escape alive even if punished, even if horribly punished. The man was determined not to die, no matter what, Raider thought.

"On the ground," Mace ordered.

Obediently Bruce dropped instantly to his knees and then to all fours near Mace's polished boots. Still he would not look at the man who had this control over him.

"No, *cabron*. Spread like the eagle, I believe you call it."

Still without protest or complaint, Bruce allowed himself to be spread-eagled and tied by hands and feet to the deep-driven stakes. He lay in the dust and manure of the corral and stared toward the slowly darkening sky.

When Bruce was tied down and completely at Mace's mercy, Miguel slipped down from the rail where he had been seated and walked toward Mace's house.

Mace looked carefully at the ring of faces on the corral rails. He motioned the two Mexican helpers back to their places and said, "There are some of you here who already know of my companion. I suspect, yes, that all of you know about her, even though we do not speak of her." He spat on the ground. "You are all pigs not fit to speak of a lady. You know this, yes?"

He waited, staring boldly at his collection of bandits

and cutthroats until he received a brief flurry of answering nods.

If that was what Juan Mace wanted them to agree to, they would agree. *El jefe* demanded it and so it was.

"Not one of you, no," Mace went on. "This one is a lady. A great lady. You whisper of her at night, and those of you who have seen her may dream of her face in the darkness and may call her to mind as a vision when you fuck some slut or when you flog your own meat in the night. An' that, that is but natural. That I say nothing to. This I would do myself if the lady she was not mine." He smiled.

"You are the sons of whores, I think, yet you know what is right when it comes to this fine lady. All of you. All but one of you, *sí?*"

Dramatically Mace stepped back and pointed an outthrust, accusing finger down at Bruce. "All of you, I think, but this one."

There was a reaction from the men now. Several of them began to look as ugly-dangerous as Raider had expected Mace to be, and several more allowed their jaws to drop open in astonishment. Clearly any violation of Elaine Volnay was beyond believability. No, Raider thought, Bruce would receive no sympathy here and no help. Whatever Mace chose to do to him now would be applauded by the very men who had been Bruce's friends.

"This one," Mace said, still avoiding mention of the offender's name, "this animal with no right to be called a man, this one has dared to violate the gracious lady who is my friend."

The response from the men was a low, growling murmur of sound, the bear-pit yammer of an enraged mob on a smaller scale. It was the sort of thing Raider had heard often enough, and he hoped he would never hear it with himself as the object of a mob's collective, unreasoning hatred, for that was what it was. Mace had his men where he wanted them now, supporting anything and everything he might choose to do to this offender and thirsting for more.

Bruce, Raider realized, would be required to pay for all the men's secret fantasies, and they would be taught a lesson of warning themselves at the same time.

Juan Mace, Raider thought, you're a damned clever man, and I salute you.

Mace was allowing himself to show expression now. His voice became louder and more strident. His carriage became even more erect, and he began to wave his arms. He began to exhort the men to greater emotion.

In Spanish and in smatterings of English he built on the themes of hate and betrayal and revenge, asking the men over and over again what he should do to this animal who had betrayed womanhood, who had betrayed Mace's trust, who had betrayed these very men who had been his companions.

By now, Raider realized, it was the men themselves who were supposed to have been violated by Bruce, and Elaine's violation was only an instrument of the crime.

Jesus, Raider thought in admiration of Mace, the man's as clever as a tent-show Bible thumper.

Mace had them with him now, ready to snarl and rip Bruce into pieces with their bare hands if Mace only gave them the word to pour down off their top-rail perches.

Bruce, Raider noticed, looked even whiter now. His eyes were closed and he was lying unnaturally still, as if he were afraid that any chance motion of his might touch off an unstoppable flood of mob violence. In spite of what he had done, Raider could not help but pity the man. And now, with Bruce tied firmly to the stakes, it was too late for any last-gasp attempt to free himself or to escape or at the very least to ensure that he would be quickly gunned down and put out of his misery. Even that was denied to him now, thanks to Mace's controlled cunning that had led Bruce to participate willingly in his own complete subjugation.

Jesus, Raider thought again.

As the crowd was reaching what almost had to be its final heights of fever pitch, Miguel returned to the corral.

Elaine Volnay, cool and serene and as beautiful as every queen should be, was on Miguel's arm.

The men became silent, as much with awe as with respect, Raider thought.

CHAPTER SIXTEEN

For several long, slow heartbeats the men stared until Raider began to wonder whether Mace's deliberate raising of high-pitch emotions would backfire on him and the men would vent their feelings by attacking the woman themselves. But then, unexpectedly, and quite out of place, Raider thought, the collection of Mexican and gringo bandits burst instead into a rousing cheer for the lady, for Juan Mace's lady, for *their* lady.

By God, Raider thought, he's done it. He's turned each and every one of these greasy, louse-ridden low-lifes into a personal champion of Elaine Volnay's honor. It was all Raider could do to stop himself from raising his hat in a salute to the old man's mastery of human nature.

Elaine took the cheers in stride, as her proper due. Graciously, she turned her head along the line of worked-up bandits to view them and to accept their homage to her elegance and her beauty. Delicately, she touched fingertips to rose-hued lips. Modestly, she dropped her eyes away from the line of worshipers.

Hell's bells, Raider thought, she's almost as good as the old man.

The cheering and the few remaining growls stopped with knife-edge suddenness, and the men sat on the fence gazing with obvious reverence at this beautiful woman. The sight of a woman like that would be enough to command instant fealty from such riffraff as this crowd of bandits. She was a woman on a plane far above anything any of them could have imagined in their sorry pasts.

Elaine had changed clothing since Raider had last seen her and had obviously been hard at work on her makeup as well.

The riding skirt and torn blouse were gone. In their place was a gown of lace and satin, a fragile and delicate thing of great beauty. The woman's own considerable beauty, the elegance of the gown, and the soft, eggshell-white color of its material combined to give her an appearance of virginal loveliness that no sane man could ever have dreamed of violating. Which undoubtedly was why Mace would have chosen to put Elaine into that particular gown, for the occasion. After this, the men would almost certainly regard Elaine Volnay as being as beautiful—and as unattainable—as the stars in a velvet sky.

Mace stepped to the side of his lady and with all the grace of a highborn Spanish grandee offered his arm. Elaine placed the tips of her fingers above his wrist and allowed the old bandit chieftain to lead her beside Bruce's immobile head. She seemed to float rather than walk when she moved, but where Mace led her was a reminder of their purpose here. The looks of wonder and awe began to leave the men's faces, to be replaced once again with anger—this time a cold and bone-deep fierceness as the crowd of rough men looked down at the one among them who had dared to violate this creature from some higher existence than theirs would ever be.

"This is the man?" Mace asked in a voice just barely loud enough to reach all who were watching.

Elaine looked down at the redhead—very coldly,

Raider thought, even considering what had happened before—and said, "It is." She too spoke just loud enough for all to hear. It was obvious that she had been coached in advance.

Mace nodded. Ceremoniously, he took her slender hand and lifted it from his wrist, placing her fingertips on Miguel's arm in as formal a changing of the guard as ever took place outside Buckingham Palace. "There are things a lady should not see," Mace said.

Miguel nodded and led the woman away. The eyes of the men followed her through the gate and across the yard to the house. Not until Miguel and Elaine were inside the small house did Mace move or speak again.

"Ai, *cabron,*" he said then, looking down at Bruce, "the time has come that you must pay for the pleasures, *sí?*" He was smiling again. It was not a pleasant smile.

Mace wrung his hands together. He was beginning to look positively eager now, Raider thought.

To one of the yankee toughs—a pale, thin man with a drooping mustache and a revolver with a barrel nearly as big around as its owner's waist—Mace said, "Bring me your toy, Reilly. I would borrow it for only a small while, *por favor.*"

Reilly hopped down off the fence and began to walk toward one of the huts.

"Now!" Mace called impatiently. Reilly began to run. Now would not be a good time to anger *el jefe.*

The man returned less than a minute later carrying what appeared at first to be another coil of rope. It was not. On closer inspection Raider could see that the coil was a light stockman's whip of braided leather. The whip was small, perhaps a third the length of the more common bullwhacker's blacksnake.

Raider had seen such stock whips before, but not often and not around this part of the country. They were fairly common in California, where a few of the old-fashioned diehard *vaqueros* still favored them, and they were quite popular in the swamps of Florida, where cattle could not be worked with horse and rope the way they were in more open country but had to be rooted out of their hock-deep tangles of water and roots with dogs and short whips. Come to think of it, Raider decided, Reilly looked like he might have come from that malaria-ridden and almost unknown section of beef country where their trade was more with Cuba than with the stockyards of Chicago and Kansas City.

Reilly handed the whip over to his chief with a respectful bob of the head and hurried back to his perch on the fence. Raider did not blame the man for not wanting to be singled out in Mace's attention.

Mace inspected the slim coil in his hands and slipped his right fist through a rawhide thong attached to the buttstock. He flipped the thin twist of leather out onto the ground between himself and Bruce. Even from ten paces' distance, Raider could see that the whip had been fashioned with care and much skill, built up from many extremely thin strands in a basketweave pattern instead of being braided from four or six wide strips. The careful work had resulted in a product that was virtually round and as solid as a machine-woven cable. It tapered down pencil-thin at the tip, where there was a flat popper. A whip like that would be extremely heavy for its size and could probably slice flesh to the bone if the man wielding it knew how to handle it.

Mace seemed to know how to handle it. He waggled his wrist to get the feel of the braid and the lifeless material twisted and turned snakelike, as if it were alive itself and not being directed by the man, until it slithered onto and across Bruce's belly. Mace grinned and turned his wrist. The braid wriggled gently down until the cruel popper was nested in Bruce's mat of dark-red pubic hair. Still the redhead did not move, but the watchers could see his body tense, and sweat began to roll down his sides into the dirt.

Lord A'mighty, Raider thought. What a position for a man to be in.

Mace lifted his arm and the whip snapped obediently away from Bruce's body. The captive groaned. It was the first sound Raider remembered him making since Miguel had brought him back.

Mace stepped away from his prisoner and then turned his back on the man. No one believed he was ignoring Bruce, though. Mace walked calmly toward the fence rails beyond where his men were seated and began to practice with the borrowed whip, learning the feel of it, giving his arm and hand the knowledge of where the lash would bite with each choppy, snapping stroke forward and back. He spent several minutes at this practice, seemingly without hurry, his men waiting with forced patience behind him. For the moment, he continued to ignore Bruce, but Bruce could not have avoided hearing the pistol-shot cracks of the soft leather popper at each swing of Mace's arm.

The sweat was running heavily from Bruce now, and for the first time he tested the strength of the ropes and stakes that bound him. He pulled until his arms corded and his face darkened from the effort, but all he got in return was a slight loosening of the stakes in the soil. The ropes had been tied to the stakes at ground level, and the stakes had been driven deep. It would take an awesome amount of power to break the ropes himself. And if he did that, he would still have Mace and the full complement of his riders to contend with before he could get free. He was without hope, but still he tried.

Mace turned and saw what he was doing. The old man walked back to stand over his victim and watch the man's struggles. Mace seemed to be enjoying the sight.

"Yes, again. Try again," he encouraged. "Struggle all

you will. It will do you no good." He said it softly, almost kindly, and he was smiling when he spoke.

Raider was beginning to get the idea that this was an evil old man running the show. Not just a thief or a murderer. Raider had dealt with his fair share and more of those in the past and knew them as criminals, some of them bad men and others criminal but in their own way respectable and at times even admirable. He had begun earlier to think that Juan Mace might have been in that category from which legends are created and public affections given, but now he was not so sure. More and more Raider was thinking that Mace was also an evil man. And evil is a completely different thing from crime.

Mace smiled gently down toward Bruce again and then stepped back half a pace. He was not leaving the man alone by doing so but was judging the distance of the lash.

With a smooth, fluid motion of his forearm, Mace sent the whip sliding forward through the air, curling neatly back on itself and then flickering abruptly down and instantly up again. It was done slowly for the most part and without great effort, but the whip left behind a small, tidy red stripe on Bruce's ankle.

The redhead gritted his teeth; although the sweat poured from him more freely now, he did not cry out.

The whip arm moved again, and again there was a neat red line left in the wake of its travel, this one half an inch away and precisely parallel to the first.

Juan Mace knew how to handle a lash very well indeed.

Within a few minutes it became clear what the old man was doing. Patiently, with no show of anger or malice except in the depths of his eyes, Mace was shredding the redhead's skin, a half inch at a time.

The blood was flowing freely now in the earliest

wounds, although Mace applied the whip with care, never allowing it to bite deep. Instead, it struck lightly and repeatedly, only hard enough to split the skin but never enough to slice into the meat of Bruce's still-living flesh.

Bruce began to scream, his voice a high, bright bell of terror more than of agony. His voice became hoarse as the line of red stripes moved steadily up his calf and across the inside of his thigh toward his balls.

Mace smiled at him again and moved around to the other side. Again the old man began at the ankle and worked his way up Bruce's other leg until the insides of both legs were raw and bloody. The ground between them was becoming soaked with dark, red-brown mud from the blood collecting there.

Mace tossed the lash out without force or snap and allowed it to uncurl of its own weight and fall on Bruce's unprotected balls and limp, shriveled cock. There was no damage done by the light touch, but it drew a more frenzied howl than had yet been heard from the man. Several of the watchers, Raider noticed, turned their eyes surreptitiously away. Raider knew because his own eyes had long since been diverted from the scene Mace was playing out before them.

Mace resumed his efforts with more light slashes along Bruce's arms and down both his sides.

"But there is so little left, *cabron*," the old man said at one point. The words drew the attention of his men back to him, and Mace stared at them one by one as if daring them to turn away from him again. He wanted each of them to see.

Mace walked casually around behind Bruce's head. "Hold very still now," he said pleasantly. Bruce, in pain though he was, was twisting his bloody torso and neck in an effort to see Mace and to know what the old man was doing there where Bruce could not see him.

"Very still," Mace repeated.

Quickly, this time with power as well as precision, the short whip snapped forward. This time it popped loudly, and when the blood-darkened tip fell back at Mace's side, Bruce's right ear lay on the ground several feet from his head.

Bruce screamed, and his body convulsed against the grasp of rope and wood; but even the awful strength of panic was not enough to break his bonds, and almost as quickly he fell back in limp exhaustion, weakened by the slow but constant loss of blood.

"Once more," Mace said. Again he drove the whip with speed and power, and Bruce's other ear was ripped from his scalp. The pain and shock and loss of blood combined so that this time there was scarcely a response from Bruce.

Mace walked forward until he was standing directly over Bruce. He called to the nearest of the men who were watching, a tough-looking youngster who now looked as if he would rather puke than move, and had the man bring a dipper of water to pour over Bruce's head to help revive him. The unwilling helper ran back to the fence and stood leaning against it rather than climbing back to the top where he was supposed to be.

Mace waited until there was a semblance of awareness in Bruce's eyes again and told him, "So little left now. But I save the best for the last, yes?" He laughed, and walked around to stand between the stakes holding Bruce's feet.

Bruce screamed as shrilly as a spinster librarian could have done and tried to struggle against his bonds, but he had no more strength left. He screamed until he could force no more sounds from his throat, and then he gagged and whimpered. His body was bucking up and down in its terror, an ugly parody of the act that had caused this vengeance.

Still calm and with his face displaying no apparent emotion, Juan Mace again began to apply the whip with skill and force, the lash leaping out with awful accuracy to cut and tear and leave behind a raw, red, spongy mass of mangled tissue.

It continued for what seemed a long, long time.

CHAPTER SEVENTEEN

Raider was sick to his stomach and even sicker down deep inside. What he had just seen was not human. It probably was not sane. Certainly Raider would have doubted his own sanity if he had been able to watch what Juan Mace did to that man and, as the others seemed to be doing, accept Mace's idea of punishment calmly and as a matter of course.

Juanito. His good and trusted partner in crime. Jesus, Raider thought, *no*body deserved that. Shoot the man, sure. Have him flogged within an inch of his life, sure. Have twenty gun-toughs hold him down while Mace beat him, fine. Raider could have understood all of those but not this.

Raider barely stopped himself in time. He had been about to shake his head in disgust and confusion. That would not have been a good idea at this time and place, with all the others gathered close around. As it was, though, he had his best poker face firmly in place. He was sure that no one could tell what he was feeling, not just from looking at him.

The thought made him wonder about the others. How many of them were hiding disgust and revulsion behind phony facades, the same as he was? He looked at the faces around him and found only stony indifference reflected in the men's blank expressions. But then that was what they would be seeing on his hard-set face too. He wondered. This might not be the peaceful, cooperative camp he had thought it was. The whole crowd could be quietly boiling beneath the surface, ready to explode when Mace built the pressure finally to the bursting point. If so, that might raise some interesting possibilities if a man could help determine when and where the blowup should occur. It could even turn Juan Mace into a Pinkerton ally when it came time to break up this gang, Raider thought.

He smiled to himself slightly, not minding if anyone saw. So much for temptation.

It was a bit difficult at this point even to remember why or how he had been tempted to participate in Juan Mace's planned history-making robbery. In fact, Raider was not at all sure he had been tempted. There never *really* had been any question about whether he would throw in with them. Not really.

Anyway, the point now was to get word to Doc. Once Weatherbee knew what was going on here, he could handle the outside end of it in preparing a surprise for Señor Mace and his bucko boys.

Now that Raider was doing some serious thinking on the subject, he realized that the tricky part might lie not with handling Mace and his crew of happy cutthroats but in dealing with John Law afterward. Because if the Pinkerton Agency was to collect a fee for all this excellent work Raider was putting out, there should first be a robbery. You can't collect on a recovery until there is something lost for the Agency to recover. Prevention is all very well from an altruistic point of view, but Allan Pinkerton was not exactly renowned for altruism. For efficiency, yes, but not for public-spirited benevolence. And for that matter, railroads were not much known for a sense of gratitude either. Stop a robbery in the planning stages, and they would probably send a beautifully worded letter expressing their thanks.

Let the flippin' thing take place and then return their loot, and they would pay ten percent of the amount recovered. That would be *much* better from the Agency's point of view than a letter, however lovely.

That was settled. Raider would continue in his make-believe role as John Slocum, boy train robber, and he would try like hell to get word out to Doc Weatherbee down in Santa Fe. Get old Doc to put his inventive mind to the task while, as usual, Raider handled the field work.

Raider sighed. He wondered whether in the strictest line of duty he would be forced to pay court to the fair Elaine. After all, the lady might well be his very best source of information. . . .

There are nearly always a good many ways to go about getting something you want, and quite often the simplest and most obvious is the best. After breakast the next morning, Raider drifted over to the house and knocked at the side door. Mace, alone in the room, answered it.

"John, come in. You would like coffee? Or a brandy so early?"

Raider shook his head. "Not right now, Juanito. Thanks. What I wanted was to see if it would be all right with you if I was to go into town." He grinned. "There must be one somewhere around here."

"Not so close, but there is one, yes. You have business there?" Mace did not look actively suspicious, but there was a hint of tightening at the corners of his eyes. If Raider had not already known enough about his host to make him cautious, that would have done it.

"Hell, I don't even know what the town is, Juanito. But, uh, Angelica ain't much, you know?"

Mace laughed. "I do know. Can you believe it, I myself have known that one. Before, uh . . . before."

"You? Hell, Juanito, I thought you had better taste than me even."

Mace shrugged. "What can I say? But it was not so bad then. She was clean and not so ugly. More meat to her then. I think she has a sickness."

"I think she prob'ly has every right to have a sickness," Raider said. "The point is, she ain't much right now, and I'm getting just plain horny sitting around here with nothing to do but be tempted by the things I ain't got. But I don't know the rules, and I figured I better check with you before I went riding off somewhere."

Mace nodded. Raider hoped it was an approving nod. "The rule is, no one goes out without permission. And now. . . ." Again he shrugged.

"No problem," Raider said with a smile. "For what we've got in mind, I can wait. A long time if it comes to that."

"Good," Mace told him. He hesitated. "There might be. . . ."

"Yes?"

"It is a personal thing and a foolishness no doubt."

"But?" Raider prompted.

"It is my son. He did not come in last night either." He spread his hands in apology. "What can a father do but worry?"

"I don't have any kids, Juanito, but I'd guess you're better off worrying than not having anyone to worry over."

"You are a wise man, John, as well as a quick one. This I had always heard about you, and it is true. You are right. But this does not lessen the pain in the heart of a worrying father."

"No."

"I tell you what we shall do, John. You want to go to the town, and I want to hear if my boy is there. This you can do for me."

"I never met your boy, Juanito. I don't know if it

would be safe for me to be asking around for him,"
Raider protested. He hated to do it, but he had to if he
did not want to arouse Mace's suspicions. Ignorance
was not in order here.

"I have thought of this," Mace admitted. "But I
think perhaps Miguel too would enjoy a few hours to
himself." He touched Raider's arm. "An' I want you an'
Miguel to know each other better, *sí?* It is the two of
you upon whom I must depend when our moment ar-
rives. Men who have shared a bottle and perhaps a
woman or two will work better together than strangers."

Raider nodded. "I agree, Juanito. And . . . how
should I say this? I respect Miguel. He has your respect,
and I am sure that was not lightly given. But I think
there is a distance between us. I agree it would be good
for us to know each other more closely."

Mace smiled, and this time it was an open smile of
real pleasure. "*Sí,* John, my friend. A man of intelligence. This I admire in you. When you leave, John,
please find Miguel. Ask him to see me. Then . . . we
shall see."

"Good enough," Raider said. You're going to talk it
over with him, he thought to himself, and probably
sic him on me as a bird dog. And if you don't, I'm betting that Miguel will be the boy to think of it on his own.
I think what I'd better do is to damned well watch my
tail when we get into that town. Because getting a message out to Doc isn't nearly as important as keeping
this battered hide of mine intact.

CHAPTER EIGHTEEN

The town was called Florence, and there was not a lot to it. With the arrival of the railroad, the citizens, judging from the signs they had erected so hopefully, were expecting quite a boom. It was clear from the age and condition of the few buildings that Florence had been there before the railroad, although Raider could not imagine why. There seemed to be little justification to put a town here except for the fact that a couple of creeks joined the Arkansas at the spot. Maybe that was all the excuse a budding boomer might need, Raider thought.

Miguel had been cheerfully friendly in the few conversations they had had on the long ride from Mace's Hole to Florence. So friendly, in fact, that Raider found the change odd enough to form a left-handed sort of warning. Miguel and/or his bossman probably were up to something.

"There are two cantinas here," Miguel said as they entered the town. "There were more, tent saloons selling Indian whiskey, until the railhead moved on. Now jus' the old places again, I think. If the boy is here, he would be in one of them."

"I always like an excuse to see the inside of a bar," Raider said lightly. "Don't *need* one, you understand, but I always like an excuse."

"But of course, *amigo*." Miguel's smile looked positively oily in Raider's opinion. His opinion was, after all, honed to a fine edge by his desire for self-preservation.

"How 'bout the cathouses?" Raider asked.

"Two of them. One over each of the cantinas. There are a few cribs in the alleys but," he shrugged, "for them a man would not leave the arms of Angelica."

"Lemme ask you a favor then, buddy. If I start to get so drunk that I want to head for one of those places, lay a gun barrel upside my head or something. I'd hate like hell to pay good money for the same kind of stuff I could get back at the Hole."

Miguel grinned and nodded, "*Sí, amigo*. If you will do as much for me."

"That's a deal."

They tied their horses in front of the nearer of the two saloons and rattled their way through the strands of hanging beads suspended in the open doorway. That, Raider knew, was a sign of sheer laziness, having the beads still hanging so long after the fly season was ended.

The saloon was a homey sort of place, the like of which Raider had been in in a hundred different places in a hundred other towns both large and small. It smelled of beer and tobacco and sweat, the individual odors mingling to form the distinct blend that was friendly and welcoming in spite of the separate ingredients.

There were no niceties here, no formal elegance of the kind that would have pleased Juan Mace or the jaded gentlemen of Denver and Kansas City. Instead, this was a workingman's saloon where a fellow could spit on the floor and slap his partner on the back and bray as loud as any Rocky Mountain canary and still feel as comfortable and contented as in his own home. Maybe more so.

No niceties? Hell, there wasn't even a free lunch, Raider noticed. Just nickel beer or dime whiskey out of a bottle the label of which would have no possible relationship to the actual origin of the liquor it held. Raider nodded. He could get along with this as easily as with the other, fancier kind.

In spite of the late afternoon hour, the place was far from booming with business. There was a card game in one corner attended by five men dressed for long riding and hard work. Half a dozen more were propped on the long, unpolished hardwood rail along the front of the bar. Another table was occupied by three men who had the appearance of store clerks or some such town occupation. None of the men seemed to be of Mexican ancestry, and none were as young as Mace's boy would be.

It was unnecessary, but Raider asked it anyway. "Is Geraldo here?"

Miguel shook his head.

"Then I reckon we'd better try the other place before we light into any serious drinking."

Miguel nodded abruptly and spun on his heels. He was out the door and back onto the board sidewalk almost before Raider could respond to follow him.

"I take it you aren't fond of that place," Raider observed when he caught up with Mace's lieutenant.

Miguel gave him a sharp, quick look. "Juanito keeps telling me you are not so stupid for a gringo."

"And you keep forgetting?"

The man shrugged. "So he tells me. Yes, I do not like that place. Our people, sometimes we have trouble there."

"Mace's crew, you mean?"

This time the look Miguel gave him was one of disgust. "No, I do not mean my *compadres* at the camp." He touched the dark skin of his own forearm. "Greasers, *amigo*. Greasers." He made a face as if to spit.

Raider grinned. "Some of the laziest, dirtiest, sorriest bastards I've ever known have been Mexicans. But then I've known some 'Mericans that was worse. You know what I mean?"

"I know. But the fact, it remains. You are a gringo. I am a greaser."

"If you'd rather. Me, I don't care."

"The other place is just over there," Miguel said, changing the subject. Together they swung to their left and crossed the soft, dry dust of Florence's main street.

The second bar was almost a duplicate of the first, except that it had a few more people in it and maybe a few more lamps burning. Since it was the more prosperous place, the owner probably figured he could afford to burn a little more coal oil for his customers' pleasure, Raider decided.

In neither one of them were there any women. And in neither one did Miguel see Geraldo Mace.

"Not here either, huh?" Raider asked.

Miguel shook his head.

"Do you think we should check the cathouses now?"

The Mexican bandit cocked his head thoughtfully and stared out the open doorway—no leftover fly curtain at this door—to check the remaining daylight before he answered. "I do not think so. If the son is in town, he will be sleeping somewhere. We will give him more time to come out if he is in the arms of las' night's woman, eh."

Raider nodded. That sounded fine to him. He was ready for a drink. "Then I'll buy the first round for us, *amigo*."

They drank a couple of beers and carried their third mugs of warm, slightly sour brew to a table where a low-stakes poker game was in progress.

Two hours of play with men whose names Raider never did get straight—nor cared to—left Raider a few dollars ahead of where he had started and Miguel a good twenty dollars behind. With a quarter limit to the raises, that had to have been hard to do, Raider decided. Miguel was either the worst poker player Raider had ever sat at a table with or was deeply in thought somewhere else. Raider gave the man the benefit of the doubt and decided that Miguel must have been worried about Geraldo. No one could be that consistently stupid and continue playing the game.

"I am hungry now," Miguel announced out of the blue as the deal reached Raider again.

"Okay." Raider passed the deck to the next player, a heavyset man who looked somewhat foolish in his hard hat and sagging bow tie but who played carefully and well. "Reckon that does us for a while, boys, but keep our seats warm. We might wanta come back after supper."

The heavy man, ahead by more than Raider was since they had joined the game, nodded agreeably and began to shuffle the cards. One of the other men, though, a slender, bearded fellow who looked like a professional gambler but played like a drummer fresh from New Jersey, began to scowl.

"Bullshit," the unhappy one said. "You're ahead, an' the game is going on. Set where you are an' have some chow sent to the table if you want, but, by God, you're staying in."

Raider gave him an odd look that held no immediate menace. "Mister, my partner here is down further'n you are, and I'm only a couple dollars ahead. If you want to push a quarrel, why don't you wait till it's over something worthwhile?"

"I said you're gonna stay, an', by God, you're gonna stay," the man insisted. He took a swallow of the bar whiskey in a glass by his elbow. The man had been drinking steadily throughout the game but not in heavy amounts, a birdlike sip at a time. Surely he could not be drunk, Raider thought.

Raider would have been content to jolly the fellow out of his unhappiness, but Miguel was as quick to heat up as their recent opponent at the poker table.

The man started to say something else but did not have a chance to finish. As soon as he started to speak, he was interrupted by a flashing knife blade that stopped barely short of his Adam's apple.

The man blanched and seemed to wither in his chair. He began to sputter some sort of denials or apologies, but too softly for the faint, mewing sounds to be understood.

"Miguel, my friend, I think you're feeling a bit peck-ish tonight," Raider said. "Put the knife away 'fore we have to go take a bath before supper."

Miguel grunted something unintelligible. But he removed the knife from the vicinity of the other man's throat and replaced it in the sheath at his belt.

"Neighbor," Raider told the poker player, "you're a pretty lucky man. Stupid as a cow in heat but lucky." He scooped up the handful of coins that represented his winnings and dropped them into his pocket. "I think if we come back to play some more after awhile," he said, "you oughta excuse yourself from the game. I don't believe you're in shape to be playing with the grown-ups tonight. C'mon, Miguel."

They left the saloon with Miguel still angry and on edge.

"Damn, but you're touchy as a rattler with poison ivy rash," Raider said once they were back onto the now dark sidewalk. "What is it?"

"Fucking gringos," Miguel muttered.

"I could take offense to that myself, you know," Raider said mildly.

"I know." Miguel was not backing down a bit.

Raider shrugged. It was better to let it pass for the moment. "Let's get a bite to eat and see if we can find Juanito's boy somewhere."

Miguel grunted.

"Whatever you say." Raider led the way toward the nearest lighted storefront. A sign painted on the window glass claimed "Eats." Jeez, Raider was thinking, with the Mexican in such a fine humor, it was going to be hell trying to get away long enough to send Doc a message.

CHAPTER NINETEEN

Dinner did nothing to give any apparent relief to Miguel's mood. The meal was greasy and foul-tasting, which would have been all right, but it was also inexcusably scanty in the amounts served. Short servings were downright unpardonable, and downright surprising in a railroad town where they must have been used to serving hardworking men who cared more about quantity than quality.

Raider paid for both meals and led the grumbling Mexican away from the restaurant. "Where next, Miguel?" he asked.

Miguel grunted and mumbled a few oaths in Spanish that Raider was not sure were directed toward the eatery's cook or toward Raider himself. At the moment it seemed like either might have applied.

"Look," Raider said. "Bitching and fussing isn't gonna get the boy found nor us taken care of. Where's the nearest cathouse?"

Miguel pointed with his chin in a vaguely delineated direction.

"All right, so you lead the way. Damnation, man, cheer up."

"Bullshit," Miguel said.

"That sounds kinda familiar." Raider was beginning to get into a mood quite as foul as Miguel's. He needed to do *some*thing to make Miguel content, and to let Raider have a little time to himself.

Raider began to get the first glimmerings of an idea.

They reached the cathouse—a very ordinary structure outside and in, with none of the fancy appointments of the better Denver houses—and Raider was glad to see that they were early enough to find more girls in the place than customers. That was just what he wanted.

"Miguel, *mi corazon*." The stringy-haired old bawd who seemed to be in charge greeted Miguel as an old and apparently valued customer. She threw her arms around him and playfully patted the buttons at his crotch. "Too long, Miguel. It has been too long since you have been to see us. And who is this handsome friend of yours?" She gave Raider a wink.

Jeez, Raider thought. Her mustache is heavier than that gappy line of teeth in her gums. He hoped she would not try to kiss him the way she had Miguel.

Miguel performed a grudging set of introductions. The old scag was named Madam la Rosa, and she was filled with honor to be the hostess for a fine gentleman like John Slocum, of whom she had heard so much and so well.

She knew about Slocum, did she? Raider thought. It had not occurred to him before, but now he began to hope fervently that none of her girls had ever met the gentleman whose name Raider had borrowed for the occasion. Wouldn't that be a kick in the teeth? Fingered by a dollar whore when there might be literally millions at stake. Raider began to sweat lightly. If anyone wanted to assume it was in anticipation of the thrills Madam la Rosa's girls were about to provide, that was just fine.

The introductions were completed throughout the room, to men and camisoled whores alike, and Raider began to breath a little easier when no one popped up with a challenge to his identity. None of the others even indicated that they had heard of Slocum before.

The girls were about what Raider would have expected in a dive of this caliber. A bunch of slatterns, most of whom would have looked a hell of a lot more alluring without their rouge than they did with the caked layers of ochre and scarlet that smudged their cheeks and lips. They ranged from fat to scrawny. But, hell, they were all smiling and available, and once the lamp was blown out it would be hard to tell them apart except by smell. Anyway, there were a couple of them who weren't completely hopeless. One, older than most but with a hint of fading elegance in her hollow cheeks—or was that only a lingering bout with the consumption that was taking overlong in killing her?—seemed almost attractive. Raider immediately gave her a smile and a nod to reserve her for the idea he had in mind.

"What's the normal tariff here?" he asked Madam la Rosa.

She gave him a look that was somewhere between a smile and a simper. "Don't tell me you've been rich so long you've forgotten how things are for the working boys, Johnny?"

He smiled back at her. "You just had end-of-track here, ma'am, and I hear the railroad pays mighty well. An' I *sure* wouldn't want to do anything to insult you or this, uh, fine establishment here."

She chuckled and left Miguel to slip an arm around Raider's waist, which was perhaps half as thick as her own. "Ain't you the gentleman now, Johnny. But end-of-track's on down the road now, and we ain't uppity here. Never was." The old bitch smelled worse than a boar hog. Raider wished she would reattach herself to Miguel, who didn't seem to mind the strong odors. "A dollar a throw, Johnny, French or straight. If the girls like you," she pinched him, painfully, "and I'm betting they will, you can prob'ly have it half and half for the same, dearie."

"How much for all night?" Raider asked, resisting an

impulse to pull away from the old bat and run like hell for a tall glass of whiskey.

"Ooo my, Johnny. I like the way you think. Five dollars for the night, sweetie. Busy nights I don't allow that, but. . . ." She shrugged.

"You don't expect to get real busy tonight, do you?"

"Naw. Ever since end-of-track moved, the men in town here've gotten scared the money is gonna be cut off. Or else they've all gone limp an' useless of a sudden. I don't expect we'll be all that busy."

"Good." Raider forced a leering grin. "I just won a couple bucks at the poker table, and my friend Miguel there's been in a bad mood lately. What I thought I'd do is set the both of us up for a night of hard ash-hauling. Something special. Like, say, two girls apiece. Can you handle that?"

"Two girls, Johnny? You bet your sweet pecker we can handle that. And I'd just *love* to be one of them if I wasn't so busy. A pretty thing like you." She sighed with raw envy of the lucky girls who would be sharing Raider's bed that night. At least that was what Raider thought she was trying to do with the drawn-out snort that passed her lips.

So much for flattery. Madam la Rosa got down to business. "First the money, Johnny. Twenty dollars right here," she held out an open palm, "an' haul 'em off."

Raider pulled out the money. Twenty dollars, even with the addition of the several dollars he had won at the table, was going to wipe out nearly everything he had in his pockets. And he sure could not wire Pinkerton's for an advance against his expenses. Come to think of it, they still did not even know that he was on a job. As far as the Pinks were concerned, he was probably absent without authorization and would be subjected to a dock in his pay until he reported in. Damn them. And

damn Miguel and Madam la Rosa and ninety percent
of the rest of the world to boot. He gave the old bawd
the money.

She tucked it efficiently away and gave Miguel another friendly pat on the crotch. Good grief, Raider
thought, if she was that attentive to him *after* the money
was in her hands—no, even if he was blind drunk, surely Miguel wouldn't be pig enough to bed the old bitch
herself, not on the busiest and horniest of nights when
the working girls would be soaked with the last twenty
customers' sticky leavings.

"You are generous," Miguel said. It was the first he
had spoken in some time.

"Hell, we can both use it."

"Then the first choice is yours, *amigo*," Miguel said.

Good, Raider thought with relief. He isn't going to
argue about it or question the gift. Thank goodness.

Raider immediately nodded toward the slender, almost elegant-looking older whore who was hovering
hopefully nearby, and she drifted to his side and into
the curl of his right arm with a smile of quite evident
gratitude.

Miguel crooked a finger at a giggly, plump little thing
with a head full of frizzy, henna-red hair, and Raider
raised an eyebrow toward the woman who was already
with him. She nuzzled his ear and whispered, "Take
Suzanne too, honey. She's the tall girl in the corner
there."

That was fine by Raider. He really didn't care who
the second whore was. The fact was, he was more interested in a veteran's judgment—or disinterest—than
he was in the prospect of superior sex. He didn't really
expect to find that here anyway. And Suzanne looked
like she had been in the business nearly as long as the
first one had. Raider gave Suzanne a nod, and she
looked almost as grateful as the first girl.

Without waiting to see who Miguel picked as his second bedmate, Raider took a whore on each arm and sashayed up the stairway toward the bare little cubicles that Madam la Rosa provided for her customers' privacy.

CHAPTER TWENTY

It was an interesting problem Raider had set for himself, made all the more so by the fact that Suzanne and the first girl, who said she was called Nellie, were so obviously eager to complete their appointed tasks. As soon as they were locked safely into the room and out of sight of the rest of the horny herd, Nellie led the way and Suzanne quickly followed in a determined assault on Raider's fly buttons.

"Slow up there, ladies, we got all night," he suggested. A grin from Suzanne and a licking of Nellie's lips was the only response he got.

"Damn it now, I'm serious, girls. I mean, I want to lay back an' enjoy this the way it oughta be done, you know."

"Oh, we do know indeed," Nellie assured him.

"Cut it out now, will you? No. *Quit!*" He was becoming annoyed and a little bit worried. Now that he had gotten rid of Miguel, he still had to get rid of the two excessively willing whores. Without, he hoped, doing anything to make them talk about it afterward. "Looka here," he said, "I want to be able to *really* relax through all this. You, uh, wouldn't have any peyote handy, would you?" It seemed a safe enough request. Liquor they would have in abundance if he asked for it, but the town should be too far north and too far off the beaten track to have a Southwestern delicacy like the dream-making peyote buttons on hand.

"I can check," Suzanne offered quickly. "We might could have some downstairs."

"No, wait a minute. I, uh, I'd just as soon not have anyone know I like the stuff. You understand?"

"Sure." Both women shrugged. At their ages they would have been in the business long enough that Raider doubted he could have come up with *any* request that would genuinely startle them or so much as mildly surprise them. Asking them to perform with a troop of elephants before an audience probably would not be found objectionable as long as they were paid up front.

"I really want to keep this on the quiet," Raider went on. "And I think I spotted a fella in town who could fix me up. Why don't you girls wait right here while I slip out and find the guy. I won't be long, and you can prob'ly use the rest." He grinned. "Getting ready for me, see."

The professional animation left their faces, and Suzanne turned wearily to slump on the sagging edge of the one small bed in the tiny room.

"Whatever you want, honey," Nellie said. She too turned away and took a seat to wait for him.

"I won't be long," Raider assured them. He gave Suzanne a wet kiss on the lips and Nellie a longer and deeper one. "Just make sure you're here when I get back. I mean I am *really* looking forward to this." Which was no lie. After Angelica, he really was.

Raider slipped out into the dimly lighted hallway. Either business was poor enough to warrant oil savings, or some of the establishment's customers preferred not to be recognized; the place was downright dark and dangerous. He felt his way in a direction opposite that toward the main stairway they had come up a moment earlier.

He heard voices inside one of the rooms he passed

—a man's voice that he thought was Miguel's and a high-pitched giggle that came from a woman's throat. He did not hear the voice of the second woman Miguel had taken with him, but maybe she was already too busy to talk.

Raider had hoped for a doorway and an outside set of stairs at the end of the hall. Instead he found a window.

He eased the sash open and leaned out. The window opened onto a small roof, apparently over a back-door stoop or some such thing below. Fair enough. He climbed out onto the wooden shingles—mercifully tight —and let himself over the edge. The small back porch had a handrail he would be able to climb onto to regain access to the second floor of the whorehouse once his business in town was concluded.

The railroad depot and office was only a block and a half away, and he had no trouble finding it. The hour was late enough that he had little worry about being seen on the streets, but his luck was not running entirely good. A light showed in the railroad dispatcher's office. Either the dispatcher or a telegraph operator seemed to be working late, damn the luck. Raider had no desire to be seen by anyone. He could not afford to be associated with any strange message leaving the town of Florence, because for all he knew Juan Mace had half the population of the town and three-quarters of the railroad employees here on retainer as paid spies. It was a most unlikely possibility, but who the hell wanted to take chances with his own life?

He stopped well back in the shadows from the lighted depot and found a comfortable spot to hunker next to a tree trunk while he found a scrap of paper and a pencil stub in his shirt pocket. Doc Weatherbee had tried over and over again to drill into him the necessity for keeping such articles handy. Maybe for once Doc's suggestions were paying off.

Normal procedure would be to send a message to Doc in Phillips code, a sort of telegraphic shorthand, but lately the damned operators had begun using Phillips themselves. And Western Union had begun charging a regular word rate for the messages, even if they were put into Phillips by the sender. Predictably enough, Allan Pinkerton had begun to balk at its use by Pink operatives, basing his objections on the ever-important expense figures. The man was an out-and-out tightwad.

Pinkerton's did supply several other code possibilities, and Raider and Doc had a version of their own. But Raider always had trouble remembering the damn thing.

Now he was berating himself for that occasional lapse of memory. He sure could not send the message in clear language or in a Phillips form that the local operator might understand. He had to get word out but preferably, almost necessarily, in a form that only Doc or another Pink would be able to translate into any meaning.

For about fifteen minutes Raider hunkered against the base of the tree, chewing the wooden end of his pencil and racking his memory in search of the right words and letter combinations. Finally he began to write.

> HOW NOW GRAY COW QUERY ALL THE EGGS IN THE GRINDER ARE ABOUT TO BE BROKEN SOONEST STOP TWO BASKETS FULL STOP OP STOP EAST PTOGNMSG STOP OP STOP MOONLIGHT STOP OP STOP LONESOME STOP WITHOUT FAIL

If anyone but Doc could make sense out of *that* mess of gobbledygook, Raider would recommend that Pinkerton's hire him. "Grinder" was a steam engine, "eggs" a boodle of money, "op" meant to reverse the meaning of what came next, "ptognmsg" was the message's point of origin, and so on. The question now was whether

Doc would receive the message and what he could do about it if he did.

Since Raider was not sure yet about the exact train Mace intended to hit, there was little more he could do at the moment except hope. And wonder.

There was also the question, of course, about how Pinkerton's would want to handle the whole affair, assuming that Doc could manage his end of the deal. There was even the possibility that Allan, pennywise little cretin that he was, would cheerfully stand aside and watch the train being robbed, then wait until the Denver and Rio Grande had made its best recovery offer before any action took place.

Oh, well. Raider sighed. That part of it, thank goodness, was not his to worry about. He rolled the penciled message into a cylinder, reached into his pocket for his bit of remaining money, and grinned. The hell with it. He unrolled the message again, wrote "send collect" at the top in parentheses, and slipped a quarter tip into the package when he rerolled the whole thing.

He slipped cautiously toward the still-lighted depot and left his wire balanced on the doorknob, where the operator was sure to find it coming or going. That done, Raider grinned into the chilly darkness and headed back for the ladies who were waiting for him.

CHAPTER TWENTY-ONE

Raider was barely inside the door when Nellie and Suzanne descended on him like a pair of milk-pail calves looking for their artificial nipples. The two whores dropped to their knees and flipped the buttons at his fly open so fast that he was not sure they could have done it any quicker if they had yanked them off instead. In fact, for a moment he was not sure they hadn't. They reached inside and pulled him out into public view, and he was just about the right size and shape and consistency for a calf nipple. But that didn't last long. One good flick of Suzanne's tongue and a hot, wet slurp into Nellie's throat, and Raider's organ more closely resembled a stove poker than an India-rubber nipple.

"Jeez," he yelped. "Do you girls always greet your customers like this? Hell, I'm gonna be back, you can bet on it."

Nellie mumbled something in reply, but he could not make out what she was saying.

"It isn't polite to talk with your mouth full," Raider told her.

"What she's saying," Suzanne told him, "is that we were getting worried about you, Johnny. You been gone so long an' all."

He shrugged. "I couldn't find the fella I was looking for. Hell, though, you're more interesting than anything

I could get from him anyhow. It was a lousy idea. Forgive me?"

Two eager pairs of hands helped him out of his clothing and shoved him down onto the bed, where they could work on him better.

For long moments Raider felt as if he had been set afloat on a sea of moving tongues and lightly caressing fingertips. He closed his eyes and gave in to the swirling flow of warm, moist sensations.

He did not know and did not really care which of them was doing what at any given moment. Their tongues and hands and dangling, silky breasts roved up and down the length of his hard-muscled body, building him slowly toward a feverish pitch and letting him down again just as gently until he began to wonder whether this was really happening or whether he had simply drifted off to sleep and was in the midst of the finest wet dream a grown man had ever known.

Lordy, he thought, these old broads are *prime*.

He felt one pair of lips nipping the loose, sensitive skin of his scrotum while another pulled him deep into her throat.

Raider moaned.

They lifted his legs high into the air and doubled them back toward his chest, and for a moment he wondered what they were up to. Leave them to it, he decided. They're the pros here.

He felt the bed shift as one of them left him for a moment and turned around, straddling him while she faced the other way. She lowered herself onto him, a surprisingly tight pussy sliding down the hard length of his tool while the other one guided him inside.

If that did not feel good enough, the other girl quickly jumped from being a guide to a participant, running her tongue over his balls and down to his anus while the topside girl began to pump slowly up and down.

"I could get addicted to this," he murmured.

"Us too, Johnny," one of them said. He thought it was Nellie. He wasn't sure and really didn't care. Whoever was wherever, he was content with the way things were.

As if on some kind of cue, both girls disengaged themselves at once and again shifted positions. He opened his eyes and smiled as Nellie lay atop him, her body light and warm and dry against him. He kissed her and felt Suzanne tonguing his balls and guiding him into an amazingly tight, rather dry recess in Nellie's slim body.

Raider drew his face a few inches away from Nellie's and cocked an eyebrow at her. She grinned and nodded confirmation of what he had guessed.

"It feels kinda good back there for a change," she said. "But you are a big one, Johnny. Mmm-um!"

Nellie raised herself from him slightly to spear him all the deeper into her and then smiled at the look on his face.

Raider grinned and reached between them, his fingers finding and lightly brushing the hard, tiny button that would produce the woman's pleasure. She looked shocked at first and then quickly pleased, delighted. Within a few moments the focus of her eyes left Raider's face and drifted toward some distant place. She bit her underlip slightly and shuddered under his touch.

"My God, Johnny, I haven't done that in years. Not with a man I haven't."

"Then I'm glad to've been of service, pretty thing," he said.

Nellie slipped away and let Suzanne mount him in her place, and Raider repeated the courtesy for her.

If Raider thought they had been good before, he was astounded now. The pair of veteran bawds carried him to heights he had not known he could reach. Carried him to the tops of the distant mountains and sent explosions rocketing through his balls like Fourth of July fireworks on a hot, still night. And then pulled him right back up to the heights again to start the whole thing over anew.

It was dawn before the two women finally conceded that they could get him off no more, and by then Raider was tender, almost sore the full length of his still-willing but quite unable cock. He was as completely satiated as he had ever been in his lifetime. Or more.

"Damn," he muttered. "If it wasn't for the incest laws, I swear I'd adopt the both of you an' take you home for good."

They quit covering his hard chest with light, butter-fly kisses and nuzzled against him, one on each side in the curl of Raider's arms. Their quiet little mewings of pleasure sounded almost like purring, and Raider felt very much like what he imagined a tomcat must feel at the end of a long and pleasant night in the alleys.

Damn, he thought as he was drifting off into sleep, why didn't I think of this before? He smiled to himself with his last hold on half-wakeful consciousness. All in the line o' duty too. He knew nothing more.

CHAPTER TWENTY-TWO

"I haven't felt this pussy-whipped or this satisfied in a helluva while," Raider observed as they rode. They were traveling at a ground-covering road jog and had been for more than an hour. It had been somewhat longer than that since Miguel had last spoken. If Raider had expected his generosity of the previous night to make Miguel his instant buddy, he was sorely disappointed. On the other hand, the gesture had indeed served its purpose. It had allowed him to separate from the Mexican long enough to get his wire sent. He hoped.

That was still in doubt. Ever since he had left the rolled message at the depot door, he had been fretting about whether it would be sent, whether it would be received, whether it would do any good.

Well, almost ever since that time. Since he had awakened late in the morning, anyway.

Raider smiled to himself. He was still more than a little tender and had that hollow feeling of complete satisfaction deep in his lower belly, somewhere just about where his balls took root. Damn, but he did feel pretty good in that respect, and the hell with Miguel.

He knew, of course, what was bothering Mace's lieutenant. They had had themselves a fine night on the town, but they had not accomplished what they had come in for. They still had no idea where Geraldo Mace was, or the kid who had been with him.

Not that Raider really cared. His absence had been of service. Now the boy was Miguel's worry, and Mace's.

They made good time getting back to Mace's Hole. When they did arrive, Raider was pleased to be riding close to the still-silent Miguel. Even knowing where he should look for the guards at the narrow entrance to the Hole, he almost missed seeing them. They had long since detected the approach of the riders and stayed well hidden until they could clearly see who was trying to enter the gap they guarded. Anyone who tried to get through there without their consent would be in for a bad time of it, including, Raider reflected, an army of Pinks. He hoped Doc Weatherbee would be damned well careful this trip. He did not want the old grayhead perforated by Juan Mace's efficient sentinels.

It was past the supper hour and nearly dark when they reached the corrals to unsaddle their horses and turn the road-weary animals loose to ravage the hay rick.

"Should I come with you to check in with Juanito?" Raider asked. He had given up trying to make small talk with Miguel several hours before.

"*Sí*. Come along."

They walked in silence to the house, and Miguel paused to knock at the side door before they entered. Behind them, Raider could smell the tantalizing odors of cooked meat and some other spicy dish, but he doubted that anyone would have thought to save any for them. Oh well, he decided, he had missed a meal before and survived the experience. No doubt he would be able to suffer through until breakfast yet again.

Mace answered the knock with a call for them to come in. The man looked older than Raider remembered him, old and somewhat haggard. But then, Raider realized, what they had to tell him was already obvious. Geraldo was not with them.

"Sit," Mace invited.

They observed the formalities of accepting a drink from the old bandit and took their first sips in polite silence before speaking of the thing that had brought them there. Miguel, Raider noticed, was waiting for his boss to make the first conversational move, and so Raider did the same. It was several long minutes before Mace inquired, "You have heard nothing? Seen nothing?"

Raider looked at Miguel and waited for him to speak. It was, after all, his place to make the report.

Miguel shook his head. He added a flow of words in rapid-fire, liquid Spanish, but the shake of the head had been enough. There really was no need to add more.

Mace received the news with stony indifference feigned on his face, Raider saw. The man would have been quite a poker player the way he could hide his feelings. There had been enough hints already for Raider to guess how deeply Juan Mace felt toward and about this beloved son of his. For him to accept the negative report from Miguel so calmly was a mark of Mace's control, not of indifference.

Once that was disposed of, Mace became again the polite host instead of the chieftain.

"You have been on the road for too long," he said, "and you have missed your supper. Permit me to serve you here."

Mace led the way into the elegant portion of the little house and back to the kitchen area, which Raider had not seen before. It was as finely appointed as the main part of the house, with ornately carved chairs ringed around a massive table that would have looked much more in place inside a formal dining room three times the size of the little kitchen. The stove was in its own way an excellent piece, with carefully blacked ironwork and highly polished nickel plating on the trim and the tall, warming oven. Once again Raider had to shake his head at Juan Mace's odd sense of taste in this virtual wilderness so far from the degree of cultured civilization Mace so obviously admired.

There was no sign of Elaine Volnay. She was in the still-unseen bedroom, Raider assumed. Mace pointed them to their seats and excused himself for a moment. He disappeared into the end of the house Raider had not yet seen and returned soon, still alone. He said nothing about his departure but began to serve them some leftover beef from a platter he took from a cooler box and a pot of stewed tomatoes and onions that had been in the warming oven. While Miguel and Raider ate, Mace built the oven fire anew and put a pot of coffee on the stove to boil.

"Mighty good, Juan," Raider offered when his plate was empty for the final time and had been set aside in the copper-lined sink.

"It was my pleasure," Mace insisted.

"Look, you fellows prob'ly have a lot you'll want to talk about. And I'm kinda tired after last night."

That brought a slight smile and a lift of the eyebrows from Mace. For the first time Miguel's expression relaxed from the harsh frown lines he had carried all through the day.

"It was a night to be remembered," Miguel told his boss, "thanks to our *compadre* John."

"Tell me."

Miguel did. Apparently he had been quite as satisfied as Raider with the dual performance of the night before.

Mace smiled, fully this time, when the explanations and bragging were done. "This was good. I am glad now that you have gone, even if you looked in the wrong place for the son. It is good." He sighed. "Ah, to be young and vigorous again. How fine this would be. But no matter." He waved his hand in the air. "An old man, he has memories of his past, and while there is life, there are yet pleasures. Remember this, you young ones, and do not disdain the coming of age and wisdom." He sighed again, and it was obvious from the distant expression he wore that he was viewing memories in the privacy of his mind. And some of them perhaps were not so distant.

Raider coughed and looked absently at the dark grounds in the bottom of his porcelain coffee cup.

"But I have been keeping you, John, and you said you were tired. By all means, you may be excused. We shall see you in the morning, yes? And, John . . . thank you for assisting in this search. I had no right to ask it of you, and I thank you for your help. Yes?"

Raider said his goodnights as politely as he knew how and let himself out the way they had come in, through the side door that at least some of Mace's crowd got to see from time to time.

It was cold when Raider stepped into the night. The late season and high altitude combined to put a sharp bite in the air, and he wished he had not left his blanket-lined coat tied to the back of his saddle. He stepped off the low porch and angled his path toward the corral where his saddle was slung over a rail.

"Psst!"

Raider stopped, dropped into a crouching spin, and palmed his revolver even before he had time to register the thought that the sound was a deliberate one intended to get his attention. He felt more than a little foolish standing there shivering with a gun in his hand and no idea what or who he should shoot at. He chuckled out loud and put the gun away. "Sorry," he said softly into the inky darkness that faced him. "You startled me. Whoever the hell you are."

"Over here." The voice was a whisper, but it failed to disguise the speaker. There were only two women in this camp, and the skinny Angelica certainly did not possess the throaty, velvet tones of those two softly uttered words. It was Mace's beauty, Elaine, who had spoken to him. "Over here," she said again.

Raider moved forward slowly and feeling his way cautiously as he entered the deep shadows behind Mace's house. He was completely blinded here, so dark was the sheltered area, and would have been at the woman's mercy if she had intended to do him any harm.

She did not. He sensed her presence when he neared her. He could smell the fresh, clean odor of her skin and hair and would have sworn he could feel the warmth of her body as well. Her hand found his and tugged him forward.

Without warning, the full-bodied voluptuousness of this magnificent creature was pressed against him and he felt her arms wrap around him. Arms, he noted, that were comfortably enclosed in a thick coat of some kind. Raider wished he could have said as much for his own arms, despite the fascinating implications of finding the Volnay woman here and suddenly having her superb form plastered against his body.

Her face socketed into the hollow of his throat, and he could feel her rise on tiptoes—she was a big woman and needed little extra lift—to place her lips against his right ear. Her breath was hot against his cold skin, and he began to become erect in spite of his discomfort.

She started to say something, then stopped and pulled back from his ear a fraction of an inch. He felt more than heard the chuckle deep in her throat, and she reached between them to draw the front of her coat open and press herself more firmly against him.

"Do I feel something there, John? Yes? Oh, certainly I do. And from the size of the bulge, I would say you are a stallion to be reckoned with, John Slocum. Mmmmm. A stallion fit to satisfy any mare in heat."

Her hand dropped away from her coat and moved

none too gently to his crotch. Through the cloth of his trousers she began to tug and pull at him.

"That isn't a lump of dough there, you know. You don't have to knead it to get it to rise."

"Oh, but I do need it, John. Mmm, yes, I would say that I do."

"Then maybe we should find us a place that isn't so, um, exposed to the elements, let's say."

She laughed lightly, and more loudly than he found comfortable, and said, "But, John, my sweet, have you never bundled a girl into the woods in wintertime and spread her legs in a drift of new snow? Surely you have not missed out on this treat?"

Raider laughed. "Yeah, I guess I have at that. But it was a hell of a long time ago. I was prob'ly fourteen at the time and randy as a damned billy goat."

"Of course you have. And so have I, although in the less comfortable of the two positions. But you are telling me that this was long ago and now you are too dignified and bent on the creature comforts, no?"

"No. Hell, lady, if that's the way you really want it, I'll oblige you. But I don't mind admitting that I'd enjoy being able to take my time about it. If I remember correctly, that ol' game is kinda on-again, off-again, an' head for the stove. Remember?"

"Indeed I do, John Slocum. And you are right. Come with me. Carefully. There are some loose billets of firewood on the ground back here. Please be so kind as to not trip and fall. I do not think you want Juanito to join us."

Raider shivered, and it was from much more than the temperature. No, he had not forgotten Bruce or the horrible way the man had died.

For a moment he had to wonder whether Elaine had led Bruce too into a sheltered place to give her satisfaction and then gained another kind of satisfaction afterward from Mace's reactions when she told him about it.

No, Raider decided after a scant moment. It had not seemed like that at all.

Of course, his opinion on the subject could well have been influenced by the rising surge of desire he felt when he thought about the creamy texture of Elaine Volnay's flesh and the ripe fullness of her figure. The woman was a genuine, by-God beauty, and he meant to have her. He had known from the first time he saw her that he would, he must have her. And he was not going to turn fainthearted now when she was leading him to the hay.

CHAPTER TWENTY-THREE

Quite literally into the hay as it turned out. She led him around behind the house and across a starlit expanse of rock and grass to a thick grove of aspen. There seemed to be a path through the slender trunks and lacy leaves, but it was a good thing she knew the way because Raider would have been blundering around like a bull buffalo in rut if he had been left to find his own way. Still, it was probably a good thing there was no moon yet, he decided. If Mace or Miguel happened to be wandering in the vicinity of a window, it would not do for them to see him here with Mace's woman.

Behind the aspen grove they came to a low shelter. Elaine opened a door and drew him inside. She let go of his hand, and a moment later he heard the scrape of a sulfur match. The lucifer flared, and she used it to light a lantern hanging from a support pole.

The shed was a small barn. Elaine's sleek horse was stabled in a box stall in half of the small building, and her tack and a set of grooming brushes hung neatly on pegs driven into the back wall. Most of the floor in the remaining half of the building was covered by a deep pile of grass hay. Elaine slipped out of her coat, gave Raider a coquettish smile, and arranged herself in a lovely but hardly demure pose on the hay.

159

"Now, John. If this is comfortable enough to suit you. . . ."

It was.

He lowered himself beside her and took her into his arms. Her mouth was hot against his and just as fiercely eager in her desire for him. Her tongue plunged deep into his mouth and traced the hard line of his teeth. He met her tongue thrust for thrust, and the woman began to moan.

There was no heat inside the building except that provided by the body heat of the horse, but Raider found that he was no longer cold. He was not cold in the slightest. If anything, he was burning up now, but the temperature outside his body had nothing to do with that. Elaine Volnay had everything to do with it.

The hell with caresses. The hell with gentleness. Not now. Not yet. Raider's groping hand flew down to the hem of Elaine's skirt and hauled the material up to waist level, exposing pale, soft skin that he should have savored with his lips and tongue but did not. There would be time enough for that later. Now he wanted to grab her, to knead her most private flesh as she had been pulling and tugging at his cock a few minutes before, and to plunge himself deep into her.

His hand found the wet depths of her and rudely shoved her legs apart. She responded in kind, throwing her head back and moaning aloud while she clutched at the bulge in his trousers and began to fumble at the buttons of his fly.

Raider had not felt so intensely, agonizingly horny since he was a teenage kid with pimples where his beard should be. He helped her yank the last of the buttons free and grinned at the look of excited pleasure that crossed her face when his prick sprang free and hard and upright into view.

"Now. Please. Now."

He nodded. He could not find and did not need

words. Not at that moment. He flung himself onto her and felt her hands, as eager as his, cling to him and guide him in a swift plunge that enveloped him in the heat of her loins.

Their coupling was quick and frenzied, a mad ride on a madly bucking animal that was this beautiful woman with the golden hair and the flesh like superheated silk.

Elaine shuddered and climaxed as rapidly and as intensely as Raider did. For a long, powerful moment they strained against each other, rigid from necks to toes with the intensity of that first release.

Only later, with the initial passion spent, did Raider lie beside her to cuddle and pet the golden sheen of her hair, to run his tongue over the exquisite length of her neck, and to gently remove the layers of cloth that hid her perfect breasts.

She closed her eyes and gave herself to him then, allowing him the full use of her body—and her body was perfection. He had never seen any female form in any idealized saloon painting that so perfectly exemplified what a woman could and should be. Elaine Volnay made Venus de Milo seem no better an example of womankind than Angelica.

Raider paid homage to her perfection with his lips and tongue, finding and tasting every part of her. Long before he was finished with his explorations, she was aroused again, moaning softly and moving her hips with every flick of his darting, gliding tongue.

"Oh, my sweet, sweet John. This, yes . . . this. This is what I have wanted. This is what it should be with a man. Oh, yes. Mmmmm. Yes." She shuddered, more softly this time, and arched her back as the climax built its fire inside her and swept through her body. She lay back against the hay, limp and for the moment satisfied.

"Don't go to sleep there, girl. I'm a long way from being done."

"Believe me, I know." She pushed him flat against the hay and slowly began to remove for him the clothes he had not yet gotten around to discarding. "Now it's my turn, sweet. Lie still and let me do the work, yes?"

"Yes." Yes and yes again, he thought.

She was gentle now, giving to him as he had given to her, lingering over each touch and each taste, using her hands and her lips and her tongue.

She drew away from him and sat up beside him. She lifted her arms to unpin her hair, and he thought he had never seen a breast before this moment, because in comparison any other breast was no more than a beef cow's teat to be used for the production of milk. But none other could have this beauty of symmetry and firmness, this tip-tilted perfection capped with the palest of rose-hued nipples.

Raider sighed loudly and lay there enjoying the sight of her, unhurried, content to wait as long as it took, enthralled by the sight of this woman's loveliness.

"There." She withdrew the last of the pins that had been holding her hair in place. With a toss of her head she shook her hair free in a cascade of shimmering gold. "Now."

She gave him a hoyden's smile and bent over him.

With her nipples she lightly traced the lines of Raider's chest. She allowed the soft, curling ends of her hair to follow the insides of his thighs lightly.

The soft, cool touch of her hair seemed to take on a life of its own, tracing the outlines of his body, bringing him to a renewed surge of excitement, gently moving across his balls and up and down the length of his cock.

The touch, light though it was, was almost too much to bear, and he began to pump his hips to meet flesh that was not yet there, meeting, instead, the teasing, tantalizing, yielding flow of gold that was her hair.

"No, not yet," she whispered.

He thought it would never end, and the weightless

hint of touch went on and on until he thought he could not stand it a moment longer without grabbing her and forcing himself into her.

At the last possible instant Elaine bent swiftly to claim him, taking him deep into the heat of her mouth.

Raider cried out with a pleasure that was almost pain and on the third thrust into her throat, spewed a gout of hot come.

She felt the pulsing spasms that racked through him and pushed herself down farther over him, taking him even deeper and staying with him until the last sticky drops had been pumped from him.

Still she stayed with him and milked the last possible juice from his body, ingesting it into her own body.

Finally she lifted her head from him and smiled. She licked her lips and wiped her mouth with the back of her hand.

"There," she said cheerfully. "I think that should take care of the hurry-up part of all this. Now, sweet, let's get down to some serious screwing. Okay?"

Raider grinned and held his arms open, welcoming her into them. "Yeah. Let's get serious now."

CHAPTER TWENTY-FOUR

Raider was nervous when he woke the next morning, satiated but uneasy. If the woman had told Mace . . .

There was no way he could know, though, until he showed his face outside. Or until they came for him. And lying in bed would not make troubles go away if he had any.

He took little time pulling his trousers on and fastening the buttons that had given Elaine so much trouble the night before. That delay seemed funny now, although it certainly had not at the time.

Damn, but she was good.

He buckled his gunbelt into place, feeling infinitely better with the weight of the dark-blue Colt at his hip, and stamped his feet into his boots.

It was funny, he reflected, how much better a man can feel with his gun close at hand and his boots on his feet. Without them, he felt naked and vulnerable. With them, he would face whatever came.

He finished dressing at a slower pace and stepped out into the angled, early morning sunlight. It was still cold enough to give the bracing air a brittle feeling and to give everything he could see a curious, almost unnatural clarity. And he still had not gotten his jacket from his saddle.

At least, he noticed, everything he could see seemed

quite normal. Everyone was beginning to get up and move about, hunched against the cold, with their faces showing the vestiges of sleep. The camp seemed perfectly normal.

Raider hunched his shoulders in a futile attempt to defeat the cold, no doubt looking exactly like all the rest of the men as he scurried along with his hands thrust into his pockets. He headed for the corral.

He reclaimed his coat and pulled it on with a grateful groan of anticipation. In another moment he would be warm. He pulled his deerskin gloves from the side pockets of the coat and drew them on too. They provided little protection against the weather, but at least they did not too seriously interfere with his ability to use a gun.

The very finest gloves, and Raider's were as fine as money could buy and leathercrafter could make, would interfere. Anyone who did not believe that might well find himself unexpectedly dead one fine, cold day. But there was a choice that had to be made, and a hand numbed by cold will not act swiftly either.

Raider looked around. It seemed, judging from appearances, that he did not have to worry about that choice this morning. No one seemed to be paying any attention to him whatsoever.

Warmer now, his shoulders relaxing inside the protection of the coat, he turned away from Mace's house and relieved himself in the dust of the corral.

Feeling considerably better, he ambled at a normal relaxed pace toward the chow hall and was rewarded with the clear, ringing sound of a spike being struck on an iron triangle.

Angelica would have been up for several hours already to prepare the meal that was now being offered, he thought. He wondered why she continued to accept the miserable life she was given here, if she had any choice about it.

Had he somehow been thrust into her position, Raider knew, he would have had to rebel. One way or another he would have to get out, get away. He shook his head. He honestly did not understand people like Angelica, people who would stay on and take everyone else's dirty water time and time again. He would have thought she could have, and would have, run like hell at the first opportunity. Or at none. Certainly *he* would have done so, but then, he was not Angelica.

Hell's bells, he remembered, Mace had said that she had been his own private stock at one time. That must have been quite a while ago, judging from what the woman looked like now and from what Mace's tastes so obviously were. So she had been here for a long time, possibly for a *very* long time. He just couldn't understand that.

He joined the line of men moving into the chow hall. He was not sure until they all sat down at the long table, but there were fewer of them now than there had been when he and Miguel had left for Florence. A good many of the men were missing, which meant that something was probably up.

Mace had said he intended to let things cool off until the big job, and so it was not likely that they were off pulling some nickel-and-dime haul. Whatever they were up to, it must have something to do with Mace's history-making robbery plans. And if that was correct, the time for the job was coming near.

Raider began to worry all over again about whether Doc had gotten his message. And if he had, what the old boy could do about it. All of a sudden Raider began to feel very much alone and vulnerable among this crew of thieves and layabouts.

He ate his breakfast in silence and was sitting over a barely warm cup of coffee with his thoughts in Santa Fe when the other men finished wolfing their food and filed quickly out. Neither Miguel nor Mace had showed up for the meal.

Raider sighed, tasted the nearly cold and now quite bitter coffee, and made a sour face.

"Here, lemme freshen that up for you." He had not noticed Angelica at work in the long room, but she had been paying attention to him. She was at his side by the time she finished speaking and took the coffee cup from his unresisting fingers. "I've got some fresh in the kitchen."

She fairly flew in her effort to serve him and was back almost immediately with two freshly poured cups of steaming coffee. She pulled out the chair next to his and perched on the forward edge of it as if she were ready to spring to her feet and make a show of being at work if anyone walked in on them.

"Thank you, ma'am." Raider raised his cup toward her in salute and took a sip. "That's better."

"I haven't seen you much for a couple days," she said.

"No, I been busy. Had to go into town for the boss-man."

"Oh, I know where you went. An' why. I hear lotsa things, you know."

"Really?" Raider was more annoyed by the woman's presence than interested in anything she might have to say. But after the way he had treated her before, he felt an obligation to at least be polite to her and pretend an interest he did not feel.

"Sure I do. Why, I even know where you was till so early this morning."

Raider's eyes turned cold. He gave her a look that sent her physically reeling on her chair and made her slop coffee onto the remains of someone's breakfast.

"My God, John, don't look at me like that. I didn't mean anything by it."

"How do you know?" he demanded, his expression

still as cold as if his face had been carved from a block of ice.

"Please, John. I *swear* I only meant to be teasing you. I wouldn't tell a soul. That's the truth." She was clearly frightened of him. She did not try to shrink away from him, but her eyes were wide with fear and she was even paler than normal. She began to quiver.

"I asked you. . . ."

"I know. I know you did. I was awake already, fixing to start my cook fire. I went out to do my business." Her eyes left his, embarrassment conflicting with fear. "I don't know why I oughta care. There ain't a man here that hasn't had me but them two queer ones, but I still find that a private thing. Anyway, I went over into the woods, an' I seen you and her walking together. That's all there was to it, John. I *swear* I only meant to tease you about it. Nothing more."

"Then you didn't hear anybody talking about me?"

She shook her head violently from side to side in her denial. "No, nor I won't say anything about it to anybody neither. I can promise you that. I swear on it and," she swallowed hard, "hope to die if I ain't telling the truth."

Raider sat for a moment in uncomfortable silence. There was no question that she was frightened of him. But she was probably in mortal terror of Juan Mace or she would not still be here. So the question was not what she *intended* to do at this moment but what she *would* do at some time in the future.

What it came down to was that this slatternly female held Raider's life balanced on the tip of her tongue. She had had reason to be grateful to him before, but he had turned right around and abused her. She could damned well go either way on him.

The only sure way to keep her quiet was to kill her, and he could not do that. It was one thing to kill a man in self-defense. But to kill a woman, even one with as little value as Angelica, simply was not in him.

He could try to get her out of the camp, but that just opened up another risk of discovery. Besides, she would take her mouth with her wherever she went, and it was pretty plain that old Mace had a most efficient network of informers. Outside, the woman could tell by accident a story she might refuse to deliberately tell here in Mace's Hole.

Christ, he thought, what do I do now?

"John."

"What?" he barked at her.

"I'm sorry. I'm truly sorry. I never meant to worry you. I only meant to play some fun with you. I guess . . . I guess it's been so long that I've forgot how." She began to cry.

Cursing himself and her too beneath his breath, Raider put an arm around her skinny shoulders and did his best to comfort her. It was not a thing he was practiced at, but he made the effort.

CHAPTER TWENTY-FIVE

A grinning Juan Mace called Raider inside the little house late that morning. Miguel was there too along with a man Raider had not seen before, a burly, good-looking Black Irishman who was introduced as Bert O'Something-or-other. O'Meara, Raider thought.

"Sit, my friends and companions. Sit. Drink. Here, have some of this brandy." He smiled. "Bert brought it in with him this morning, and he swears it to be the finest to be found between San Francisco and Boston."

Mace poured for the four of them, and Raider decided Bert might well have been correct in his judgment. It was indeed an exceptional brandy.

They sat for a while in Mace's study, sipping their drinks while Miguel and his leader made small talk. The new man, Raider noticed, said little but seemed quite comfortable in his silence. He gave an impression of being a bright and competent man who would be a handful if anyone tried to take him with either fists or firearms. He gave no hint of where he had been recently or what he had been up to, although it was fairly obvious that it would have been on Juan Mace's business. Raider supposed that everyone in the room except himself already knew the details.

After the obligatory period of social conversation— there were times when Raider found Mexicans to be about as "polite" that way as Indians are—Mace sat his glass aside with a smile of satisfaction and laced his fingers together across his stomach.

"I believe, my friends, that we are very nearly ready for our great adventure to begin. Bertram has done some excellent, uh, *discovery* work for us." The aging bandit gave O'Meara a bright smile of thanks and nodded to him. "Thanks to his excellence, we have located and sent for the mules we will need to complete our job."

That explains the missing men, Raider thought. They were on their way to find, or more likely to steal, a herd of mules to carry all the loot Mace expected to extract from the railroad on this deal.

So O'Meara was the gentleman in charge of the organization's intelligence. *That* Raider definitely meant to keep in mind. There were still a good many Irishmen connected with the railroads this side of the big river, Raider knew, and by now many of them were in responsible positions, after starting with the young lines back during the railroad boom days of the 1860s. If O'Meara was buddies with some of them, it would be a fine source of information for Juan Mace. And if Raider could confirm that and find out where to point the finger, it could be of interest to Allan Pinkerton.

"The mules," Mace went on, "will arrive within the week, possibly sooner, yes?"

Mace paused and got a nod of agreement from O'Meara. "Call it five days' time," the Irishman said.

"Good," Mace said. "Miguel, how are the men?"

"Fit enough, *jefe*. Enough rest to be sharp, I think. Enough boredom to be eager. Yes, I would say they are ready."

"*Bueno*. Today I want you to begin examining their arms. Ensure, please, that every pistol, every rifle is in good repair an' the ammunition is fresh. You will do this for me, Miguelito?"

"This or any other thing you wish. As always."

The pledge of loyalty—and it was no less than exactly that—was received by Mace with a broad smile.

"And you, John, our new *compadre,* for you also there is a thing I wish you to do."

"Name it," Raider said, trying to put as much conviction into that short declaration as Miguel had into his.

Again Mace seemed pleased. "Bert must go outside again. I want you to accompany him. I will give you money to buy the supplies you need." He held a warning finger into the air. "Mind now, I want them purchased. It would be foolish to try to steal the exact things you must have. You will know more better than I what to get."

"Will they have it around here?" Raider asked.

"Whatever you require, in Colorado City they will have it."

Raider nodded. The town was virtually the capital city of the high-country gold mining, and they would damn sure have everything he needed . . . which was, plain and simple, enough explosives to blow up half a mountain. "If that's where we're going, all right. Give me a wad of money and we're all right."

For a moment, a fleeting moment, Raider had the hope that he would be left alone once he and Bert O'Meara got to Colorado City. If that was the case, he could probably find time to get in touch with Doc Weatherbee and perhaps with Allan in the Denver Pinkerton office. But Mace quickly dashed his new expectations by adding, "You will have a great deal of equipment to bring back with you, John, so I shall send with you two of my better men, yes? Two men and, would you say, three pack horses?"

Raider nodded. "Three should do it easy enough. Hell, if they have what I really want, one animal will be enough."

"Take the three then. To be safe, yes?"

"I agree."

"*Bueno*. Miguel will assign the men to you later if that is to your liking."

"Whatever you want. You're in charge of this show." Raider grinned. "I sure as hell don't have any complaints to this point. Reckon I'd be pretty foolish to start tellin' you what to do now, Juanito, *mi jefe*."

Mace seemed pleased with his arrangements. He poured each of them a second glass of the truly superior brandy, and a short while later the meeting broke up to the sound of the dinner gong.

"Miguel and I shall be remaining here, my good friends. We will talk again later if you please. An' you, Bert, an' you, John, can leave in the morning's light, yes?"

Raider and O'Meara left the pair of Mexicans behind and walked slowly toward the chow hall. There was no need to hurry. The crowd of men they could see jammed up at the doorway in a rush to get inside showed that they were already too late to grab the first seats for the meal. But anyway, there would be enough for all. Raider felt no particular desire to rush in with the rest of the herd, and apparently O'Meara was in no particular hurry either.

"I haven't seen you before, Bert. But then there's a lot I don't know about Juanito's operation. I sure have to admire him, though. He gets things worked out to a fare-thee-well, for a fact."

The Irishman pulled out a plug of tobacco that was black and none too clean-looking. He gnawed a chew off for himself and offered it to Raider.

"No thanks."

"Suit yourself." O'Meara shoved the remains of the plug deep into a hip pocket and continued to walk at the same slow pace toward the chow hall.

"Regular chatterbox, ain't you?" Raider observed when they were nearly there.

"So it's been said."

They drifted into the low building together and sat together through the short meal, but O'Meara remained silent except for an occasional request that a particular foodstuff be passed his way.

That was a shame, Raider thought. If the man would open up to him, it could be damned well informative. But Raider could not seem to pump him for information. Maybe on the trip north. . . .

Raider had nothing he needed to do that afternoon. His horse and his always-ready war bag were all he needed to travel. He stopped at the supply shed to pick up an extra box of .44-40s and drifted up the stream, away from the bustle of the camp where Miguel was beginning his chore of inspecting the firearms—and making the men nervously excited by doing so. Anyone who hung around there, Raider decided, was apt to find himself in a pointless brawl, now that the crew was getting the bit in their teeth with the prospect of facing some action soon.

Raider walked farther than he had the first time he went that way and found a delightful, shaded pool in the slow-running creek. In the spring, he was sure the run would have been a regular torrent, but at this time of year it was easy-moving and lazily peaceful. The stream put him in a very similar mood himself, too relaxed and pleasant to break the quiet with the hollow thump of gunshots. He stepped into the pool to bathe and stretched out on the sandy gravel bank to let the sun and the mountain air dry him.

It felt good to lie there. The sun had warmed the hole sufficiently for real comfort in the middle of the afternoon, although a fresh breeze or a step into the shade would have brought a quick chatter to his teeth and a layer of goose bumps over his skin.

Upstream of where he lay with his head propped on his cupped hands, he could see and occasionally could hear the light spurt and spreading ripple of a trout rising to some real or imagined morsel. Downstream, just below the pool, a jumble of rocks in the creek bed lent their delicate music of falling water despite the low condition of the little creek.

It was such a delightful afternoon that Raider found it quite appropriate and in keeping with the mood of the day when he heard Elaine's sultry voice speak softly to him from the bank nearby.

"That was just the way I wanted to find you, John. Naked and beautiful. No, don't protest. I know it is not supposed to be a manly thing to be called beautiful, but that is the way I think of your body. Beauty the way a woman sees it. Do you understand that? No, John. Lie still. Right there the way I saw you when I arrived. I like seeing you that way." She laughed. "No, not *that* way either. I was enjoying watching you limp and spread on your belly like that. *Quit* now. Make it go down."

"I'll try."

"Yes, that is much better. Thank you. Later we can think about the other. Not now."

"You were out riding again, I suppose, and just stumbled onto me here?" Raider asked.

Her laughter came easily and without care. "No, not this time, I confess. I saw you walking this way and thought I might find you again. But you almost fooled me. I crept through the bushes down below, where I saw you before, like an Indian making war. Imagine how surprised I was when all I surprised was myself."

He grinned. "Sorry about that. Come join me?"

"Ah, I wish that I could. But if one of the other men came along. . . ."

"Pity. It feels good here like this."

"I should imagine."

"Perhaps another time then."

"Yes, perhaps." She sighed. "Soon all the men will be gone except for one or two. Miguel, of course. Few others."

"Juan really intends to retire then?"

"But of course. What could he do afterward that would have nearly so much meaning as this? And why would he need the money? No, this life as we have known it is to end. And I must say that I am glad. I will like having the greater freedom when this is done."

"But I'll have to be leaving too, I would think."

"Yes." She laughed. "Not right away, though. Not until I have come here with you to lie naked outside the stream while you say deliciously lovely lies to me."

"Lies?" He shook his head with mock vigor. "Never. With one so beautiful as you, Elaine, a lie is not needed. Worse yet, in order to lie to you I would have to call you ugly. Because any ravings about your beauty will fall short of the truth, but they will most assuredly *not* be lies."

"Flatterer."

It was his turn to laugh. "Isn't that what you came here to hear?"

"You aren't supposed to know that."

"Even though it's the truth?"

"Yes, even though." She took a step out of the screen of trees in which she had been standing and held a hand out toward him. "You've taken the sun long enough, I think. And I've let you hang limp and beautiful quite long enough. Now I want to see the way you can grow and become so hard and throbbing. Would you do that for me?"

He did. Almost immediately. The invitation from Elaine Volnay's lips was a more powerful stimulant than a bushel of Spanish fly could have been.

She did not wait for him on the bank but turned away and plunged into the thick, streamside growth. He could see as she turned that she was already unbuttoning her blouse, and Raider was not a step behind her when she reached the protective shelter of the brush.

CHAPTER TWENTY-SIX

They rode out early the next morning, as soon as they were through with a hurry-up breakfast. The three others —O'Meara and two of the Mace crew named Gonzalo and Luis—seemed cheerful and ready to go. Raider felt like the only thing keeping him in the saddle was a distaste for bashing his head on the rocks if he should happen to fall. When it came right down to it, he probably would have preferred falling anyway. At least then he could have stretched out flat and maybe caught a few minutes' sleep.

He had spent most of the previous afternoon with Elaine, then met her in the horse shed again that night, after she said Juan Mace would be asleep and she could slip out to join him. Well, she had joined him all right. Not that he was regretting those hours now, but having to get up again an hour after he had gone to bed . . .

With O'Meara leading, they made good progress. Raider was content to get behind the other riders and the pack horses Luis was leading, put his horse's nose into the tail of the last pack animal in the short string, and doze while the others found the way. They held to an easy jog that fortunately took no concentration, and he was almost rested by the noon stop.

"Quiet today," O'Meara observed while they chewed some cold beef they had packed along from the Hole.

"I thought you'd be happier that way," Raider said.

"Uh huh." O'Meara seemed quite content to let it go at that.

"I wasn't exactly serious, you know."

"All right."

"I swear," Raider said. "You're the damnedest Irishman I ever met. I thought you people were all of the Blarney variety."

O'Meara grunted. "Shows you can't believe everything you hear. 'Sides, I never seen that particular rock. Just a bunch of little ones in the land I tried to farm." The man got a surprised look on his face, as if amazed he had opened up and said so much at one time. He clamped his mouth shut and ducked his head, contemplating the chunk of dry beef in his hand and ignoring Raider.

Raider smiled to himself. It was a start.

They took little time at the noon stop and were in Colorado City before dark.

Raider remembered the place, if not with any particular fondness, from his last time through. It was a small, ugly community dominated by the stacks and acrid smoke from the smelters, the streets a bustling confusion of people and freight teams and the clanging ring of steam hammers forcing reluctant metal into shape for one obscure purpose or another.

O'Meara, leading their tiny caravan, pulled to a halt before they splashed across Fountain Creek into the town.

"Slocum."

For a fraction of a second Raider forgot whose name he was carrying. He remembered, he hoped, before any of them might have noticed, and reined his horse around the pack animals and the two Mexicans to join O'Meara at the lead. Inside, he was cursing himself rather forcefully. It would not do to make that mistake again, and tiredness was no excuse. There were no excuses here.

Just bullets if he managed to blow it with his own stupidity.

"Yeah, Bert."

"I'm going into town alone from here. Give me a start before you come in. Take care of your business and get the hell back down to the Hole. And, Slocum, if you see me on the street here, you don't know me."

"All right."

So much for Raider's hope of getting close to O'Meara and finding out more about his—and Mace's —sources of information here. But at least he knew now that O'Meara wanted his connection with Mace to be a secret. That was something to go on if or when he found the time to pursue it.

Raider had to admit that Colorado City was a logical place to pick up the kind of information Mace would be wanting. The town fed on the mining industry. Anything and everything happening in the tunnels up in the high country could be heard about here. And a few miles away were the hotels and spas that were the watering holes for all the fops and swells and dandified businessmen who ran the railroads.

Yes, Raider thought, it would be a fine place for the job they wanted done. And for the job he had to do for Mace. If he remembered correctly, one out of every three stores here had a full line of mining equipment, including explosives. The other two of every three, of course, were saloons or lowbrow cathouses. All in all, Colorado City was one hell of a town.

O'Meara nodded and bumped his horse forward, down a low bank and across the shallow flow of the creek. A few minutes later he was among the town buildings and out of sight.

Raider watched him go, then turned in his saddle to Gonzalo and Luis. "We'll rest here a minute or two, then go on in. O'Meara said if we see him in town we aren't supposed to know him. Okay?"

He got a couple of bored nods in return. It was obvious he was not telling them anything new.

When he thought he had given the Irishman enough of a lead, Raider took the lead of their small group and splashed through the icy flow of water and onto a side street of the town.

The main drag wasn't much, but what it lacked in class, it made up in busy. Evening here had nothing to do with closing stores, merely with lighting lamps. The place had not gotten any quieter in the few weeks since Raider had last seen it. One thing was for sure. A small pack string of men picking up explosives in this town would be nothing out of the ordinary.

Raider did not particularly care where he spent Mace's money, so he stopped at the first mining-supply store he came to, which was practically the first store to be found on the city streets. The proprietor, a balding fellow with a fringe of white hair that would have made him look like a Dominican friar if it had not been for an ugly red scar across most of the left side of his face, did not give Raider and the Mexicans a second look when Raider laid down the supply list he had composed at the breakfast table that morning.

"Uh huh. Got it all except the ten-second fuse. I'm outta that. Could you take twice as much five-second? I'll make you a price on it."

"I won't quarrel with you over that, mister. Put it together for us, ready to travel."

"I got a good deal right now on drill bits too if you need them. First-quality stuff it is too."

"Oh, I think we have all we need in the hardware line," Raider lied. Or maybe he didn't. The cache of new firearms Mace had stored in that supply shed back in the Hole might qualify on that count.

"Suit yourself. I'll have this ready in half an hour. You wanta wait or stop back?"

Raider grinned. "It's been a while between drinks. I think we'll stop back later."

"I ain't amazed," the storekeeper said. "I'm open late, so don't rush."

Raider and his two companions had only a few steps to go to find a suitable bar. There were three of them in the same block as the mining supply store, and one seemed as likely a place as any other.

Raider was frankly hoping he would get a chance to get away from Mace's men long enough to make another contact with Doc or with Allan, but when he suggested to the men that they leave the pack loading to him and meet him in the morning, he got an overlong hesitation in response. It seemed fairly obvious to him that Mace or perhaps Miguel had given them instructions not to let him out of their sight for the evening.

He wondered whether someone back at the Hole was becoming suspicious of him or whether this was just normal procedure. But he was not likely to learn anything by asking. If anything, it would tip them to him, and it probably could not help. He kept his mouth shut and pretended not to have noticed anything odd about their refusal to go off and have themselves a high time on the town.

Nor did either of the men—each about as talkative as O'Meara had been—show any sign of getting happily drunk and forgetting their instructions. After an hour of slow drinking, Raider led the pair dutifully back to the supply store, where they picked up their goods, loaded it into the packs the spare horses were carrying, and set out to find a flophouse for the night.

Colorado City, as far as Raider was concerned, was a bust.

CHAPTER TWENTY-SEVEN

"John Slocum, you're a son of a bitch."

Raider was still undecided about just how much of a son of a bitch John Slocum was, but in this case the words were being directed toward him, not his temporary namesake. The speaker was a squat, powerfully built man named Bill—or Will, Raider was not sure which—Decker.

"Do you wanta discuss this now or wait till breakfast is over?" Raider asked. They were all filing into the chow hall.

"Later. At the corral."

Raider nodded. "Soon as we're done eating, then. Mind telling me why?"

"You're an ass licker, that's why. Sucking up to ol' Mace, buying whores for that greasy Miguel, coming in here trying to take over. What it comes down to, I just don't like you."

Raider grinned. "If that's the way you feel, then I guess I'll have to lick your ass. After breakfast."

Decker nodded. "No guns is the rule around here."

"I don't mind."

Oddly enough, now that the challenge had been issued and accepted, Bill Decker seemed calm and even friendly. The conversation had drawn them face to face in the moving line of men, and now Decker stayed with

Raider as they entered the low building and chose seats. They sat side by side through the meal, with Decker eating an enormous quantity of the poorly prepared food while Raider limited himself to much smaller portions.

Angelica was barely in evidence during the meal and pretended not to notice Raider when she did come into the room. Raider was just as glad not to have to confront her. She made him feel embarrassed somehow. Certainly he seemed always to be at his worst when she was anywhere near.

She also, by merely being a woman, reminded him of Elaine Volnay's presence nearby. And thoughts of Elaine made him downright, dangerously horny. Damn, but that was a lot of woman. They had gotten back to the Hole too late the night before for him to expect her to know and to respond. Even so, he had hoped. He had slipped out to the small stable and waited for her but had wound up with only her horse for company. After an hour of waiting for her and thinking about her, Raider had come close to wishing that the damn horse was a mare. Now even Angelica was reminding him of Elaine, and if that wasn't a sure sign of impending insanity caused by excessive pressure in the balls, Raider didn't know what was. Maybe he really *needed* a friendly scrap with Bill Decker to get his mind off the more important things. Like pussy.

Raider sighed. He reached for the nearest of several coffee pots Angelica had placed on the table. He poured for Decker first and then for himself. "I sure am looking forward to our discussion, Bill," he said cheerfully.

"As a matter of fact, I am too."

They squared off in a small catch pen adjacent to the main corral. Some of the men had been thoughtful enough to clear the pen of the horses it had been holding, although not of the damp, green apples they had left behind, and the entire crew seemed to have gotten the word in plenty of time to assemble as spectators. The rails on all four sides were liberally decorated with bandits' butts, and behind them, Raider could hear some enterprising souls offering bets to anyone who wanted to place them.

It was a bit disquieting, though, for him to notice that the odds most frequently shouted were 3½ to 1. Favoring Bill Decker.

Raider handed his gunbelt and knife to Luis, who happened to be perched beside the corner post Raider was claiming as his own, and stripped off his shirt and hat as well.

Decker was also down to britches and boots by then. With his shirt off Bill Decker looked like he was wearing a heavy winter coat, tanned with the fur on.

The man stood a full six inches shorter than Raider but was built something on the order of a hogshead full of nails, low and heavy and solid. His arms did not seem particularly long for his height, Raider was glad to note, but the muscle they carried was impressive. He looked like he could slug it out with the back end of a mule and not necessarily come out on the short side. Through the thick mat of hair on his torso Raider could see a number of old scars crossing his chest and belly where someone with a knife must once, or more often, have taken offense to Bill Decker's ways. All in all, Raider decided, the man looked downright competent.

On the other hand, Raider had fought some pretty good scrappers in the past himself, and he had found that speed was often a whole lot more important than power. Raider was definitely quick. It would be, Raider knew, a contest between speed and power.

He grinned and windmilled his arms to loosen the long, clean pads of muscle that bulged at his powerful shoulders and biceps. Raider felt good, better than he had felt in quite some time now, and his grin grew wider. Across the way he could see Decker reacting in much the same way to the coming bout, and that pleased Raider. Right then he felt closer to Bill Decker than to anyone he had spoken to in weeks. He positively *liked* the man and knew that Decker was feeling exactly the same way about him.

Yes, by damn, Raider decided, this was a fine idea.

Miguel—Raider hadn't realized the top brass knew anything about their little show and had not seen the lean Mexican until that moment—stepped forward into the center of the pen, drawing the attention of the crew and bringing a dozen conversations to a sudden halt.

"You have finished your betting, yes?" He paused briefly but did not really wait for an answer. The fact was that they had finished their betting. Yes.

Miguel grinned. Raider was surprised, but he thought most of that grin was directed toward him. Hell, he hadn't thought Miguel liked him all that much.

"It has been a long time," Miguel went on, "but now again, *mis amigos,* we have foun' a man to face Señor Bill Decker in his pen, yes? So, now we are to have some fun." He turned and mostly to Raider explained in a loud voice, "The rules we 'ave here are most simple. No gun. No knife. When a man is down, you go back to the corner an' wait until he gets up again to begin the fight again. When he don't get up again, you are the winner. Okay?"

He was looking directly at Raider, and so Raider nodded. Fair enough. And he would show these boys a thing or three. A long time since anyone was willing to fight Decker, huh? Well they'd find out something now, by damn. He smiled to himself. Or his name wasn't John Slocum. Oh well, they weren't going to scare him into giving it less than his best.

"I'm ready any time," Raider said.

"*Bueno.*" Miguel backed toward the railing, his eyes shifting from one man to the other in the opposing corners. When he reached the side of the small pen, perhaps twenty-four feet square, he said, "Begin."

Raider thought Miguel sounded awfully pleased with that single word.

And he kept remembering those odds. They were, he recalled, offered *after* the men had seen him take out the now-dead Bruce not too awfully long before.

That was all right, Raider decided. Speed against power. That was the ticket. He'd give them all a lesson in how it was done. You bet, boys. It was just a shame he hadn't gotten any money down himself.

Decker hunched his shoulders like an ornery old boar grizzly and dropped into a crouch, shuffling forward into the middle of the pen with a grin on his face.

Raider began to grin again too and moved lightly forward to meet him, stalking him like a huge, lithe cat creeping through the grass to take down and devour a tough old bull buffalo.

CHAPTER TWENTY-EIGHT

Raider had his strategy locked firmly into his mind before the fight even began. Speed was what he wanted. Once Decker began his rush, there would be no time to evaluate each attempted blow, decide what to do about it, and then react appropriately. Raider did not intend to take that much time. Each rush and bulldog attack had to be met immediately, before Decker had time to think or change his tactics or alter the rhythm of his punches.

Well before the first punch was thrown, Raider had figured the probabilities, judged how best he should respond to each, and imprinted in his own mind the reaction he should make. That way he needed no time to consider and none to respond. He could let his muscles respond to the subconscious instructions he had already given.

The fight should take no time at all.

Speed against power.

Now, as they neared the center of the pen, eyeing each other like a pair of fighting roosters with their steel spurs in place, Raider knew he could soon expect Decker to drop his chin toward his chest and charge forward with his fists pumping up hard toward Raider's gut or to throw a single, wild whistler high and fast toward Raider's jaw.

Raider had seen those two openings a hundred times before in a hundred barroom fights, undertaken by bull-like men very much like Bill Decker here, who seemed to be the pugilistic champion of Juan Mace's bandit camp.

And either one was fine with Raider. He knew exactly what he should do to counter them, exactly how to slip away from the fury of the oncoming fighter and to land his own punishment while easily escaping what Decker would otherwise do to him.

Speed against power. That was the ticket. Scientific knowledge and learned cunning against brute force and animal will.

Raider had watched the best of them, the professional prizefighters who could take on an amateur twice their own size and weight and come out unscathed. Because they *knew*—knew what they were doing, what they intended to do, how they should best go about it. They knew that speed can defeat power ten times out of ten if the bearer of that speed is knowledgeable and capable. And Raider was both. He had watched the best of them, and with one or two he had stepped into the ring on a friendly basis to learn from them. And learn he had.

Speed against power.

Raider smiled as he lightly cat-footed close to the shuffling Bill Decker.

Tell the nice people bye-bye, Bill, Raider thought to himself. You're fixing to take a little nap soon.

Decker's chin dropped toward his chest in exactly the way Raider had expected, and Raider felt his chest and shoulders swell like a stud horse in rut. He could feel his own power and his own competence, and he liked the feeling. He felt as if he could have floated over, through, and around the unsuspecting Decker, stinging him at will like a hornet attacking a sloth.

Damn, but Raider was enjoying himself.

Raider saw Decker's chin drop, and then the much

shorter man pulled himself lower into his crouch. Raider set his feet, standing loose and light on the balls of his feet, ready to react to Decker's rush, to slip and turn like a dancer in a New Orleans ballet, or like a master of the foil and rapier, because he too had the weapons he needed.

Raider saw all this and waited, ready, and for a fraction of a second he realized that something—he did not have time to think just what it was—was not quite right.

He thought it had something to do with Bill Decker's feet.

He almost had time to realize what it was. Decker was not planted quite the way Raider had expected.

And there was no rush as of a black Spanish bull toward the red cape. Instead there was a flicker of motion, too quick for him to see, and Raider felt the left side of his cheek go numb.

It really did not hurt at all. There was the flicker of movement, the quick sensation of numbness, and then his brain registered that it had heard the sound of hard flesh striking other flesh. He definitely heard the punch more than he felt it.

"Back to your corner, Bill. G'wan back now."

That was odd. Why would they be saying that?

And why was he looking *up* toward the men who lined the fence?

It took Raider a moment to realize that he was on the ground.

Christ! he thought. Speed against power *and* speed. He hadn't thought *any*one could be that quick with his fists. Not that quick and *look* like such an overmuscled, syrup-slow bear as Bill Decker did.

Raider shook his head once and bounced to his feet, amazed more than hurt but certainly wary now.

He would not be caught like that again. No siree Bob, he wouldn't.

Decker shuffled forward again. Like a damn old boar grizzly. Slow and easy to sting.

Raider didn't believe it. Not any more.

This time Raider acquitted himself much better. Much better. As soon as Decker was the right distance away, Raider dropped into the prizefighter's Marquis of Queensberry stance, knees flexed and fists ready. *That* should show Decker something.

Decker adopted the posture himself. He looked awkward in it with his barrellike build, but he certainly held himself comfortably in the stance. And he was no longer shuffling, Raider could see perfectly well this time. He stood easily balanced on the balls of his feet.

The man surely was smiling, Raider saw.

Decker flicked a straight left jab forward, and Raider's right parried it easily aside.

Another jab, and the same result. Now, Raider knew, he could expect the flashing hard right. He set himself ready for it.

Decker's left hooked swiftly under Raider's guard, catching him hard in the gut and bringing to Raider's lips a grunt of surprise.

While Raider's attention was momentarily down below, Decker's right caught the exact same spot on Raider's left cheek that he had hit before. The result was predictable.

"Back to the corner, Bill."

Raider returned to his feet.

Raider ignored the all-too familiar left hook to his gut and lashed out with his own hard right. This time Decker was not quick enough to parry, and Raider's fist, hard as a slab of walnut, landed where it was supposed to.

The flat of stubble-dotted skin over Bill Decker's cheekbone split, but the man was like a rock. He neither went down nor so much as staggered at a punch that would have put most men on their knees and no small number flat on their faces and counted out.

Lordy, what have I got here? Raider asked himself.

Decker did not even pay him the courtesy of shaking his head.

They circled and feinted, trying to draw each other out of position, each wary now, each catching the rhythm of the combat, each completely unaware of the swell of sound from cheering, jeering voices that ringed them so close but could have been a dozen miles away for all they heard of the men who watched and encouraged them.

A Decker right missed at the last instant as Raider rolled his head to the side and responded with a straight left of his own that caught Decker on the mouth.

Raider's guard drifted a hair too high, and Decker bulled close to him, clinching with him and pummelling his belly with a rapid tattoo of lefts and rights until Raider could recover and bounce back out of the way, much more slowly now than he might have done some minutes earlier.

In a flurry that used up more of his precious strength than Raider could ever have expected, he bored in and overwhelmed Decker's guard, somehow was able to land a combination of right-left-right and right again on Decker's head and hunched shoulders.

A madly looping right—a man of Decker's ability just didn't *use* wild punches like that; who the hell would ever have looked for one?—took Raider on the chin, and again he was on the ground.

It was—he wasn't quite sure—the eighth or maybe ninth time he had been down. He took his time about getting up again, frankly needing the breather and admitting it to himself. But he did get up.

A Raider left got through to Decker's breadbasket and pulled his guard down. Raider sidestepped enough to take himself to the side of Decker's right and launched a hard, straight shot that took Decker flush. For the first time it was not Bill Decker who had to go to the corner and wait.

It felt almighty good. But that blocky, tough little man was grinning when he stood up again, and it was Raider who felt a weariness as they closed again in the middle of the pen. But it *did* feel good.

Raider changed his tactics. He tried boring in close, smothering Decker with his superior height, leaning on him, making Decker carry the weight of both fighters for a while.

What that got him was a steady ripping in the guts from Bill Decker's seemingly never-tiring fists. *No*body could be that tough, but Decker was.

Raider hung on the outside. He had a solid reach advantage on Decker. *That* was the ticket. He could not believe he had been so stupid, had taken so long to realize the perfectly obvious.

Decker drifted with him, picking off Raider's by-the-book jabs, sliding inside to counter with agonizing speed and devastating results.

Raider found himself on his butt again. He shook his head and once again—he was getting used to it—saw the droplets of bright blood splatter the dust of the horse pen.

He had no idea now how long they had been at it—forever or very close to it, he was sure—but the horse apples that had been fresh when they started had had time to glaze and darken now. They were damn near dry.

He got up again. His knees weren't working like they were supposed to. They felt mushy. No spring in them anymore. He knew he was staggering as he headed back toward the middle of the pen.

Decker did a curious thing. He paused and held both hands stretched forward, waiting, obviously intending to throw no blows for the moment. He motioned Raider forward and again offered his hands. Raider caught on. He stepped up, and they touched knuckles briefly. Raider did not know what the bull-like little man meant, but he accepted the gesture. It was, he sensed, a courtesy of some sort, a salute to a respected foe.

This time there was a difference as Decker hunched himself deep into his shoulders and moved forward, still fairly light on his feet while Raider's boots were dragging in the dust.

This time Bill Decker was serious.

His fists pummelled Raider's guard, knocked it down and broke it apart, crushed his defenses and sent the breath wheezing out of puffy red lips, and—finally—landed the one final, perfect right that rose out of nowhere and exploded like a howitzer shell against Raider's jaw.

Now, for the first time since the amazement of that first joining of the two, Raider was surprised to discover that he was once again down in the dirt. He hadn't known when he went down, had not felt it or realized it.

He must have been there for some time, too, because Decker had his shirt draped over his shoulders and was bending over Raider, offering him his hand to help him to his feet. He was smiling, but it was a smile of joy, pleasure with no hint of arrogance or superiority in it.

"Ay-God, Johnny, there's no man *ever* stood in with me so long since I left the ring an' took up the free life. Ay-God, boy, I like the way you fight. An' I sure had fun today. Thanks."

Raider shook his head. He still felt wobbly. But not nearly as bad as he might have.

Decker was right. It *had* been fun.

"Bi—" He coughed, spat to clear his throat. "Bill, I tell you what. I'd be right proud to pour you a beer." He grinned. "If you'd give me a hand with walking that damned far."

With their arms around each other's shoulders, the two men limped toward the storage shed, where they would be able to find something sudsy to drink.

Behind them, Raider could hear the shouting of the excited crowd, and for the first time in quite a while, he was aware of the press of men around him.

He felt pretty darn good, he decided. Considering.

CHAPTER TWENTY-NINE

Even though he had lost the fight—and Lord, hadn't it been a long time since Raider had had to admit to that? —the fight seemed to gain him a lot of respect and friendliness from the men. And most of all from Bill Decker.

Raider was too sore and miserable to want any dinner that day, but at supper and thereafter Decker was his mealtime companion, and it was clearly understood as well that any time Raider wanted company, a drinking companion, or someone to talk to, all he had to do was look for Decker.

The man was not a nuisance about it, though, thank goodness. Raider's first fear had been that Decker would hang too close for him to be able to see Elaine. And in spite of the battering he had received, he still very much wanted to see Elaine Volnay again, as quickly as possible.

The mood of the crowd at the evening meal was positively cheerful throughout the room. Mace and Miguel sat for half an hour over coffee when the eating was done. Mace joked with his men, bantered back and forth with them, and seemed to have caught their relaxed and casual air. When he finally left to return to his own house, he gave Raider a wink. It was plain that Miguel had given him a full report on the matter, or that Mace himself had been watching it all.

The man was no fool when it came to the welfare and morale of his gang, Raider was realizing more and more as time went on. Nor about any other aspect of his illegal business for that matter. The simple truth was that Juan Mace was a thief but certainly no fool. Hell, he was doing very, very well in a hard and often dangerous business. Where other men had gone to the gallows, Mace sat secure and happy in the beautiful high valley he had named for himself. And where others starved themselves into prison or, worse, honest employment, Mace had prospered and grown fat in his old age.

He was a canny old rascal, as his plans for the D&RG might soon prove to the whole world. Almost literally to the world. Because it was certain that if Mace succeeded in pulling off the job he had detailed so carefully in his plans, he was going to go down in the history books as the most inventive and successful of all robbers, of all time.

Raider shook his head in admiration for the old devil. With something as daring and as well conceived as this, he could *almost* wish Juanito success. If it hadn't been for Bruce, Raider probably would be rooting for him, to himself at least, and maybe even in fact. It was impossible to judge that now, but the possibility had certainly existed. It was strange for him to reconcile that now with his own basic honesty, but he could not deny it even for his own peace of mind. There were things, quite enough of them, that Raider had done that he later regretted, but he was not going to start trying to lie to himself. Not that. Not ever.

He sighed and left the table. The mood of the evening was such that a number of the men had chosen to linger where they normally would have eaten their food and bolted for their own small shelters or for the relaxation of the beer keg.

Now they were not even giving Angelica a hard time as she gave up waiting for them to leave and came out among them to begin clearing the table so that she could get her pitiful few hours of sleep before she had to begin building the cooking fires for their morning meal.

Raider let himself out into the crisp, cold night and headed for his cabin, where he had left his coat.

He was almighty sore and knew he would be stiff as a Sunday-morning collar come the dawn and aching in every battered muscle, but he could still walk and intended to do so for as long as he could—right back to that horse shed in the pretty little grove where Elaine sometimes went to walk, and to play.

Someone had already lighted the lantern in the small cabin when he got there to fetch his coat from the foot of his bunk. That bunk was a temptation that drew him like cows to a cornfield, but he was sure that if he once gave in and stretched out, it would be tomorrow morning and maybe later before he got up again. Almost sadly he turned his back on the blankets and left the cabin again, without pausing even to sit down for a much-needed rest.

It was early, but most of the men were still inside the chow hall and not milling about in the open yard, and so Raider took the chance and went straight from his cabin into the shadows at the rear of Mace's house.

It was a dangerous thing he was doing, and he knew it but did not really care. Elaine was more woman than he had ever come in contact with, and if there was a chance he could have her again, he intended to take it and hope for the best afterward. Whatever the risks, she was worth them.

He reached the safety of the shed and found it empty except for the patient horse that stood chewing hay in its stall.

The lantern had not been lighted, and Raider debated whether he should give himself that luxury. Showing a light would tell Elaine he was there. But if anyone else saw light seeping through the cracks where there should have been only darkness, it would be entirely too much of a risk, and an unnecessary one at that.

Instead, he slumped gratefully into the soft comfort of the hay pile where so few nights before he had lain locked in a sweaty, hard pumping embrace with a naked, gasping Elaine.

The place did not feel so inviting now as it had then, but still it was damned pleasant to be able to sink into it. It did feel good.

He sat for a time propped against the board rails that separated the storage area from the stall. The smell of warm, living horseflesh was strong in his nostrils, but it was a smell that was pleasant to him and comforting in its own way. He liked the smell of a horse, did not even really mind the odors of sweat and manure. And somehow the ammoniac barn odors made the place seem warmer.

After a while he slumped farther down and then still farther until he was nestled deep in the softness of the hay, and soon he was asleep.

Hot. Wet. Engulfing. Making him harder and ever more ready. Lifting him slowly, gently, toward a climax that was quiet and down-deep satisfying.

Dimly he felt the soft, mellow release. Felt the flow of his own warm come rise from his balls and flow soothingly out into the wet heat that held him so tenderly. The whole thing had a dreamlike quality to it, and for a time he was not at all sure it was really happening to him.

It was really happening.

He came fully awake then and tried to bolt upright,

only to wince from the pain of a thousand previously undiscovered sore spots and sink back down into the yielding hay.

Jesus, but he hurt. Everywhere. All at once.

"Lie still. It's all right. I know how you must be feeling. I saw it, you know. I was watching through the window with Juanito's field glasses."

Elaine sighed. "You were magnificent, Johnny. I've seen a lot of men fight Bill Decker but never anyone like you."

"I got whupped." The words came out as a croak. His mouth and throat felt dry and sore. He must have been sleeping with his mouth open, probably snoring to boot. He must, he thought, have made a hell of a pretty picture for Elaine to walk in on like that.

Still, it hadn't stopped her any, and so it was all right.

"No," she insisted. "You were wonderful. Fourteen times you got up again and went after him. And you knocked *him* down, John. No one has ever done that before or stayed with him half so long. I was serious, you know. You were magnificent. Believe me."

"I don't feel so damn magnificent, let me tell you. Fourteen times? Christ, I hadn't any idea it was that many. I'm more of an idiot son of a bitch than I thought I was." He started to laugh, but that effort petered out into a groan.

"Hush now, John. Lie still. Let me. There. That's better."

Her face, dimly sensed in the deep darkness of the shed, disappeared, and again he could feel the sweetness of her mouth engulf him and the soothing touch of her tongue against his already reengorging shaft.

Now that she was no longer close to him, he remembered with pleasure the scent of his own come on her breath. Damn, but he had liked that.

And he liked what she was doing now. Oh, yes, he was ready again.

The explosion would not come so rapidly this time, and he was glad, for he had no desire to end this pleasure. Not now or at any time in the future. He would gladly have lain here for days under her touch and basked in the joy of her.

For a delightfully long while, she tongued him, moaning her pleasure in tune with his, until he threatened to climax again and she pulled quickly away from him.

"Not yet, Johnny, my dear. Not so soon this time, hear? This time I want to join you."

He could hear the faint rustle of cloth and felt Elaine shift beside him on their bed of sweet-smelling hay.

He began to move, reaching for her to draw her down beside him so that he could roll over atop her, but she stopped him with a hand pressed against his chest.

"No, sweet. I know how sore you must be. Not this time. Just lie still and let me do it."

She straddled him and lowered herself gently over him until he slid into the wet depths of her. He groaned, but it was a sound of pleasure rather than pain, and it brought a happy chuckle from her. The sound reached him softly through the darkness.

"I agree," she whispered. "I love it."

Slowly, so slowly that at first he was not positive she was doing it, she began to rise the full, enormously long length of him, bringing him to the moist, lightly haired lips of her pussy and then lowering herself again to pull him deep inside her.

"Lovely. Just lovely," she whispered.

"Umm, you are indeed."

"Ah, thank you, sir. For a compliment I'll do anything. What would you like?"

He laughed. "Anything will do just fine, thank you, ma'am. With you, anything."

Ever so gently she rode him. Slowly up and down. A

little faster. And faster still. Soon she was thrashing and twitching like a mare in heat, driving herself harshly, grunting with the mingled ecstasy and effort, her breath coming ragged now, her own responses rising to meet his, until with a shudder that might otherwise have been mistaken for agony, she climaxed and yelled and ground her mound against the tangle of his pubic hair.

The feeling of her climax was so strong that it drew Raider into his, and for the second time in so few minutes, he bucked beneath her and spilled his come into her like lava spewing out of a superheated volcano.

Raider sighed and went limp against the hay, and Elaine collapsed against him, allowing herself to rest against his chest, his sticky cock remaining sheathed in the warm protection of her body while they rested.

This, *this* was the best reason of all for living.

CHAPTER THIRTY

"All right," Mace told them. "We're through farting around. It is time we do our work, yes?" He grinned. "Yes."

The old bandit had the whole crowd, minus those who had gone to bring back the pack mules, in the chow hall on a cool midafternoon. No one was grumbling about the disruption of their routine, though. Not now. This, after all, was why they were part of the gang. When Juan Mace laid out a job, they were fixing to make some money.

"Some of you have heard what it is we are about to do. The rest," his broad grin got all the wider, "will be pleased to know we are all to be rich men. You, me, each of us."

Briefly, and with practically no detail at all, he gave them a rough idea of what was to come. Even that sketchy report was enough to bring the men to their feet with loud yells and huzzahs for the grizzled old veteran of so many high-country raids. Many raids in the past, it was true, but never anything to compare with this, and each one of the men knew it. Those who were not bright enough to realize what they were hearing in terms of history were at least sensitive enough to catch the mood of their fellows, and that mood was one of jubilation.

Even Raider found himself caught up in the excitement, yelling along with the rest of them, cheering this sometimes genteel, sometimes brutal old man who had made a place for himself in a wilderness and had held it long enough to become probably the most successful brigand there had ever been. And now with one final stroke of genius, Mace was about to surpass everything he had done in the past all lumped together.

It was, Raider had to admit, brilliant, and seemingly foolproof. Unless, of course, the Pinkertons should happen to get in the way.

That was still an interesting and disturbingly unanswered question. Had Doc received Raider's wire, and were Doc and Allan able to do anything about the small amount of information he had sent?

He would find out soon enough, he knew.

It took five minutes or more for the sudden tumult to subside, and by that time Mace looked like he had just been elected president of the world. He stood before his men, smiling and nodding, luxuriating in the praise they were heaping on him.

When finally they began to grow quiet, Mace raised his arms and got immediate silence in return.

"Tomorrow," he said. "Tomorrow early. We *ride!*"

The cheering swelled up anew, and Mace moved regally to the doorway and out, the sound following him as he moved and swelling to a fever pitch for as long as he was in the room.

Bill Decker was at Raider's side, in his happiness punching Raider on the shoulders nearly as hard as he had punched him in the pen so few days before.

"Isn't this grand, John? Isn't it the finest thing you ever heard?"

"There's never been one to beat it," Raider agreed honestly enough, "and never will be again, I'd wager."

"Aye, that Mace. He's a caution, an' that's a fact. He'll make the lot of us rich old men before he's done."

Miguel jumped up in front of the group and began to point to men near him. "You. You there. Esteban? Yes, you. An' you right here. Go bring us a barrel of beer, *sí?* Put it here. Right here. This day we celebrate, but tonight we do not. Tonight we go to our beds with the clear heads and the prospects of wealth. You understan' me? You all understan' me?"

They did, and for several hours they were as cheerful a crowd as any Raider had ever seen, bar none.

Come morning, they crawled out of their bunks earlier than usual but also, thanks to the way Mace and Miguel had handled things, more sober than usual. Raider did not think he could see a single hung-over face at the breakfast table where he would be sitting, he hoped, for the last time.

Most of the men had gotten their gear together the night before in readiness for their travels. Others, like Raider, never needed more than a moment's warning before they were ready to ride.

Raider threw his few possessions into his war bag and rolled it with his sugan and bedroll, ready to be tied behind his cantle. It was still dark when he left the tiny cabin he had been using, his gear in his hand and breakfast still warm in his belly. Actually, he realized, he felt pretty damn good.

"John!" The whisper came from over his shoulder, behind the grassy hump that marked the cabin's low roof. "Over here."

His first thought was that it was Elaine, and he rushed toward the softly whispered sound before he realized that the voice was not hers, that it would have been foolhardy for her to try to slip away from Mace on this of all mornings.

"Yes, Angelica?"

She had been watching him closely, but as he came near, her eyes fell away and she looked down toward the ground as if she were overcome with shyness.

"Before you go, John, I . . . wanted to tell you something. Do you mind? Please?"

"Mind? Hell, I don't mind, girl. Say whatever you like."

She nodded, but for a moment did not speak. Finally she said, "You ain't been here long, John, but I got to tell you. You're . . . the first man has . . . well . . . has treated me decent in a long while. I just wanted to . . . to tell you I 'preciate that. I won't be forgetting it neither. I got an idea I won't see you again, John. I got it in mind that you won't be coming back here again. So before you go, well, I just wanted to tell you that. I 'preciate it. An' I thank you."

She sounded perfectly miserable by the time she was done, as if she expected him to explode with anger because this poor, scrawny slattern had had the audacity to pay him a compliment.

Raider did not really know how to respond. She was thanking him for having treated her so well, yet this was the same woman he had not just once but several times treated worse than he had ever treated any human female in his entire life. Her compliment and her thanks were difficult for him to take. They made him feel like a complete heel under the circumstances.

He shook his head. He did not know what to tell her. Instead, he reached for her and drew her to him and wrapped his arms around her thin shoulders, holding her tight against his chest, gently rocking her to and fro as if she were a child to be cradled and petted instead of a grown woman who had spread her thighs for the smelliest and worst animals in these high mountains for more years than Raider could probably guess. He held her like that for what seemed a long time until finally she slipped away from him and darted off into what was left of the morning shadows.

Most of the men were already at the corral by then, and Raider joined them there.

They were a jovial lot, cracking jokes and trying to bugger each other's horses as they mounted, few of them looking or acting as serious as the nature of their business would indicate.

They were certainly a well-armed crowd, Raider could see. In battle dress, which they virtually were, they were more heavily armed than any military troop would have been.

Cavalry troopers would be issued a revolver, a single-shot carbine, and a saber. Nothing more. But these boys carried, at the very least, two revolvers apiece, and some had as many as four Colts slung on their saddles and another brace of the weapons on their belts.

Raider was sure, too, that there was not a single-shot carbine or rifle among them. A single-shot weapon is more durable and more powerful than a repeater and is far more accurate at any great distance, but what this crowd wanted was not a marksman's accuracy but awesome firepower, and they certainly had that. Most carried Winchesters or Henrys, a few had old Spencers or the more modern Kennedys, but there was not a Sharps or a Springfield to be seen among them.

As for the sabers, what these bandits lacked in long steel they made up for in short, for each was now bristling with knives, and a handful of the Mexican riders were carrying the long, slender lances that the south-of-the-border cavalry and the Comancheros were famous for. Raider wondered briefly whether some of these men with whom he had been living were or at one time had been Comancheros themselves. There was nothing that he could think of that was lower than a Comanchero, and when Raider thought about the surprises Doc might have waiting for them at the end of their journey, he almost hoped that those Mexicans were indeed carrying that unsavory brand.

The men were all mounted and ready before Juan Mace made his appearance among them, and instantly another round of wild shouting and cheering split the first light of the new day.

The men milled about Mace as if he were Robert E. Lee or some grand, conquering hero from a distant time and a long-dead army. He might have been one of the Caesars judging from the welcome his men gave him, and his expression reflected the pleasure this gave him.

"*Muchachos, mis muchachos*. We ride. Now!" Mace waved his arm toward the north, toward the high rim where Raider knew there was supposed to be a pass that he had never seen, and the group of men moved out at a brisk jog, their accoutrements jangling and clanking as vigorously as those of a real army.

For better or worse, whatever lay ahead, they were on their way now.

CHAPTER THIRTY-ONE

They met the mule train late that afternoon, and even Raider, already fully briefed about how much loot they would have to haul away if they were successful, was impressed.

The mules, long-legged stout animals each and every one, were strung in a line that stretched for more than a quarter mile along the narrow, winding switchback trails in the nearly barren mountains where they made the rendezvous. Held in tight nose-to-tail line, of course, they would have presented a much more compact appearance, but strung out they were impressive indeed, and the sight of them seemed to lift the men's spirits even further.

For safety's sake, Raider's packs of explosives were transferred to the mules, and the horses that had been carrying them were taken along as spares in the event they might be needed to replace injured or otherwise disabled mounts. That was a measure of Juan Mace's foresight, Raider thought. The man seemed ready for any emergency. Or *almost* any.

That night they pitched a camp that Mace laid out in a nearly military fashion close to a pool of clean, clear water, high in a rocky bowl on the side of the Wet Mountains.

Decker pointed out where Florence lay in the distance, not visible from inside the bowl, although the few lights of the town were quite clearly seen from the rim above the water, and Raider realized that they could have reached the same position hours earlier by a more direct route if Mace had been willing for the party to be seen on the trail. The point was that again the wily old fox had not tried to buy convenience at the price of increased hazard.

The men drank from the pool and filled their canteens, and the cooks who had been idle back in the Hole filled canvas buckets ready for morning coffee before they led the horses and mule train in to drink and soon to foul the clean water.

Raider liked that touch on Mace's part, because it takes very little mule piss to ruin a man's enjoyment of his morning coffee.

There was no liquor in this camp and no rowdiness whatsoever. The men were quiet, almost contemplative, and Miguel cautioned them to remain so. Sounds can carry far on the thin air of the high country, and a little thrashing of metal against metal could easily have led to their discovery, even if it looked like there should be no one around for miles in any direction. Certainly they had not seen anyone outside their own group since leaving the Hole that morning, but the precaution was taken anyway.

Raider spread his bedroll early and lay on top of it with his coat still on and his saddle for a back rest.

"You all right, John?"

"Sure. You, Bill?"

"Yeah. Say, I'm sorry about askin', you know? I mean, you been there a hundred times before. You got nothing to prove. I didn't mean anything by the question."

"Hell, I know that."

"You want a chew?"

Raider shook his head. "Thanks, though."

Decker bit off a hefty wad of tobacco and squatted beside Raider. "I ain't been at this so long myself," he commented.

"No? I wouldn't have guessed it. I figured you'd been with the bunch for years."

"Naw, just for a few months. Never on anything like this."

"Bill, there's never been *any*one in on anything like this, not ever."

"Yeah, well, that makes me feel a bit better, maybe."

"How'd you get in with them? If you don't mind my asking."

"I don't mind." Decker sounded, in fact, like he just plain wanted someone to talk to, about almost anything. "I used to be a fighter. A pro I was, too. You know, go into a town an' put up the posters and handbills. Draw 'em in and offer to pay any man could go five rounds with me. Of course they couldn't do it. I wasn't ever good enough to get any prize matches, but we made out all right on the small-town circuit. Least I thought we was making out good. Then one morning I woke up an' found that my manager and some saloon gal—Lordy, that man was old enough to know better'n that too—was both gone, leaving me with a bunch of bills we'd run up and no money to pay them. The hotel man got after me about it, but what could I do? Nothin', that's what. He made a big stink about it, so I guess I beat up on him some, an' he died. So I took out running. Met up with a couple boys that put me in touch with Mace, and here I be."

Raider nodded. He was half asleep already. He wondered if Decker was going to face a long jail term when this crowd got rounded up. He hoped not. Things would be bad enough just from this job without adding more to his burden. That was one thing for sure. Jail was a hell of a lousy place for a man to take up housekeeping. Even a queer was bad off in the *juzgado,* and a normal man could hardly stand it. Sometimes Raider wondered why they took the risk.

Decker chattered at him for quite a while more, and eventually Raider nodded off to sleep, never really knowing when it was that Decker realized he was no longer listening and went to find his own blankets.

It was already fully daylight when Miguel walked among the men to kick them awake. A good many were still sleeping heavily, a sure sign that they had had trouble getting to sleep the night before. They came awake readily enough, though, and were quick to pick up the mood they had let go the night before. This was *the* day.

Mace himself went among them to divide them into groups and to give them their instructions, taking his time about it and making sure each man understood what was expected of him. The instructions were given in both Spanish and English to make sure there was no problem there. Then Miguel went to each group and had them go over their plans to his satisfaction.

Finally, shortly after noon, they saddled their horses again and began the final descent of the mountain slopes toward the tracks lying in the arid basin below.

"Slowly now. Slowly," Mace and Miguel warned. "Do not raise the dust now. It would not do. Slowly. Yes."

Raider wondered what lay ahead of them now. He swallowed hard and held his horse to a slow pace behind the man ahead of him in their long, long line of armed riders.

CHAPTER THIRTY-TWO

"On time," Mace said with a satisfied look on his face. He snapped the cover of his watch shut and sat back with his hands comfortably crossed on his saddle horn, watching the Denver and Rio Grande engine approach from the direction of Florence just a few miles to the east.

The train was not much for appearances—a single engine with its tender, four flatcars piled high with tarpaulin-covered materials, one closed boxcar, and a half-assed second tender that must have been intended to serve as a caboose of sorts. The tarps were effectively covering whatever materials were stacked on the flatcars, but Raider could not help wondering whether they were also hiding a crew of Pinks and maybe a posse assembled in Florence. No, he decided quickly. If that were so, Juan Mace probably would have heard about it. Or would he? They would find out soon enough.

The engine chugged slowly up the slight grade of the Arkansas River bank, the tracks following the river's course almost exactly here. There was nothing human in sight except the train and Mace's crowd of men, for the moment hidden behind a pair of bluffs north of the tracks. When the train was stopped, the cars and crew would be caught between the raiders and the river, blocking any escape on foot to warn railroad officials in Florence of what was going on so near their town.

"Stay near to me now, John," Mace reminded Raider for the tenth or twelfth time. His repetitions were a good indication that the old bandit, now that his finest hour seemed to have come, was nervous despite his long history of pulling off successful forays against those who had the money and the goods he coveted.

Miguel was a half mile to the west of where Mace, Raider, and a dozen of the other men waited. The D&RG work train moved nearer.

"We show ourselves now, I think," Mace said. He gigged his horse and let it prance into the open, where even a half-asleep engineer would be sure to see him against the starkly arid tan gravel that covered the land. Raider and the other riders followed, keeping a respectful distance to the rear of the leader.

"Jorge, Stan, over to the other side now," Mace ordered, and half the group split away, racing their horses across the tracks ahead of the train so that the engine would be blanketed on both sides by heavily armed riders when it reached them.

From the engine came a shrill whistle and a puff of escaping steam. All right, Raider thought, the crew had spotted them. The question was whether that signal was intended for the raiders or for a group of hidden defenders.

"Now," Mace said softly. "Forward." He spurred ahead, and Raider jabbed his horse and galloped after him.

They merged with the still-chugging engine, Juanito riding like a youngster, light and easy in his deep-seated Mexican saddle with its huge dinner-plate horn, reins knotted and dropped loose on the horse's neck while Mace guided the handsome sorrel with his knees alone and held a .44-40 Colt in each wrinkled fist.

"Allo, Señor Engineer. Please stop your train for me to talk with you." Mace was laughing and smiling and brandishing his pistols. He made a hell of a sight, Raider had to admit, riding like a damned centaur, paying no attention at all to the footing his horse was able to find alongside the roadbed, concentrating instead on the engineer and fireman now beside and above them in the cab of the light engine. It would have been funny as hell if the horse took a header right then, Raider thought, but both mount and rider were too good for that. Juan Mace was in his element and seemed as happy at this moment as any human being Raider had ever laid eyes on.

"Go to hell," was the engineer's response.

Mace shrugged. He grinned up at the man and waved his right arm in a circle over his head. A quarter mile ahead of them, the rest of Mace's small army swept out of hiding and onto the tracks immediately before the oncoming train.

"As you wish, señor, and most assuredly I cannot stop the engine without your assistance, eh? But I think you an' your people there, I think you will not survive the bullets. Do you agree?"

The engineer agreed. Raider saw the man look ahead of him at the mob of men waiting with rifles and pistols held high, saw the look of bleak dismay cross his whiskered face, saw the capitulation in his eyes.

"Don't shoot," the engineer hollered down to them. "My God, don't start shooting."

The engineer dropped down out of sight behind the steel wall of his cab, a wall that might have looked like fine protection but that both sides knew would act as a rebounding board for ricocheting bullets if the bandits opened fire. A moment later the sound of the driving engine changed and slowed. A series of short toots on the steam whistle signaled the brakemen to set the screws. Before they reached the main group of riders, the train had begun to slow. Raider's horse did not have to stretch itself out so much to keep pace with the engine.

"Stan, stay with these fine gentlemen, please," Mace ordered over the sound of squealing brake shoes behind them. With a shift of his weight alone—and damn, but he was a fine figure of a man on horseback, Raider thought—Mace checked the pace of his horse and began dropping back along the length of the moving train.

They were among the others now. The full length of the train was covered on both sides by yelping riders who were waving their weapons menacingly in the air. Still, though, there was a carnival atmosphere to the whole thing. These robbers were having themselves a good time, threatening violence but anticipating riches, and they were in fine humor. They had been warned beforehand not to shoot into the air or make any really loud noises that might carry all the way back to Florence. Not, of course, unless someone needed to be shot. That would be all right.

The flatcars slipped forward of where Raider and Mace were riding. Others of the men galloped past them, holding their positions relative to the train, while Mace and Raider loped to bring the boxcar next to them.

As the tarp-covered flatcars pulled alongside them, Raider could not help himself. He flinched. He examined the roped-down coverings and finally had to condreds of other items needed to build a railroad through protective coverings thrown over stacks of rails and ties and boxes and barrels of spikes and sledges and the hundred of other items needed to build a railroad through rough, virgin country. There were no possemen hidden under those tightly secured covers.

Raider began to wonder all the more whether his message had gotten through to Doc.

When they were beside the boxcar, Mace stepped up the speed of his horse to match it, and more than a dozen of the men near him moved in close to cover their leader as well as the car.

"Open the door, please," Mace called politely. "If it does not open before she stops, señors, I will have my men fill the car with bullets before we open her, yes?"

There was no answer, and the train was moving very slowly now.

"Very little time is left now," Mace called cheerfully. "Look out the cracks, señors. You see me here, no? Ay, of course you do. You see my men? Yes? You see the guns? We are now to use them if the door, she remains as she is."

The squealing and clanking had subsided enough by now that Mace was speaking to the hidden guards in a practically conversational tone of voice. He still sounded quite cheerful.

"You think I do not know you are there? You think I am bluffing, yes? Ah, but I do not, *mis amigos*. No-no. Willy Radhahn, you are the leader of these guards, yes? And Curtis Reed. You are there too. You think I do not know? Ah, my friends. I do not wish to hurt you. Please open now, or I mus' tell my men to do a very bad thing."

The door slid open. Inside, Raider could see a group of very unhappy-looking men and on the floor, in plain sight, a small pile of very wicked-looking shotguns and carbines. Under the circumstances, Raider was delighted that the railroad guards had decided to offer no resistance to the grinning bandit who now shifted his horse onto the treacherous gravel footing immediately beside the tracks and stepped lightly from his saddle to the open doorway of the still-moving boxcar. The man was beautiful in his own way, Raider thought. A showman as well as an accomplished robber.

Mace stood in the doorway and waved triumphantly to his men as the train rolled finally to a halt three-quarters of a mile west of where the engineer had decided to put on the brakes.

The horses were winded now after the hard run, some of them sweating heavily, but Raider had seen no mishaps in the run, and all the men seemed to be accounted for.

From their concealment not 300 yards away, the final contingent of Mace's riders broke out of cover and led the mule train forward. Mace had figured that almost to perfection, Raider thought.

The men had been strung out along the tracks for more than a mile to begin with, and now they all came together neatly and easily, everyone where he should be, lines of riders spread out along both sides of the stopped work special, others scurrying to meet the mule train and bring up the animals they had been assigned to load.

It was a neat operation, militarily precise somehow, in spite of the seemingly casual approach Mace had taken to his men at home in the Hole and when preparing for the raid, and it had gone as well as if it had been planned and rehearsed for weeks in advance. Raider was impressed.

He was also worried. Where the hell were Doc Weatherbee and Allan Pinkerton? Where are you when I need you, boys?

Mace signaled to him. "Now is the time for your talents, John."

Behind him Bill Decker was leading up the mules

packed with his explosive and, separately, primers and fuses and oilcloth sacks of drillers' mud.

Now would be the real test for Raider. If he failed to remember the little he knew about blasting, he might well find himself exposed as an imposter. Raider did not think he would like the results if that were to happen.

CHAPTER THIRTY-THREE

There were eight men inside the boxcar. Eight men and enough firearms for three times that number. Seven of them looked livid with frustration and barely controlled anger.

The eighth man in the guard detail was none other than Bertram O'Meara. He looked quite smug.

That answered that, Raider thought. For this robbery of a lifetime, the rat had come out of the woodpile.

They weren't trying to keep the association hidden any longer, it seemed. Juan Mace embraced his informant with a hug of pure joy and gave O'Meara back his weapons. The two spoke briefly in Spanish, O'Meara's nearly as rapid as Mace's, and the Irishman took up a position to guard his recent companions.

At least, Raider thought, the railroad guards were no longer glaring at him or the other Mace men who had joined them in the boxcar. Their anger had a new and even more intense focus now.

Raider sighed. Soon enough, if Doc had gotten the message, he would be getting some very similar looks himself, but from Juan Mace and Miguel and probably from Bert O'Meara too.

Well, that was all right. It seemed pretty reasonable for a fellow to be unhappy with you if you were in the process of putting him behind bars. That kind of went with the territory.

For the moment, though, Mace and O'Meara were the ones in charge.

"Out now. Take them out," Mace ordered.

With the muzzle of O'Meara's shotgun pointing the way, the dispirited guards filed docilely to the car's door and out into the harsh afternoon sunlight.

The other bandits followed, leaving only Raider and Juan Mace in the boxcar.

"You can bring the stuff in now," Raider called, and Bill Decker began moving the blasting gear inside.

The object of Raider's attention now was a blocky steel safe that was a cube of hardened metal about four feet on a side. Massive ring bolts were cast into the sides of the thing, and a series of heavy chains ran over the already stout safe and down into the floor of the rail car, presumably wedding the safe to the frame of the car.

Raider bent to examine this formidable enemy, snapped his fingers, and went to the open doorway.

"Bert!" he called.

"Before I start in here, I want to ask you a couple of stupid questions."

O'Meara shrugged.

"First, man, is the payroll in that safe?"

"Are you daft, man?"

"Nope. This thing is so secure it makes me wonder if it's for show or for real."

"The money is there. I saw it loaded myself."

"One more then." Raider grinned. "You wouldn't happen to have the combination, would you?"

O'Meara shook his head. "None of this lot does. To remove temptation, you see. The combination is waiting for us at the railhead."

It was Raider's turn to shrug. "It was worth asking."

"Aye, I expect it was."

Well, shit, he thought. Guess I have to do it after all.

There were things he was better at than cracking safes. Cracking safecrackers for one. But if Slocum would know how to do it, so must Raider. He wiped his palms against his pants legs and bent to the task.

"This one looks like a son of a bitch," Raider said absently to Juan Mace, who was hovering over his shoulder. "But we'll see how it holds up to the powder. It kind of depends on how big the lock cavity is."

Working quickly with the high-quality tools he had bought in Colorado City, Raider bored four holes into the safe's door, one at each corner. The metal, he was amazed to discover, was much softer and more easily drilled than the impressive appearance of the safe would have led him to believe.

"A little mud now," he said when the bottom holes were done. Decker handed him one of the oilcloth bundles of drillers' mud. Raider used a fingerful on each of the two bottom holes.

"Why you drill the hole an' then plug it?" Mace asked.

"It gives the blast a place to go," Raider said. "Holds it in enough to be good an' powerful but gives it a weaker direction to go in." He grinned. "We want to blow the door outwards, you see. Otherwise we might could blow up the payroll along with the safe."

Mace nodded.

With a scrap of wire for a probe, Raider felt inside the top two holes. He had cut through the outer sheet of steel on the thick door but was careful to not harm the inner slab. The space between them contained the modern lock mechanism with series of tumblers so cunningly designed that Raider was sure they would have defeated him for days if he had tried to open the safe that way. Good enough that they might have defeated even a professional for hours. And they could not afford to spend hours with this train stopped, or they would arouse suspicions and blow the rest of the plan.

"Help me pour, please, Bill."

Carefully, using slender funnels and a fair amount of patience, Raider and Decker began to pour powder into the space between the front and rear door plates. It took most of a twenty-pound keg of the blasting powder to fill the gap.

"That's all she'll hold," Raider said finally. "I reckon it's enough."

He used another dab of the gray, claylike mud to fill one of the upper holes and—very carefully—crimped a blasting cap onto a length of fuse. He shoved the cap into the final hole and cemented around it with more of the mud.

"Pack the rest of these blow-up-ables way the hell an' gone away from here, Bill, but don't lose 'em. If I've messed up this shot, an' that can happen to anybody—" an insurance policy he thought he should throw in for Mace's benefit, just in case—"we want to be able to try again. Right?"

"Right. But it looks good to me, buddy."

"Fire in the hole!" he shouted as he leaped out of move everybody back some. When I come out of here, I don't want anybody in my way 'cause I won't be stopping to visit."

Mace nodded and followed Decker outside.

Alone in the car, Raider took a deep breath. Doc, you ornery old bastard, he thought, I wouldn't be doing this if you'd set this up the way I'd have done it. Now I don't know for sure if this thing's going to fizzle like a cork coming out of a beer bottle or blow this car and half the rest of the train to slivers.

The hell with it, he thought. There was only one way to find out for certain.

He measured off thirty seconds' worth of fuse, gave

himself another six inches of primer for safety's sake, and clipped it off there with a stroke of his knife blade.

Raider stood and checked to make sure the path between himself and the car door was clear. Only then did he strike his match and touch it to the fuse.

"Fire in the hole," he shouted as he leaped out of the boxcar and began to gallop toward the men who waited a hundred yards or so away.

CHAPTER THIRTY-FOUR

Juan Mace was overcome with another fit of grinning and backslapping, and he concentrated both of them mostly on Raider.

"John, my friend, you are a genius," he insisted over and over again.

Actually, under the circumstances, Raider was inclined to agree with the old bastard.

The safe door had been peeled open as pretty as a sardine-can lid. Two tugs with a pry bar were all that had been needed to clear away the sagging inner plate.

What was exposed inside was enough to make a man catch his breath, or quit breathing altogether. If that happened, at least he was sure to die happy.

The whole inside of the big safe was stacked nearly to the top with neat, orderly steel trays, and in each long, lovely compartment of those trays were racked row on shining row of beautiful gold coins.

"Oh my. My oh my," Raider muttered. Talk about your basic temptation. This had to be it. He had no idea how much money was in that safe. All the money in the world it looked like, or at least a healthy percentage thereof. He truly did not understand how anyone human could stand to work in a mint day after day and not go mad. He wanted to plunge his hands into the stuff, to pour it all into a pile on the ground and roll in

Miguel," Mace shouted. "Hurry. We are here too

it the way a kid will roll in a haystack. Lordy! He sighed. He also sneezed.

The boxcar was still foul with acrid smoke. It filled his nostrils, and he would be smelling it for days, he knew. There is little that smells better than a whiff of black-powder smoke in the open air but equally little that smells worse than a heavy dose of it in closed quarters. At least it would clear out once they started moving. They could ride with the door open until they got close to the railhead.

"Miguel," Mace shouted. "Hurry. We are here too long already."

Again in an orderly flow without apparent confusion, the men led the waiting pack mules to the boxcar doorway, stood only long enough for the golden contents of a tray to be dumped into the packsacks, and moved out of the way of the next mule. The men did not take time to comment on their loads, but their jubilant expressions and the way their eyes bugged when they saw the trays of racked coins were enough to prove that no one was unhappy with the haul.

Damn, Raider thought to himself again and again. Damn, damn, *damn!* No wonder a man could turn to a life of crime.

With the men so well organized, it took only minutes for the entire haul to be loaded onto the mules and for the mules to be reformed into a pack train and led away toward the nearest safe crossing on the Arkansas.

"I kinda hate to let those longears outta my sight," Raider said.

"Ah, but they carry the smaller part of our work," Mace reminded him. "Now we do the rest of it, eh?"

"You bet," Raider said cheerfully. "Now we get the good part."

A good many of the men, and virtually all the Mexicans in the band, accompanied the mules under the command of loyal, dependable Miguel. They took with them, Raider noticed, all the captured guards and all or nearly all of the train crew. Those who remained, except for Mace himself, were Anglo. The presence of a Mexican crew on a D&RG train would have been certain to arouse suspicion down the line.

"We are ready now? Good. O'Meara!" Mace was not one for resting laurels when there was more loot to be taken. He was back at work already.

O'Meara was put in charge of the phony guard contingent in the boxcar. Others were detailed to act as brakemen and to ride—their weapons concealed but handy in the event of need—as deadheaders in the caboose.

A man named Henry Something-or-other had once worked on the B&O and now became an engineer on the D&RG. Raider and Mace joined him in the engine cab, the aging Mexican cheerfully covering himself with soot and grime as a disguise and becoming for the time being a fireman.

For the kind of wages he expected to make, Raider thought, the job could hardly be considered demeaning.

Henry puttered for a moment with the various gauges and levers, said something—Raider was quite sure he did—to the hissing engine, and reached to give a cheerful little tug on the whistle. He tugged on the throttle, and the train began to come to life.

End-of-track was a shambles, not a town. It was a collection of tents and tar-paper shanties strewn over a rocky, yucca-spiked landscape that had nothing to recommend it except the work in progress and the money that the work put into the hands of the graders and spikers, laborers, and gandy dancers.

There was another kind of dancer present too, of course, the dance hall—in this case dance tent—women who earned most of their income doing a horizontal version of the bump and grind. Most of them would be pretty disgruntled right now, Raider knew. It had been so long since the men had been paid that nearly all the free cash of the whole camp should long since have been in the hands of the professional gamblers, who also haunted these work camps as a source of dependable income. Except for the Chinese, and there were none of them here, there never had been a track layer born who believed that his pay was meant for anything except blowing, and that well before the next pay call was due.

Someone, Raider thought, was in for a large surprise.

Juan Mace managed somehow to hide the grins that had been pulling his face out of shape ever since they had watched the tail end of the mule train disappear into the Wet Mountain foothills behind them. The old scoundrel bent to his temporary fireman's task with a burst of energy that could have come only from his anticipation of the riches yet to reach his hands.

Idly Raider wondered just where the old boy kept all his loot. Surely a man of Mace's broad beyond-the-law experience would not trust his money to a cheesebox bank in Pueblo or some such forsaken spot. Yet surely he would not want to risk it all in a hidey-hole back at the headquarters camp either. He was not, after all, surrounded by the most honest of men.

That, Raider thought, was the sort of thing Allan could worry about if or when he had the opportunity. And if the opportunity arose, Raider was certain that Allan would take the trouble. After all, if he could recover a healthy amount of stolen funds, he could reasonably claim a percentage of the recovery on behalf of Pinkerton's. And he most assuredly would.

The train was slowing now, and end-of-track was coming near. The new "engineer"—and he did seem to know what he was doing—shut down the power at the marker pole a good half mile back and called for the brakemen to set their wheels. Raider wondered how close Henry would come on his stop. A good engineer could set his engine and brakes a mile away from the stop and come within a dozen feet of being right on the spot when the train finally quit moving, but that would be with an engine and a car makeup with which he was already familiar. How Henry would do remained to be seen, and if he was too far off the target, he might well give them all away as imposters.

Normally Raider would have no serious compunctions about a band of robbers being caught, but this time he happened to be among them. If some serious shooting got started, he might find it a bit awkward to try to switch sides in the middle of the fray. He really did not fancy being shot by either the good guys or the bad. So at least for the moment, he was hoping that Mace managed to get away with his plans.

The short work train shuddered and lurched its last and came to a halt about thirty-five feet short of the tent that seemed to be serving as a trackside office.

"Nice job, Henry," Raider said.

"Nothin' to it," he answered, but he was smiling proudly.

Raider looked up and instinctively recoiled from what he saw.

From up ahead, on the sections of track still being laid and spiked into place, there were men swarming like rats coming out of their holes. They were yelling and shouting and waving tools in the air.

"My God, this must be what an infantry charge looks like," Henry said.

The track crew were throwing their hats into the air and screaming like banshees. The pay train was finally in.

"I sure am glad they ain't mad at us," Raider observed.

Mace, apparently unnerved for a moment, muttered something in Spanish.

"Careful, Juanito. Don't give us away now, or they'll get just as unhappy as they are happy right now."

Mace grunted and turned back to his woodpile. Raider thought he was swallowing pretty hard for a man who ought to feel on top of the world.

CHAPTER THIRTY-FIVE

"Sad news, buckos," O'Meara was saying with an expression to match his message. "The blackhearted bastards in Denver had some sort of breakdown an' missed the connection. Your payroll is on its way now, ye see, but we had to come on ahead to pick up th' shipment out or *we'd* a missed a connection, an' we ain't like that, ye see? Anyhow, boyos, we'll be runnin' a special in to ye tonight, no matter th' weather nor the time an' trouble, an' that's a promise. Soon as we hit the turnaround, we should be pickin' up the yaller coins an' hurryin' them to ye. Ye can take that as a personal promise from Bertram O'Meara, boys, an' ya know there's none better."

The man had a soothing tone of voice and a most sincere expression of apology plastered on his open, Irish features. Raider damned near believed him himself.

Certainly the end-of-track crew accepted what they were told. After all, why should they not? They knew O'Meara. He was a good friend and a trusted D&RG man.

They were disappointed, it was true. The word spread like wind-whipped flames through the crowd that was pressing all around the short train and, mostly, around

231

the office tent where they expected to draw their already overdue pay.

The intense jubilation of a moment before turned to disappointment and to frustration just as intense as their joy had been, but they had been disappointed before. And the delay this time would be short-lived. The special train would be in that very night. There was a good deal of cursing, and a few obvious troublemakers were muttering veiled threats, but the mood was not a dangerous one, just seriously unhappy. Thank goodness, Raider thought. He had not anticipated the danger of being mobbed by a crowd of irate and out-of-control workers when they failed to deliver the payroll that now was in Miguel's capable hands.

First O'Meara and then a pair of track-end bosses mounted to the steel roof of the engine cab to speak to the men and give them explanations and assurances. Raider did not know that he would have taken such news so calmly, but the men accepted what they were told with less grumbling than he would have expected. They were a hard lot but apparently a stoic bunch, and within minutes they began to disperse and trudge—at a much slower pace than they had used on the gallop toward the train—back to their jobs.

"It takes a hell of a lot of men to build a railroad," Raider said in a low voice to Mace.

"And much money to pay them."

"Uh huh."

"We'll be loadin' and away as quick as we can, boyos," O'Meara was saying to one of the D&RG men. "Ye do want us back the first minute we can be here, I'll be takin' it."

"Indeed, Bert. 'Deed we do." The fellow hooked a thumb toward a row of large tents down by the riverbank. "These poor souls have been most anxious for you too. I daresay they'll help with the loading if necessary to get you on your own way a minute sooner."

Raider glanced in the direction the man had pointed. None of the tent fronts over there carried signs, but then none were apparently needed. The sides of one were rolled up enough to reveal a collection of gaming tables with shirt-sleeved dealers waiting in readiness for the payroll they had been expecting at least as eagerly as the workers.

In front of several of the tents were clusters of angry whores in lacy chemises and gaudy kimonos, their rouge and lip paints bright in the late-afternoon sunshine. Most of them were pockmarked and ugly, probably eaten inside with nameless diseases, but they were available and handy, and no doubt they did a land-office business when there was money in camp to pay for them. And, hell, Raider thought, at least they were better than Angelica, each and every one of them.

Damn it, he thought to himself, there I go again. He seemed to be incapable lately of doing or saying or even *thinking* anything about that scrawny woman without immediately feeling guilty about it afterward. The hell with her. She was out of his life forever, he hoped.

One of the railroad men turned and began waving hand signals, and within a minute or two Raider could hear the approach of several heavy freight wagons through the tents.

The wagons were guarded by men perched atop their loads, carrying shotguns and expressions of sheer relief.

"We've had this stuff here for more than a day now," the railroad boss told O'Meara, "and I for one will be damned glad to turn it over to you, Bert. That's a hell of a lot of bullion to be responsible for."

O'Meara gave him a nod of sympathetic understanding. "I know what you'd be meanin', Glenn, an' I won't mind when I sign it across meself. But I'll guard it as if the gnomes themselves was after it, an' as soon as it's loaded, it's off your hands."

"It won't take long," Glenn promised.

"I been havin' a thought, though, me friend, an' here's what it be. If someone was to hit us on the way down, see, they'd be lookin' in the car. Aye?"

"Yes."

"So what I been thinkin' is this, Glenn, lad. We'll be takin' the piles o' dunnage off the flatcars anyway, an' all those lovely tarps will be just a-laying there to rot in the fresh, pure air o' this unlovely country. So what I been thinkin' is simply to pile yer bullion shipment onto the flats an' tie the tarps over. Was anybody to have a go at us then, an' sayin' they could make us stop, which as we both know they *could* do, they find us guards loafin' in an empty boxcar an' sayin' as how your shipment was late an' won't be in till we don't be know-in' when. So what do ye think, Glenn?"

The railroader shrugged. "It sounds weak, but what the hell. Do it however you like, Bert. Once you receipt for the stuff it's your worry, not mine. Me, I believe in shotguns and buckshot. But you do what you think best."

The man named Glenn was efficient, Raider saw. He had a work detail assembled and the flatcars unloaded in very short order, while the bullion-laden freight wagons stood idle with their teams twitching their tails and hanging their heads with the perennial weariness of all draft horses.

"Ready to load," Glenn said soon enough.

"Then I think, lad, I will be askin' ye to put it on the flats," O'Meara told him.

"It's your choice, Bert."

The simple truth was, of course, that Mace did not want any of the D&RG crew entering the boxcar where that explosive-mangled safe still sat. One look inside or a whiff of the stink of burnt powder would have been enough to tell the loading crew that all was not as well as O'Meara wanted them to believe.

Mace's phony brakemen and train crew had been

lounging on the flatcars and the roofs of the caboose and boxcar, their weapons out of sight but close at hand. Once the railroad guards began to load the bullion onto the flatcars as O'Meara requested, Raider could see the tension drain out of Juan Mace and his men.

Hell, Raider felt some relief himself.

"Easy as pie," he whispered to the bandit chieftain.

Mace dropped his characterization of an arm-sore fireman long enough to squint up at Raider and wink. "We have made the history, yes?"

"Yes, Juanito, I think you have."

Within an hour of their arrival Henry tugged his whistle cord and threw the long, iron lever to engage the driving wheels in reverse. The stolen train shuddered and crashed car against car as it began to push itself backward for the long, downhill run to the main line.

O'Meara, standing on the forward flatcar with his legs spread and boots planted not unlike a ship captain's at sea, gave a cheerful wave to the D&RG men who now were beginning to recede before them as the train backed away from end-of-track.

My God, Raider thought, he's done it. Juan Mace has managed to pull off the smoothest robbery—and the biggest—in the entire history of crime. And still not a peep from Doc Weatherbee or a sign of Allan Pinkerton.

Raider was getting worried. He sighed. Oh well, if it turned out that he was out of a job now, at least he could go out a rich man.

CHAPTER THIRTY-SIX

The backward run to the east, with the single locomotive shoving its cargo of men and gold bullion, was
an exercise in glee.

Juan Mace had dropped his role as a hardworking
fireman now and could scarcely be contained within
the confines of the short train. He quickly called for
one of the other men to replace him in the wood tender
and invited Raider to join him. Unwilling to wait for
the train to stop before he could examine his prize, the
old Mexican clambered over the stacked wood in the
tender and leaped across the links to the flatcar behind,
ran across it, and jumped again to the car where the
tarp-covered bullion was stored.

Mace ripped the lashings from the tarps and threw
them aside to reveal the dull, yellowish bars that looked
like so little and were worth so very much. The metal
was not the shining, gloriously beautiful stuff that a
jeweler has polished and worked on, or even the bright
yellow of a refined product. It was not even very attractive stuff, cast in rough molds that give the surface of
the bars a ragged, almost dirty appearance that also was
dulled by the intrusion of silver and semiprecious
base metals not yet separated from the gold.

Still, it was the stuff on which dreams are built.

And there was so *much* of it. Piles of the bars. Dozens

of them, perhaps hundreds. Raider did not bother to try to count them. They were stacked like cordwood on the sturdy flatcar bed, and their value had to be enough even in this unpure state to stagger the imagination. Even if they contained no more than half pure gold, there would be enough value here to buy Denver. The hell with having a blowout there. The possessor of wealth like this could buy the whole damn city, cathouses and all, and enjoy it until his heart burst from overexertion.

Mace sat on the nearest stack. He would have wallowed in the stuff if it had been in another form, Raider was sure. Hell, Raider would have done so himself.

O'Meara too was unable to wait for the train to come to a halt. He crawled out of the boxcar door and made his way hand over hand to the roof and forward to the flatcar, where he joined Mace and Raider and every member of the Mace crew who could find an excuse to make the journey behind them.

Before long the entire trainload of robbers was congregated on the flatcars, more men than the railroad bosses and work crews would ever have suspected were riding on their work train. The happy, cheering train robbers crept out of every hidden niche and cranny on the short train, bristling with weapons now that there was no need for concealment, laughing and planning a thousand ways to spend the riches that were theirs. The only ones who did not join them were the engineer Henry, the man assigned to act as fireman for him, and —after a brief period of being allowed to admire the piles of bullion—the brakemen, who still had work to do.

"Aieee! *Amigos!*" Mace went into a long speech in Spanish. He was entirely too excited to translate his feelings into English, and probably not more than a handful of the gringo robbers with him understood what their leader was saying.

They did not need to understand the words. The emotions were enough, and they understood those already because they too were feeling them.

Even Raider found himself caught up in the mass jubilation. The greatest heist in the history of robbery had been completed, pulled off exactly as planned, without a hitch or a fumble. Each and every one of these men was rich enough to sneer at Croesus.

The men danced on the flatcars and flung hats into the air without caring that they were ending up lining the D&RG's newly laid tracks west of Florence.

"Signal ahead. Signal ahead, by God," one of the brakemen called from his perch atop the boxcar.

Mace became businesslike again, racing back along the flatcars to shout orders to the engineer. The driving power of the steam engine was cut, and the brakemen began setting the screws at each car to slow and soon to halt the train.

Raider moved carefully through the crowd to the edge of the car carrying the bullion. Across the river he could see Miguel leading the long packstring of patient mules out of the hills and down toward a ford.

This was it, by God. The last step of a long and apparently successful journey into crime. And still no sign of Doc or Allan.

The train shuddered to a halt finally, a half mile past the ford where the mules were now crossing, and the bandit crew jumped down and began shouting and waving to their companions with the mules. Even with so many people to participate in the distribution of this haul, Raider realized, there was plenty for everybody. They were all, at least as of this moment, rich men.

It seemed to take Miguel and his Mexicans a long time to cover the distance between them, but it is difficult to hurry a string of mules, no matter what kind of anxiety drives the humans who think they are in charge.

Mace spoke to one of the men, and the man ran to

the nearest telegraph pole along the right of way to shinny up the splintered wood, its base still wobbly with the packed earth that had not yet had time to settle firmly since it was installed, and cut the single strand of shiny wire that linked end-of-track with Pueblo and all the points beyond.

Now it was safe to cut the D&RG communications, Raider realized. Now suspicions would not count nearly so much as before. Now the bandits wanted to keep word of their bullion pickup secret, whereas before, the loss of communication would have made the end-of-track bosses worried and ready to believe the worst, even of a man like O'Meara, whom they knew and trusted.

Miguel and his cheering crowd reached them, and the men swarmed back onto the flatcar to begin unloading the bars of bullion onto another quickly and efficiently assembled line of waiting pack mules.

There was one jarring note in the whole procedure, though, Raider noticed. Among all the smiling faces and laughing tones of voices, Miguel stood out with his look of solemn intensity. Miguel was not laughing. He was far from cheerful. He looked dark and menacing, like a man with much more on his mind than sudden wealth. And a very serious something at that.

While the men were busy transferring the bars of gold and silver amalgam from the flatcar into the mule panniers, Miguel left his horse and waded through the crush of cheerful bandits to Juan Mace.

The two men embraced there, the old chieftain throwing his arms about his lieutenant and kissing the gloomy Miguel on both cheeks.

Miguel stood stone-faced and silent while Mace poured out a flood of excited Spanish. Raider, standing at the other end of the flatcar, got the impression that Miguel was enduring his chief's happiness without in any way participating in it.

That was decidedly odd. At this moment, with all those beautiful, valuable golden bars in full view, Miguel should be one of the happiest men alive.

Raider shook his head to himself and turned away, trying to puzzle out the answer—hell, any answer—for Miguel's behavior. It might be a sadness that Juan Mace's reign over this no-longer-isolated country was about to end. But the retirement was to be a voluntary one, and surely, as Mace's most trusted companion, Miguel would be rewarded heavily. The man had to be rich.

No, Raider decided, that couldn't be it, because this was what Mace wanted and therefore was what Miguel would want. No, Raider was just exercising his imagination. The truth was that he had no idea what was wrong. He simply knew that something *was* wrong. And he had an idea he really should find out what that something was.

Glancing up again, he saw a small, ragged figure mounted on a pony at the edge of the milling, shouting mass of men and horses and mules.

Christ, he thought. Now what? That was Angelica over there. Surely she wasn't supposed to be anywhere around here. She was supposed to be back at the Hole with Elaine. But not here.

She saw him looking her way, and even across the distance between them he could see her go rigid. She seemed to become very pale, and her thin lips were set in a hard, straight line. She certainly seemed upset about something.

Looking furtively around at the men who were near her to make sure they were paying no attention to her— they were not, since all attention was centered on the stacks of piled bullion—she made a feeble come-here gesture to Raider and pointed toward the front of the train.

Raider nodded that he understood, and immediately

the homely little woman slipped awkwardly out of her saddle and began to scurry toward the locomotive.

Mentally shrugging to himself, Raider took a chance that the slattern might be able to satisfy his curiosity. He turned away from the gold and the men who had stolen it and dropped off the flatcar on the side, away from all the people and the commotion.

Angelica might have been able to explain a great deal to him, but Raider was not to find out.

Behind him a voice he recognized as belonging to Juan Mace shouted, *"Cabron!* There. He is trying to get away. *Stop him!"*

Raider turned to see what was going on. He turned to face the muzzles and the cocked hammers of more than a dozen perplexed but obedient men.

Behind them Juan Mace glared at Raider with all the intense hatred Satan might give to a Bible-thumping evangelist.

And beside the old man, Miguel stood with his feet spread and a look of evil pleasure on his face while he pointed an accusing finger straight at Raider's chest.

"What's up, boys?" Raider asked in a voice that was light and unconcerned. Inside, though, his gut had shrunk to a fist-sized block of ice and he was wondering how—if at all—he was going to wriggle out of this one.

CHAPTER THIRTY-SEVEN

"You bastard," Mace accused him. "You miserable, lying, cocksucking bastard."

Mace looked like he was about to explode from pent-up fury. His face was red, and he was breathing as hard as a man who has just outrun a horde of Blackfoot in one of their famous life-runs. The excitement of the drawn guns and now of Mace's intense emotions was enough to draw the men away from even the lure of the gold bars, and they were crowding in close in an attempt to be able to hear what was going on.

Raider wished them luck. There was a good many things Mace *could* be about to kill him for, not the least of which was those delightful rolls in the hay with Elaine Volnay, but even so, Raider really wanted to know what it was he seemed to be about to die over. So far, though, all Mace was doing was cursing and blowing smoke out of his hairy ears. At this point the old man wasn't making a whole lot of sense.

"Stinking gringo cocksucker," Mace insisted again.

"There's a lot o' things I've done," Raider returned mildly, "but that ain't among 'em. Would you mind telling me what it is you think I *did* do to get you so worked up?"

It seemed to Raider a perfectly reasonable and sensible request, but Mace did not take it as such. The old man puffed up even redder and for a moment was unable to speak. He tried, but all he managed to get out was a sound somewhere between a squeak and a growl.

Raider decided that he really had better shut his mouth again and keep it that way. This seemed a poor time to be baiting Juan Mace.

It was Miguel, as always at his leader's side, who supplied the answer.

"Maricon," he said. "Son of a long line of gutter whores. Filth! Did you think you could do what you did an' then come among us an' make yourself a wealthy man with the tears of the very man you have treated so foully? Eh? Did you?"

Raider shook his head, not in denial but in puzzlement.

"A mere child, he was. Still but a youth. Gone now. Hah! Was he a match for the great John Slocum? Pah. I spit on you." The bastard did too, and it was all Raider could do to keep himself from lashing back at the Mexican.

"All this time you have broken bread with this good man, you have robbed of his very life. From him you took his hope for immortality—for what is a son if not this?—and then you dared come to sit at his table an' to drink with him, pretending friendship, an' all the while you plotted to steal from him even more, for you have no right to anything of this camp except for the death you so richly deserve. Bastard. You should have died of syphilis ten years ago so that you would not have afflicted this good man here." Miguel pointed dramatically at Mace standing mute with anger beside him. To the crowd at large he roared, "Geraldo. Geraldo the faithful son is dead. An' this creature is the one that killed him."

Well, if *that* wasn't setting a match to the powder keg, Raider thought silently. The men had been curious and uneasy before. Now they were as furious as their master. Jeez! He could *feel* the surge of hatred flowing out of them, all of it focused directly onto him, wanting to reach into his guts and pull them out into the dirt and the gravel, where the crowd could take turns trampling them.

No one moved, though, and no one spoke. Raider belonged to Juan Mace now, and Mace's men would wait until their leader determined Raider's fate. Then they would do anything, anything at all, that Mace told them.

Geraldo? He must have been the kid Raider had seen on the trail that first day, the one who tried to gun him but had come up slightly short on the deal. But how . . . ?

"You thought you had this planned so well," Miguel said. "You thought you were so very clever, John Slocum. Aieee, what a snake you are. But no. There was a companion with the young Geraldo. You remember this, *sí?* This you should have remembered. He too was but a youth, an' a wild one at that. He left Geraldo that day at the guarding point, an' he rode to Pueblo to see a certain señorita of loose morals and open thighs. An' this you did not know, son of twenty whores. As he was leaving, he saw you on the old trail, an' he described you when he learned the good Geraldo was not returned to his father's side. An' this boy returned to where he had left that saintly young man who because of you will never know the joys of full manhood, an' he has found the body of the dear one. So now what do you say for yourself, John Slocum? Now what?"

Miguel and the crowd around him stood glaring their accusations into Raider's passive face.

And Raider had nothing that he could say in return. Christ, how do you disprove a killing that you've done or explain one away to men who will accept no explanations?

Raider sighed. It wouldn't do the least bit of good and

he knew it quite well, but he had to try. Raw brass seemed as likely to help as anything else. He cleared his throat and said, "I haven't shot anybody in three months. Maybe three and a half. Beyond that, I got nothing to say, boys. I can prove some o' the things I *have* done, but I'll be damned if I can see a way to prove something I ain't done. And that's all I got to say on the subject."

He crossed his arms and looked Juan Mace straight in the eyes. There was nothing he could say to make the old bastard change his mind, but maybe this would at least give the old man some doubts.

It didn't. In slow and deliberate Spanish, Juan Mace gave him a cursing that would have straightened the hair on a curly wolf if the thing had understood what Mace was saying. As it happened, Raider didn't understand the words any more than a wolf would have, but then, he didn't really need to. The tone—menacingly calm now—was quite enough to make exact translations unnecessary. Raider was getting it but good.

While that was going on, and afterward as they all stood glaring at him, Raider kept thinking, despite his best efforts to the contrary, about the big man named Bruce and what Juan Mace had done to him for far less than the crime Raider was accused of. And it was, Raider knew, *far* less important in Mace's eyes, because Elaine Volnay, no matter how delectable, was only a woman and a possession to the old bandit chieftain, while Geraldo had been the beloved and the continuation of the blood. Whoever took that away from a man like Mace would regret the act a thousand times over before he died.

In spite of the iron control he tried to keep over himself, Raider felt sweat begin to leak from his armpits and run down his sides and his belly, and the sweat had the same approximate temperature as a mountain stream in January.

The blunt truth was that Raider was scared shitless. Otherwise he would have been carrying an extra load in his drawers.

"Rawhide," Mace said, speaking for the first time in what seemed a long while. "Bring me rawhide. Green hide, yes, and soak it well before you bring it to my hand."

Christ, that didn't sound exactly promising. Raider's imagination leaped to think of all the things even a single thong of green, shrinking rawhide could do to a man. The possibilities were limitless. Wrapped properly, a pouch of the stuff could crush a man's balls to a squishy, useless, agonizing pulp . . . and take half a day to do it. It took all Raider's will to keep the fear he felt from showing on his face and setting his teeth and knees to chattering, shaking spasms. Somehow, though, he managed to face the old bandit with only an apparent deep calm on his features. That was quite probably the most difficult thing he had ever had to do. On the other hand, it would be nothing compared to what he would have to endure soon.

Raider's attention, momentarily locked within himself, returned to the men who stood above him on the flatcar as his accusers and soon as his murderers.

Miguel seemed to be arguing with Mace, and now O'Meara had joined them there.

"My God," O'Meara was saying, "we canna do this, Juanito. No. Please. *Think,* me fine an' brilliant man. Use the brains tha' brought you this far. You *can't* stay here to do in this Slocum. Na, Juanito, na. Kill the divil quick or carry him wi' us an' kill him slow afterward. Aye, either o' those, whatever gives you the relief you got to have. An' Lord love ya, Juanito, I understand. I do. I loved Geraldo as me own brother. You *know* that. But th' railroad boys ain't fools, ye know. The line's been cut now, an' they'll be gettin' the suspicions, they will. They'll be sending riders t' Florence, an' they canna help but see us here if here we be a-playin', but don't be askin' the lot o' us to stand here wi' ye an' risk our own deaths just so you can be enjoyin' his. Ye can't ask that of us, Juanito. Ye can't."

Miguel cut in then, in Spanish. From the impassioned way he spoke and the pleading tones of request that lay beneath the foreign words, Raider was sure that Miguel's speech was another version of O'Meara's but in a different tongue.

It was not exactly a pleasant situation to be making choices in, but Raider found himself rooting inwardly for Miguel and O'Meara to prevail. Either way would be rather hard to take, but at least their way would mean a delay. And a delay could always carry with it a glimmer of hope. Until the last bullet struck or the last drop of blood drained from his body, Raider would be looking for a way out. If in the long run he had to die hard and slow to avoid a fast and painless early death, well, that was just the way it would have to be. He would take the later death every time, and he'd find a way to cheat the bastards if he could.

Mace was responding heatedly in Spanish. Angry. His red-faced fury returned, and the calm he had been maintaining evaporated as if it had never been. He ranted. He stalked up and down the length of the D&RG flatcar, his men hurrying to get out of his way, their heads and eyes turning from him as if they were afraid to attract his attention in any way. Mace stamped his feet against the solid boards of the flatcar floor and, lifting his hands toward the heavens, seemed to be appealing to the deity for his stupid companions to understand the need to kill Raider here. But slowly.

Someone, Raider did not see who it was, crept out of the crowd on the flatcar and timidly handed Mace the wet, dripping rawhide he had asked for.

Where they would have found such an oddity at a time and place like this, Raider could not know and did not really care. The fact that they had was, simply, the shits. And rather tough luck for one apparently end-of-his-rope Pinkerton agent.

Christ, Raider thought, it was bad enough that he was going to go under. It made it somehow worse that he was doing it under someone else's name, and an outlaw's at that. Probably no one ever *would* know what had happened to him. Eventually Allan would cross him off the Agency books and scrupulously set his remaining pay aside in the unlikely event someone stepped forward with a claim against it. And Doc Weatherbee would sooner or later decide that Raider was no longer in the picture and get respectfully drunk in his honor. But that would be that. There would be no one else around to mourn.

It was odd the way a man's thoughts ran at a time like this. Raider was, he finally realized, trying to avoid thinking about the inevitable.

Hell, he decided, he was entitled. He could think about ice cream parlors or rye whiskey or the varying flavors of pussy juice. If it made him any more comfortable, fine, he was entitled. In the meantime, he kept his eyes brazenly locked on Juan Mace, still hoping against hope that he could pull it out with a show of brass balls since he didn't seem to have much else going his way.

He thought briefly, too, of the heavy Colt at his side, but he quickly determined that he had to ignore that. There were half a hundred gunhands here who would cheerfully pump their own Colts empty into his corpse if he made the first move, even if he somehow managed to hit Mace, Miguel, *and* O'Meara before the others got into the action. No, that was definitely out. Because there was, after all, that constant shred of hope.

He was still alive, and as long as he stayed that way, he would keep on trying to stay that way just a little bit longer.

Mace quit his pacing and came finally to an obviously angry halt beside his two lieutenants. He stamped his feet a little more and looked thoroughly disgusted, with them and with himself, but it was apparent that he had reached a decision.

"All right," he snapped in English. "All right. We take him with us. He is not to escape me by dying quickly. Take him and make sure he suffers when you tie him. We will find out how much of a man this child killer is."

Mace turned away, and Miguel and O'Meara jumped down from the flatcar to reach roughly for Raider's arms. Someone else stepped forward with a length of rope.

Raider felt them grab him and, somehow, resisted an impulse to defend himself.

He really did not much care for the look on these fellows' faces.

CHAPTER THIRTY-EIGHT

It sounded like thunder, and instinctively Raider glanced up at the cloudless late afternoon sky, trying to determine how in hell it could all of a sudden be rolling with such violent thunder when he had seen no signs of weather moving in.

For a moment he couldn't figure it out.

Then the throat of a man standing on the flatcar near Mace exploded in a spray of pink foam that was followed quickly by a thick stream of bright-red blood. The man fell to the car floor and began to flop like a decapitated chicken, his boot heels rattling against the wood in a gruesome dance of death.

By then, Mace and the rest of the men had dropped flat or thrown themselves behind the remaining stacks of bullion.

They looked like a bucketful of worms dumped onto flat ground as they wriggled and squirmed toward the far edge of the flatcar and dropped toward the relative protection of the cars.

By that time, more of them had been hit, and the boards they were crawling across were sticky and slick with streams of fresh blood that steamed in the chill of the approaching evening.

By then, too, Raider had identified the thunder for what it was, and he doubted that he had ever heard a more welcome sound than that .45-70 Gatling gun and its accompanying rain of carbine fire.

Lead slugs slammed into the railroad cars and went zinging off the steel wheels and running gear with high-pitched whines that diminished quickly into the distance as they faded.

Miguel and O'Meara and the few others who had been standing on this side of the cars with him were gone, disappeared as quickly and completely as if the ground had swallowed them whole.

Raider stood upright in the midst of the swarming bullets and heard them sizzle past him as they slammed into the cars and into exposed flesh. He heard the screams of agony as the fusillade of superheated metal caught first one man and then another.

There simply was not room enough behind those cars to hide everyone, and the Gatling gun's crew were directing their fire low now, aiming their shots in a horizontal pattern beneath the carriages of the cars to ricochet off the rails and off the running gear and gravel ballast and slant upward again into the bodies of the men who tried to hide beyond the cars.

For Raider, so quickly yanked from the face of death to this, there was a sense of unreality. He felt as a ghost must feel, as if he were an observer without form or substance who could see the scenes around him but was not part of them.

The shock of the rapid change left him with no sense at all that he himself might be harmed by the Pinkerton bullets that were spewing death and destruction over Juan Mace's crew.

That was who it had to be. Only Doc and a Pinkerton squad could have put this together. Armed with his telegram and a Gatling gun, they had arrived late, but they had arrived.

Raider stood quite at peace, almost serene in his indifference to the bullets that continued to whine past him, and watched the growing destruction as the thumb-sized .45-70 slugs chewed hunks of wood out of the railroad cars and added flying splinters to the lead that was whizzing through the air everywhere he turned.

It was truly amazing the amount of damage a Gatling could do, Raider reflected. He was finding it all quite interesting.

Someone grabbed his arm and began sobbing in his ear. Mildly curious but still unafraid, he turned to see who it was.

Angelica. He remembered seeing her with the mule string before all of this had started. He had been about to meet her when Mace stopped him. Of course, he remembered that quite clearly. But what was she doing out here where she could be shot?

The sight of her and his sudden anxiety about the woman's safety snapped Raider out of the shock that had thrown a veil over his emotions and his ability to think clearly.

"Christ, woman, get the hell out of here." He grabbed her by the arm and began to run, dragging her with him faster than she could possibly have run by herself, toward the locomotive and the protection of the steel sides of the cab there.

He raced past the empty flatcar and the wood tender and hauled Angelica roughly with him. As they reached the cab, Raider grabbed her around the waist and flung her up the short flight of iron stairs and onto the steel floor of the big engine.

Raider scrambled monkeylike up the ladder and shoved Angelica in a sprawling heap forward in the cab, behind the protecting wall and against the still-hot firebox.

"You're all right," she breathed as she curled into a tight ball against the control levers. "I swear, Johnny, I thought you'd gone pure crazy out there. An' I swear, I thought I'd jus' die when I couldn't get to you in time to warn you. That's what I come out here for. But I wasn't in time. Lord, Johnny, I'm sorry. I tried to get to you in time, but I jus' couldn't."

She seemed much more concerned about that than about the bullets that were slamming into the sides of the engine cab or the few ricochets that went screaming through the close space that hid and partially protected them.

Raider grinned at her. "You did just fine, Angelica. Just fine. Thanks."

The few words of praise brought a smile to her face that made her seem almost attractive, and for that brief moment Raider was able to see what she must have looked like as a girl, back when she was Juan Mace's personal bedmate, before he had turned her over as community property for his men to abuse or use in any way they found pleasant.

Raider started to tell her so, but he was cut short by the look of sudden terror in the woman's eyes. She was staring at a point just behind him, toward the open rear of the engine cab.

Raider turned, knowing even before he did so what he would see there. Miguel too had been able to reach the protection of the cab, and the Mexican bandit seemed overwhelmed with joy to find Raider there as well.

"John," the Mexican hissed. "You can hurt my Juanito no more. The bullets have found him. You understand? An' I, I have found *you*."

Miguel's hand shifted forward, and he held a big Colt cocked and ready there. He seemed quite insane with shock, much the way Raider had been moments before, and intent on only one thing now—killing Raider.

"You forgot something, Miguel," Raider said mildly. "*Sí?*"

"You boys never got around to taking my gun away."

Raider's hand palmed the .44-40 in a motion too fast for the eye to follow, and long practice let his muscles take over at a speed the brain could not have followed.

The Colt belched a spear of fire from its muzzle, and four feet away, the bridge of Miguel's finely molded aquiline nose became an empty socket of red flesh and white bone, and the right-hand man of Juan Mace was flung backward from the cab like a limp sack of grain to fall heavily into the gravel roadbed below.

The smoking Colt still in his fist and his attention on the open doorway where more of Mace's men might at any moment appear, Raider crawled backward on the steel floor of the locomotive until he was positioned between Angelica and the open doorway of the cab.

"It'll be all right now," he promised her. "It'll be all right. And tomorrow, you and me, woman, we're riding up to Denver. Why, you're gonna be downright splendid-looking in a pretty new dress with all the flounces an' ruffles a girl could ask for. You know that? It's true. I swear it's so. An' in a few minutes here, my ol' partner Doc will be walking down from that hillside up there where the Gatling gun's spitting just now, and you and me and ol' Doc, we're gonna have us just one hell of a fine time laughing an' talking an' getting things worked out in our own minds to just where we want them. You know that, Angelica? Well, believe it. It's the natural truth, I swear it."

He felt her stir behind him and cuddle forward to lean against his back and take assurance from him the way she might have taken warmth under other circumstances.

"If you say so, John."

He laughed. "That's another thing we got to talk about, Angelica. It will take some explaining, but that's all right. We've got plenty of time for that. As soon as those boys quit their shooting and walk down here, there's just lots of things we got to talk about."

He felt her nod her head. "Whatever you say, John. Anything you say."

Raider chuckled to himself. Going to Denver with a woman like Angelica on his arm was not exactly something he had ever planned for himself. But under the circumstances, he was downright glad to be doing it. He surely was. Hell, he would even be glad to see old Allan.

The shooting from the hillside stopped, and Raider gathered himself to stand upright. As a Pinkerton, by damn. As a Pinkerton.

J.D. HARDEN

"THE MOST EXCITING WESTERN WRITER SINCE LOUIS L'AMOUR"
—JAKE LOGAN